Hellenic Immortal

Gene Doucette

ABOUT THIS EDITION

As well as the new cover, I've made a number of minor editorial corrections. This should enhance your experience as a reader, and also makes me feel better as a person. The changes are not so substantive as to necessitate the repurchase of this edition if you are one of the many owners of the prior edition, but as always, please don't let me stop you if you'd like to buy it again.

As noted with Book One, some of what you come across here may seem outdated, technologically. (Adam learning what "GPS" stands for, as an example.) The passage of time between the books more or less mirrors the time in which the books were written, so in this context, the dating is appropriate.

I hope you enjoy the new edition!

Gene Doucette

Third Apparition: Macbeth shall never vanquish'd be, until

Great Birnam wood to high Dunsinane hill shall come against

him.

Macbeth: That will never be. Who can impress the forest, bid the tree, unfix his earthbound root?

—from Macbeth, by William Shakespeare

Priest: ... You are not one of the immortal gods, we know; yet we have come to you to make our prayer as to the man surest in mortal ways and wisest in the ways of god.

—from Oedipus Rex, by Sophocles

PROLOGUE

It was Liakhil who came for me.

I remember it being on a day where the woods seemed quieter than usual, but it's possible I decided this after the fact to make myself feel better. I'm the same way with volcanoes and earthquakes—the signs were there, and I simply missed them.

This was neither volcano nor earthquake, which was either a good thing or a bad thing depending on whether one was in its path or not.

I'd known Liakhil since he was a stripling, so seeing him as an adult always made me catch my breath. This was partly because the passage of time, not easy for me under normal circumstances, was even harder to gauge when living by myself in a temperate zone. Also, Liakhil had grown into the largest satyr I could remember, yet I still saw the boy I first met beneath that hard, impassive, bearded face.

He appeared in the woods behind me, said my name, and nearly caused me to soil myself. I always hated his kind for being able to do that, as I pride myself on being the kind of guy that's difficult to sneak up on.

"It's coming," was what he said, and when I asked what he was talking about, he just shook his head. "Hurry."

I'd have argued, but I try not to argue with satyrs, just as a rule. Also, Liakhil looked afraid, which was alarming because I didn't know that was one of their available expressions.

So we ran. Or rather, I ran as hard as I could whlle he sort of jogged. The destination was never really in question as their enclosure was ahead of us and I didn't know any other place a satyr would have wanted to be.

Then came the noises. A tree makes a very distinctive groaning sound when it is bent that's hard to describe, but impossible to mistake for something else. I first heard it in the middle of an elephant stampede. (Or, something approximating an elephant. A large land mammal, let's just say. When you're as old as I am, sometimes you're just waiting for paleontologists to discover things and name them for you.)

The ground shook in a manner similar to a stampede as well, except it wasn't a constant thing like it would have been with many land creatures trampling the landscape. It was the thud-thud-thud of a biped.

And while I knew it couldn't have been, it felt like it was directly behind us.

"What is it?" I shouted to Liakhil. He either didn't hear me or didn't feel like answering, but he did share my anxiety regarding its relative proximity.

Fortunately, we were nearly to the wall of the enclosure. Without breaking stride, he grabbed my arm, pulled me over his shoulders, and then jumped up into the canopy. This would have been a good time to see what was behind us, but my eyes were closed. I also may have been screaming.

We landed hard on the other side of the wall.

"What was ..." was all I could say before he had his hand over my mouth. He shook his head at me, and I nodded.

The ground thrummed. I realized the thriving satyr village I was used to seeing was silent and looked completely empty, which was new. It occurred to me that Liakhil had taken an enormous risk by leaving them—they were hiding in their homes, I later learned—to bring me over the wall.

How enormous a risk was spelled out as soon as the thing on the other side hit the wall.

It nearly buckled. I had been on the planet for a very, very long time by then and had never seen any being capable of that. And I have not since.

I held my breath, but there was no second blow. Instead, it marched off.

Once it was fairly distant, I turned to Liakhil and asked my question.

"What was that?" I asked, after cursing a few choice Minoan gods, plus a Sumerian deity or two.

"The Duh-ryadh," he answered.

I had heard this word before, but not for anything I could have imagined to be real.

In the tongue of the satyros, it meant evil personified. It meant the devil. But the devil wasn't supposed to actually walk the earth. Right?

PART ONE

Gambling With Fate

Chapter One

"Wagering is for men who can no longer hunt," said he to Silenus. "And in hunting, if your prey is as likely to slay you as otherwise, the wiser path would be to find something else to kill."

—From the archives of Silenus the Elder.
Text corrected and translated by Ariadne

Someone was following me.

It was more than a little annoying, because I'd only just re-entered society at large after a couple of years away, and I was still getting used to the idea—again—that the world was overfilled with people.

Las Vegas was probably not the best city in which to make this adjustment. Even without the crowds to consider, it's a terribly confusing place for someone my age. For instance, I was in Egypt when some of those pyramids you see on postcards were built, and I don't care if the one on the strip is made of glass and has lights shooting out of the top, it's still goddamn disorienting. And the togas at Caesar's Palace give me fits.

If I'd been smart about it, I would have dropped myself into the middle of Montana and worked my way into a city or two gradually, like a one-man Visigoth horde. But I had drinking to do, and Montana didn't seem like the place to do that. So instead I was drinking in Las Vegas and quietly wishing for a nice plague to come along and make the planet less crowded.

The woman following me was a longhaired brunette, and the first time I saw her she was dressed semi-formally in a knee length skirt and scoop-necked blouse, all just a little too classy and clean for two in the morning. She'd been standing in front of a slot machine, but when she shifted and sat down, her skirt rode up and showed off some leg. This is really what caught my eye, because I am a heterosexual male.

There are perhaps only one or two things on earth that will draw my attention more quickly than the flashing of a well-formed leg atop a three-inch heel—the flashing of a well-formed breast would do It, but that's considerably less common—and so I noticed her. I then managed to get back to my poker game, but from that point on, I made sure I kept her in my peripheral vision.

I'm something of a voyeur, in case you didn't get that.

It didn't take long to realize that my friend with the nice legs was watching me, too. This was puzzling because I frankly didn't look like much at that particular time. I had more or less rolled out of bed and directly onto the casino floor, pausing only long enough to put on shoes. And I don't think of myself as one of those guys who looks great at 2:00 a.m. No, whatever it was that had her lingering wasn't sex appeal, and it wasn't money, because despite being extremely wealthy at the moment, I was keeping that information to myself.

Possibly, she simply knew I was looking and decided to look back. I dismissed it as such.

But then she turned up the next night. She'd gone from a skirt to black slacks and a halter, and had pulled her hair back, but it was definitely the same woman. She situated herself at a different slot machine and acted as before, playing as long as I was playing and keeping me in her side view.

It didn't make a whole lot of sense. If she was following me for subversive reasons, keeping herself in my range of vision was just not the smart thing to do; she could see the back of my head just fine from behind and I don't have eyes there.

So she wanted me to see her seeing me, but why?

I considered prostitution, but a call girl would have approached me eventually; they don't usually get paid—or not well—just to be looked at from across the room, and if someone was paying her for that, it wasn't me.

I cashed out after the next hand and walked over to introduce myself, but she got up the minute I did and left out of a side door. I considered following, but that seemed a little too stalker-ish. Maybe, I told myself, she just liked playing slots before bedtime and I was misconstruing what was going on.

Except she continued to turn up: evening gowns, pants suits, bikini (by the pool), hair down, hair pulled back, glasses, no glasses. Same girl. And every time I got close, she made a hasty exit. Either she really was following me, or I'd developed some sort of psychosis. I suspected the former, but the latter wasn't entirely out of the question.

* * *

It was because of another woman that I was in Vegas in the first place. Her name is Clara, and she's currently somewhere in Europe spending money—her own, although she could have asked and I would have given her some—and probably having a fantastic time doing whatever it is twenty-five year olds do with ample funds in Europe these days. And since this particular twenty-five year old is always going to look twenty-five, she may be away for some time.

Clara, thanks to a medical procedure that is unlikely to be repeated any time soon, is going to live forever, provided she avoids sharp objects and volcanoes and the like.

I am too. I already have lived something like forever, provided one collapses one's definition down to the past sixty thousand years or so. Also like me, Clara will never age, get sick, or just die of natural causes. We can both be hurt—I mean physically, although I guess emotional pain is on the table as well—and otherwise die of exceptional or intentional causes, or so I assume.

It would have been a fantastic coincidence if the one woman on earth who could grow no older with me was also my soul mate (or true love or whatever romantic metaphor you prefer) and we lived happily ever after in a way no fairy-tale writer could have imagined. But this was not true love, and it wasn't anyone's fault except maybe whoever thought of the idea of true love in the first place, because I'm nearly positive it doesn't actually exist. Or rather, it's easily mistaken for something else, as I believe I have met my true love at least a dozen different times. And Clara isn't one of those dozen.

She also isn't the only woman on earth who doesn't get any older. She just happens to be the least complicated of the two.

Anyway, I bought an island in the Queen Charlottes a little less than two years ago in an estate sale. The last owner was one Robert Grindel, recently deceased, deservedly so. I decided to live in the modest private home that came with the island. Clara decided to come with me.

This was fantastic for about eighteen months, but things started to go downhill after that.

So yeah; she left. And I don't really want to talk about it.

* * *

Having an attractive woman play amateur espionage with me was something I would have quite enjoyed in a different time or place, but as I'd recently had a bounty on my head, I was far more wary than titillated. So I checked out of the Bellagio and into the MGM Grand, and went from poker to blackjack.

I switched to blackjack because you really don't have to pay much attention when playing it, unlike poker, which I'm quite good at when fully engaged, but which I find difficult while concentrating more on the people watching than the people playing.

Both are preferable to slots, which I simply don't understand. I mean, it's a machine. You can't read a machine for tendencies; you just have to hope it's not cheating. There's luck involved in cards too, but there's also a little skill. It's like the difference between praying for a fatted calf to walk into your camp versus going out and hunting one. You might not get dinner either way, but at least in one case you're not relying on the beneficence of fate or some random god to help you out. And yes, I know I just equated the gods to a slot machine. That was my point.

Also, and this is possibly related, one of the kicks I get out of cards and dice is that both were once used for telling the future, so the idea of employing them in games of chance just cracks me up. Every time I crap out at the table, I'm thinking not only did I lose my money, I also just foretold a drought for my village. You can't get that kind of entertainment from a slot machine.

Anyway, I was at one of the blackjack tables riding an improbable streak of heinously bad luck when I saw her again, sitting at the bar. She'd followed me to the MGM.

For this evening's game of tag, she went with a black sweater and skirt combo, with a cute little beret and a pair of those tiny oval glasses women nowadays wear because they look retro.

Wasting no time, I cashed out and headed for the bar, fully expecting her to turn and walk off like she had every other time—and also planning to chase her for a change, as I was now convinced this wasn't simply the consequence of my overactive imagination. But she didn't run. She held her ground, which was modestly exciting.

I slid into the seat next to her and caught the bartender's attention. His name was Chester, and he didn't have a lot to do because it was nearly 3:00 a.m.

Gambling at night was how I coped with the crowds.

I tapped on the bar to get his attention.

"Do you have any scotch that's of the legal age?"

"I got a twelve year old," he said.

"That's close enough. Neat, please."

14

"You got it."

Chester served my drink and then scooted to the other end of the bar to fill a cocktail waitress's order.

After a moment's pause I cleared my throat and asked, "Don't you want to run off again?"

My erstwhile stalker turned in the swivel chair and looked at me.

"Excuse me?"

She smelled like primrose. I probably smelled like the cigarettes my tablemate had been chain-smoking all evening.

"Or you could just move to the far end of the room," I suggested, pointing to the tables by the door. "To keep a safe distance."

She grinned toothlessly and sipped her drink, which appeared to be a rum and coke. "I'm sorry, do I know you?"

"Apparently yes, you do. Someone paying you to keep an eye on me?"

"I really don't know what you're talking about."

It was the first time I had heard her voice, which was deep and melodic, with the cadence of someone who might have started life in a language other than English. I decided I could listen to it all night. "Of course you don't. Well then, let me introduce myself. I'm Jason."

I changed my name before leaving the island, going with Jason Stargill. This required repeating it a few dozen times so it rolled out naturally, which is something you learn how to do when you switch appellations like other people do shoes. I felt pretty comfortable with it.

We shook hands. Finally close enough to get a good look, I noted her deep black eyes and round face that bespoke a Hellenic ancestry. She was also far more attractive than I'd realized from a distance. Sometimes this causes a bout of stammering on my part.

"Jason?" she repeated. "Funny. You don't look like a Jason."

15

"And you are?"

"Ariadne."

"Greek."

"Mm-hmm," she nodded. "My parents always loved the classics."

"That's nice," I said, downing my scotch. "Listen, Ariadne—and let's just pretend that's your real name for now—I'm the kind of guy who likes his privacy. I've been known to go through a whole lot of trouble to preserve that privacy. So as much as I've enjoyed the eye-fucking I've been getting for the past week, I'd appreciate it if you stopped following me. I'm sure you understand."

"Oh, I do," she assured me, genuinely smiling this time. She did sort of remind me of an Athenian I knew once; maybe the name was legit. "Everyone has their secrets. Your problem is that your secrets aren't really so secret anymore."

"Meaning?"

"Meaning if you think I'm a threat, you should look around more carefully."

Before I could come up with something useful to say to that, she stood and leaned in closely, tilted her lips up to my ear and whispered, "Good night, Adam."

Her hand brushed my knee as she walked off. And I was entirely too dumb-founded to do anything other than watch her go.

Adam was the name I'd been using before I switched to Jason, and there were very few humans still alive that knew this. Or so I thought.

Something was very, very wrong.

"Nice, huh?" Chester commented from a few feet away.

"I think I'm in love."

I was there to get over another woman and I was drunk, but I also may not have been kidding.

"Me too," Chester agreed. "You want another?" He meant the scotch.

I pushed forward the glass, because I almost never turn down a refill, and surveyed the room again. It occurred to me I had spent much of the last several days looking for Ariadne to the extent that I probably ignored anyone else who might have *also* been tailing me. It was a classic trick, and if it was being played on me, I was an idiot for not recognizing it sooner.

But the trick doesn't really work as well if the misdirect—the girl—tells you she's a misdirect. So she was either an unwilling participant or something else was going on, and I was too drunk to figure out what that was. I was not, however, too drunk to be paranoid about the idea.

I have been known to suffer from occasional bouts of what might be considered—in someone else—mild paranoia. It's sort of an offshoot of the I-have-a-feeling-I'm-being-watched sensation everybody gets where usually it's nothing, but the one time it isn't is the one we all remember. I've been right about that sensation hundreds of times, and not because I'm endowed with some special sort of psychic power; it's just that when you have millions of chances to choose from, you're bound to be right often enough to think there's something to it. It's one of those quirky human things that aren't much of a big deal if you're planning on a normal lifespan, but which become enormous after several thousand life spans. I have the same problem with *déjà vu*.

So while it was very likely that nobody in the vast, largely empty casino, was someone I'd seen before that evening, since I have sixty millennia of memories to pan through there was really no way to be sure. And once Ariadne put the idea of it in my head, it wouldn't leave.

I needed to get off the casino floor, and I needed to find Ariadne again. Ironically, inasmuch as I'd just insisted she go away.

"Hey," I said to Chester, "have you ever seen her before?"

"Not before tonight, no sir," he said.

I put a one hundred dollar chip on the bar.

"How about now?"

Chester smiled.

"She was cute, wasn't she?"

He thought I was looking for a date. A fine assumption.

"Honestly, if I'd seen her before I would have remembered it," he said. Chester swept up the chip anyway, and then took down Ariadne's glass.

"How about the drink?" I asked.

"Rum and Coke," he answered.

"But how'd she pay for it? Room charge?"

"Sorry. Cash."

I nodded. "Thanks. Guess I'll just have to hope I run into her again." I got up to leave, but Chester stopped me.

"There is this," he said, holding up a coin. "She gave it to me as a tip. Says it's worth twenty bucks. I think she was yanking my chain."

I took the coin from him. Larger than a quarter, but not much heavier, it was a dull gray and had the face of Athena on one side.

"It's a drachma. And it's not worth twenty bucks. Here's thirty for it. That's a better exchange than you'll get in a bank."

"Yeah, okay."

Chester looked confused, but was happy to take my money.

I covered my tab and slipped the drachma into my pocket, wondering if the mysterious Ms. Ariadne had expected me to question Chester, or if she always tipped in outdated coinage.

* * *

It took a few minutes longer than it should have to get back into the room, thanks to the electronic key card, which I'm adding to the long list of modern improvements I don't care for. I just can't get the hang of them. And by the time I do, the world will probably have moved on to something even more annoying. On the positive side, we seem to be getting closer to *open sesame* actually working, so I have that to look forward to.

The room was extremely unspectacular: a single bed, a small TV, a couple of bureaus, a tiny bathroom with a shower that was definitely for one, and a window that didn't overlook the strip. It was just the kind of room you got if you didn't want anyone to know you had access to a large amount of money.

I collapsed onto the bed in the dark.

This had not turned out to be anything like the getting-my-mind-off-things vacation I was expecting.

After Clara left, I spent a couple of days consoling my resident pixie, Iza—she was possibly more upset about it than I was—and talking to an ex-pat Russian named Tchekhy on the phone.

Tchekhy is not the best person in the world to go to for advice, unless you need advice on how to break the law without getting caught. He does my passports.

As one of the few living people aware of my unique nature, he was the only sentient being I could reach easily that also spoke in polysyllables. (Pixies are notoriously simple-minded.)

"You need to get off that island," he suggested wearily after what was the third or fourth day of hashing out my relationship problems.

"That may be a good idea. Where do you suggest I go?"

"I would recommend a place as opposite to where you are as possible."

"Europe?" Conveniently, the same place Clara went.

"No," he said quickly, clearly thinking along similar lines. "How about Las Vegas?"

In my mind, Vegas was a bright, shiny place with excitement and glamour and enough to do to keep me occupied for a good decade or two. And plenty of bars.

It had been about forty years since the last time I was in a casino (Vegas then too, in the sixties, when it was much sleazier) which was just long enough for me to forget the dirty secret—there may be no more depressing place on the planet than the floor of a casino. Although there was an outside chance I had simply forgotten how to have fun.

On top of that, there was Ariadne's warning, which only made me feel worse.

I needed to get the hell out of Vegas, but one of the cardinal rules when it came to disappearing was that you better know whom it is you are disappearing from first. And I had no clue how to resolve that.

As I lay on the bed and my eyes adjusted to the darkness, I realized there was something resting on the bureau that hadn't been there the last time I was in the room. I turned on the light.

Resting atop a silver room service tray was a bottle of red wine, a bottle of mineral water, and a small ceramic bowl. Leaning against the bowl was an envelope.

I took a look at the wine bottle first. According to the label, it was a dry red from Thessalia. Greek vintage.

It was about as subtle as the drachma.

The envelope contained a small place card, which I opened. A folded piece of paper dropped out. I picked it up and unfolded it, and nearly fell over at what I saw.

Something you need to understand about the Greeks—they liked their wine, and by that I mean they were willing to risk blindness, madness, or death in order to continue drinking it. If you think I drink a lot, that's only by modern standards. In Athens, I was modest.

The problem was the drink itself. It took many centuries for mankind to figure out how to make wine that wouldn't kill them. But since I was the only one who could wait that long, what the Greeks did was cut their version of wine with water. And then they threw parties that lasted for between two and five days in order to drink that wine. (Honestly, the word *moderation* wasn't invented until Christianity was.) It was the responsibility of the host to decide how much water to add to the wine, which was a big deal because it had to be weak enough so everyone could partake all night without dying, but strong enough so everyone got good and drunk.

That's what the water and the wine—and the bowl—were for. The piece of paper was something else.

Athenian drinking sometimes involved religious ceremonies, and in that case the wine and water had to be combined in a very specific way with some very specific chanting at very specific times. The note described one such ceremony, for the god Dionysos. The reason I almost fell over is that nobody had performed this ceremony in two and a half thousand years, and I was nearly positive I was the only one who could possibly still know about it.

In hindsight, I don't think there's any way to logically justify what I did next, but as I mixed the water and the wine in the bowl, held it up to my lips and began to drink, it made all the sense in the world.

Chapter Two

Sil.

Is it not true that a man who drinks steadily is a man who only thinks he is happy?

Dion.

It is so. But if a man thinks he is happy there need be no other expert. For whose opinion would he accept above his own?

—From the dialogues of Silenus the Younger.
Text corrected and translated by Ariadne

It may be my fault that anyone even knows about wine. Not that I invented it—I'm not nearly that clever—but I did tell an awful lot of people about it. (As an aside, I am probably not the best source when it comes to who invented what. For a long time, I thought I invented the wheel.) Wine was a good idea, and I like to share good ideas when I find them, because it means the product of those ideas are easier to find the next time I pass through town. Like cooked meat.

The Minoans *may* have invented wine, as I was on the island of Minos when I had my first taste. It wasn't particularly good by later standards. Grapes grew on Minos just fine and the concept of fermentation was fairly well understood, but Minoans were by nature an impatient bunch, and nobody there realized that the longer you aged wine, the better it tended to taste. And even with that gradual realization came the difficulty of putting it into a properly sealed

22

container. So it tasted like sour grape juice. Still, it packed a decent kick and showed real promise.

This was not, incidentally, my first introduction to alcohol. Beer showed up earlier. The Sumerians managed to pull that off which, if you have any idea what the Sumerians were like, you'd find it as amazing as I do. Their beer was awful, but beer it was. Later, the Egyptians picked up on it and did a fine job of perfecting the process. But Minos was a long way from Egypt, and I never quite got the hang of making beer, so I was grateful that somebody had come up with a new drink.

The man who handed me the wine—and who showed me how to make my own—was a slave named Argun. He belonged to the family of a person who today might be called a navy admiral, and whose name I've actually forgotten. Argun was a good guy. I never learned how he ended up a slave, but it probably came about as a result of one military conquest or another. (Back then the terms *slave* and *prisoner of war* were almost always interchangeable.) Had I been a landowner, I probably would have tried to make some wine myself right away, but I was a fisherman and the only thing I owned was my boat.

I was on Minos because it was one of the few places in the civilized world that supported a merchant class. (Another such place was— again— Egypt, but I'd been run out of there. Long story.) A culture with a merchant class was important because merchants got to come and go without any concern as to their larger status in society, since that was something determined based on familial connections. I had no connections that anybody would be prepared to recognize, so I was always on the lookout for cultures advanced enough to support trade and commerce.

Unfortunately, I never amounted to much more than a fisherman on Minos. Not because of any personal shortcomings, but because of the sudden death of the Minoan culture. This happened thanks to a very large volcanic eruption on the nearby island of Thera, and it ruined a lot of plans for a lot of people.

* * *

It's a little hard to grasp this from a modern perspective, but you have to understand that the ancient world was nearly deserted. By that I mean you could walk for weeks without coming across another member of your own species. On that same walk, you could also come across hundreds of other creatures, some of whom were quite large, a few rather fearsome, and one or two that tasted very good when cooked over an open fire. Likewise, except for the desert regions, the world was covered with plants such as trees, moss, and grasses as far as the eye could see, which wasn't very far as the trees were generally in the way.

So once I fled Minos in my little boat and landed on the shore of the southern Greek peninsula—it would be called Sparta a little while later—I couldn't just walk to the nearest village, or hook up with a passing tribe of hunter/gatherers. Statistically speaking, the odds of running into anybody who habitually walked upright were very small.

At that time in my life, community involvement of any sort was exceedingly rare, so I had no problem being on my own. If I came across a settled tribe while wandering, I might ingratiate myself, but not at the expense of hanging out with a culture I found unpleasant. I liked the Minoans, for example, and I enjoyed my time in Egypt. But the Sumerians, aside from their fantastic annual fertility rites, were a people I actively avoided—just like a dozen smaller tribes I have no name for, and who had nothing to offer me but trouble and very bad body odor.

My point is, on reaching safety and finding no welcoming party for me, I simply dragged my boat onto the beach, grabbed my few belongings, walked into the tree-line, and made do from there.

* * *

I think I must have spent over a century in the Greek woods (which, I probably don't need to point out, weren't called Greek anything at the time) living off the land and killing what I needed in order to keep going. Hunter, regardless of what you may have heard otherwise, is the oldest profession on earth, and it's something I still excel at, although my skills are rusty and rarely of use to me anymore.

My wanderings eventually took me as far as the foot of Mount Parnassus—or as the satyrs called it, Big Damn Hill—and it was only then that I encountered another human.

He had walked into one of the traps I'd set for game—a decidedly less arduous affair than open plains hunting, let me just say—and ended up hanging by his ankle from a tree, looking altogether unhappy about the state in which he'd found himself. That he'd been stuck that way for at least a half a day before I discovered him probably had something to do with his general discontent.

I came upon him in the early evening. From his upside-down perspective, I must have looked like a large upright monkey, or more likely a satyr, who also roamed certain parts of the wood. I'd done little to groom myself over the previous century, and I only cut my hair when it got long enough to impede my ability to run.

My saying hello didn't help, because the last language I'd spoken was Minoan, a precursor to the Mycenean tongue. He didn't speak either language, as his response clearly indicated.

"Do you want me to get you down?" I asked, trying to sound helpful. His reply was gibberish to my ears, but based on the delivery included a generous dollop of curse words.

"Okay. Calm down. And cover your head." I put my own hands over my head to give him an idea of what I meant, and then I untied the vine from the tree base.

He didn't cover his head, so his landing wasn't terribly graceful. However, he also wasn't too far from the ground in the first place, and he landed on soil rather than rock. (If he'd walked another thirty paces he would have been hanging from a different trap over a very large boulder). So his consternation was a bit over the edge, if you ask me.

He hopped to his feet and—gesticulating wildly—screamed in words I had no hope of grasping, although from the tone it was obvious he wasn't inviting me home for supper.

My new friend was shorter and broader than me. He wore a loose-fitting cloth that covered his chest and nether region (except for when he was hanging upside-down) cinched around his waist with a rope belt. On his feet were sandals, and that, more than anything else, suggested he hailed from someplace civilized. Contrastingly, I was almost naked and covered with nettles, and I'd given up on my sandals almost as soon as I lost sight of the shoreline. What clothes I did have were crafted from the pelt of a wolf, and I'd worn them for so long they probably looked like they were a part of my own body.

I stood still and let him yell at me. As the first human I'd seen in a very long while, I was anxious to find out where he came from and what he was doing in the woods below Parnassus.

When he paused to take a breath, I said to him, "Hello. What is your name?"

He tilted his head, almost surprised that I had the gift of speech. Possibly he thought the words I'd said earlier were just random noises, and only now was he realizing I knew an actual language. Then he made a noise that sounded something like *boogada-boogada!* and took two forceful steps toward me. He was attempting to scare me off. Instead of scampering away, I took two steps towards him, and that just about did it. He bolted.

"Wait!" I shouted. But of course that might as well have been *Die!* for all he knew, and he kept on running.

Alone again, I realized how very much I missed being able to sit down opposite another human and compare experiences.

Long periods of isolation from the tribe of Man always got me feeling this way eventually, to the extent that even the most mundane of long-ago conversations began to take on a certain romantic quality in hindsight. And when you're looking back longingly at a centuries-old discussion on the subject of who farted, it's time to go find someone to talk to.

So I tracked him back to his home, a lone settlement halfway around the mountain. Careful observation over the next few days led me to conclude he was a gardener, and—remarkably—he lived alone, which was nearly unheard of. (Man is a social animal by nature, largely because the ones who like to live alone tend to get eaten. Or they used to. Now the loners just spend a lot of time on the Internet, or on remote islands with depressed pixies.)

Employing the sort of tact people back then always responded well to, I hunted and killed a wild boar and left it on his stoop late one night. Once he was done eating It—which took several days—I left him another one. When it was time to leave him a third boar, rather than run off, I sat there and waited for him to find it. This didn't take long, as by that time he'd decided the only way to ascertain which god was being so generous to him was to stay awake and see who showed up.

His response was a bit more measured than in our last encounter. He offered the gift of a bowl of fruit and vegetables from his garden, which was a nice gesture. I mean, it wasn't a boar or anything, but it was nice.

Soon enough, he was building a fire for the boar, and we were eating the fruits of our combined labors and getting to know one another.

* * *

If there's one thing I have to be thankful for, it's that eventually people stopped coming up with new languages. It may seem like a great thing to be fluent in basically every language in the Western world, but I had to actually *learn* them, one at a time. (I also know some Far East tongues, but not as many, as I spent less time there.) Taking the time to learn each new language can be a real pain, and it's even worse without someone willing to teach me. Egyptian took forever, for example, because I ended up in the Nile delta as a slave rather than a traveler, and few slave owners are interested in teaching a slave more words than it takes to communicate tasks.

It took about four months to fully master the language of my new friend, whose name was Karyos. It would have taken longer, but his tongue shared a common root with the language of the Minoans, and so while many of the descriptive words were distinctive, the structure and verb forms were very similar. Plus, we're not talking about a huge vocabulary here.

By the year's end, we were comparing horticultural secrets and regaling one another with tales of past glory.

Karyos came from a tribe of horsemen, a fact that I found amazing as I had never seen a tamed horse, nor was I entirely certain what a horse was. His people had journeyed a vast (by the standards of the time) distance over a long span of time, starting—based on his rough description—in a region somewhere near the Caspian Sea.

As a member of a warrior tribe—there wasn't really any other kind— Karyos had fought in dozens of skirmishes before deciding he had enough.

But rather than settle down with a woman and cope with the possibility of more battles (I can't call a fight between fewer than fifty men a war) he took what little farming knowledge he had and exiled himself from the rest of his people. And that's how he ended up on the side of the mountain, happily alone and leaving the fighting to the young men.

He made for a good companion, not at all minding extended silences and happy just to figure out how to grow things that tasted good. Even when I took up residence in his little home, we often went days without speaking. Other than among the wild animals, we were unnoticed by the outside world. For a little while.

* * *

One afternoon while wandering through the woods a good half-day's distance from home, I came upon an extraordinary discovery: a grapevine. Remembering well the beneficial aspects of alcoholic beverages—and being about a hundred years overdue for one—I yanked the vine at the root and ran back to the farm.

"What is that?" Karyos asked, seeing me tumble into the clearing holding up the vine as if it had been handed to me directly by a god.

"This," I said triumphantly, "is the beginning of a remarkable thing. Do you know how to craft a pot from clay?"

"What need have I for a new pot?"

"We will need several. You will understand later. First we must plant this."

It took a little over a year to turn the one grapevine into multiple fruit-bearing plants, and by that time we'd fashioned a dozen small clay pots along with a method to seal them with beeswax.

After following the winemaking procedure laid down by the slave Argus of Minos as well as I could remember, we filled the pots, sealed them, and stored them in the corner of the building where they would hopefully remain cool and dry.

Then we waited.

By that time, Karyos was looking and acting quite old. From my perspective it was sudden, like he'd gone grey overnight. This used to happen to me all the time in the days before calendars and watches. It's a little like those time-lapse photography films of a flower reaching full bloom in seconds.

Politely, Karyos hadn't asked why it was that I still looked as hale as when we'd met. One evening, he pointed to our jars. "For which god do we make this concoction?"

The question took me by surprise; Karyos spent very little time worshipping any of his gods, or even mentioning them. I shook my head.

"None. We make it to fill our own bellies. It is a drink of celebration."

"I see," he mused. We were in the hut, in the dark, in our own separate corners of the room. "And what is it we are celebrating?"

"Friendship?" I suggested. "Life? What would you like to celebrate?"

He sat still on his mat and considered it. "Yes," he agreed at length. "I will celebrate life. Fitting to do so as my circle comes to close."

"You have much left in you still, Karyos."

The laugh that followed devolved quickly into a harsh cough I somehow never managed to notice before.

"Perhaps that appears so to one fixed as the stars," he said, once the cough subsided. "No, my very old and very young friend, I am rounding the final curve. But first, I look forward to my drink."

* * *

I should point out that just like everything else, philosophy was something that had to evolve over time, and in Karyos's day nobody in this part of the world—with the possible exception of the Egyptians— was talking about heaven and hell and being good in this life in order to reap the rewards in the next one. And while there may have been gods, they weren't particularly well defined. If, for instance, something unusually lucky happened, one might declare that a god—pick one— was feeling generous that day. And if a particularly bad thing happened, a god (usually a different one) was upset about something or other. Gods, in other words, were what most of us would now call chance or luck. And in that sense they served their purpose, by making a random existence seem less random.

Having not yet come up with a concept to explain where one might go after death, Karyos's people adopted an ingenious, if somewhat perplexing attitude that life was a circle. Not like Disney's circle of life thing, which was really just a nice way to say, "death is normal, children, so suck it up."

The belief was, when I die, I will come back around to the beginning of this life and go through it again. They didn't mean reincarnation, but literally reliving the same life from beginning to end in the same historical period. From a modern perspective this might sound incredibly silly, but consider the alternative of ceasing to exist entirely when you die. Nobody—including me—wanted to think about that, so outrageous alternatives were needed. And really, finding a better explanation than the cessation of existence is the basis for every religion.

I didn't care for the whole circle idea personally, which is not to say I had anything better to work with. I was—and am—a man of my age, whatever age that happens to be. I can't pretend I had any better ideas, in other words. But I did think it was pretty stupid, and said so a couple of times when I was sure such a declaration wouldn't get me killed.

* * *

When one year from the day in which the jars were sealed had passed (we marked time by counting moons) I carefully unsealed one jar, prepared two bowls for Karyos and myself, and we sat by the fire and drank.

"What do you think?"

"It is ... bitter," he said.

I puckered my lips. "Yes. I may have to work on that."

"But it fills my belly with a burn. It is pleasant."

I raised the bowl towards him. "Have more. It will make you feel young again."

A few hours later, we were both outrageously, stupidly drunk. I got to learn a fair sampling of songs that either came from Karyos's own culture or he made up on the spot. At the time it didn't really matter. I, in turn, taught him a dance I learned from a pre-Akkadian tribe that was quite remarkable when performed by a nubile moon priestess, but looked downright silly when done by a countrified old man. It was still fun.

The next day we paid dearly for it.

31

"Am I dying?" Karyos asked meekly as I tried to help him out of the hut before he stunk it up any further with his own vomit.

I wasn't doing all too well myself.

"No. We just need water, and rest."

"I feel hot and cold at once, which seems not at all possible," he groaned. "My insides wish to come out and my eyes are ready to burst forth from my skull. Are you certain this is not death?"

"I am."

Karyos grimaced. "That is a shame. I would very much welcome death right now."

"Forgive me. I had forgotten how important moderation was with this drink."

"I trust you will not forget again."

Karyos then fell to his knees at the edge of our camp and vomited into the brush.

* * *

Subsequent excursions into the clay jars proved somewhat less painful, and soon Karyos was as enthusiastic as I was about cultivating our little vineyard. He even considered taking a jug of it to the people he'd spurned so long ago, marking the first time he mentioned them aloud in at least a decade. So I knew I'd gained a convert.

I was off on one of my little walkabouts when things quite suddenly went horribly wrong.

Walkabout is a word I was only just recently introduced to, by Clara. I used to take nature walks over various parts of the island, and sometimes these walks took a few days despite the fact that the island isn't really all that big. When she asked about it, I explained that it helps me sometimes to reacquaint myself with nature whenever I'm fortunate to be near some. (Not so easy anymore.) She said, *oh, like a walkabout*. Which I thought was a sandwich. It turns out this is a big thing in Australia—one of the few places I've never been.

Anyway, I'd left Karyos alone to tend to things and wandered off, promising to bring back meat if I found any.

I returned to camp five days later, in the early morning. By the light of the gradually dawning sun, I noticed a few things wrong. Most apparent was the fire. We almost never kept the fire pit smoldering for the entire evening. At worst, it should have been embers, but no; it was fully aflame. Second, there were a half-dozen large animals milling around at the edge of the clearing, eating my grapes and otherwise making themselves general nuisances in the garden.

Horses, I realized. Tame ones.

We had guests.

I stepped out of the brush and walked over to the open flame, and as my eyes adjusted to the light, I saw five men lying about beside the fire. They weren't asleep and they weren't dead, but they were also not altogether in control of themselves. I could hear groans and the occasional light coughing; they were suffering from the after-effects of our wine.

Four of the clay jars Karyos and I had painstakingly crafted lay shattered on the ground beside the fire.

"What goes on here?" I boomed. A couple of the men moaned, but that was all I got by way of response.

Based on the clothing—chitons, leather belts, boots—they were members of the same tribe Karyos hailed from. Each had a crude iron sword at his side, which I seriously doubted any of them were in any condition to wield.

"I say, what goes on here?" I repeated, louder.

A sixth man stumbled from the hut. Standing, I could see he shared ancestral roots with my friend as well, being similarly squat and sturdy.

"Who are you?" he growled.

"I live here with my friend Karyos," I replied angrily. "Who are you?"

He spat on the ground and staggered toward the fire. I realized with growing horror that the sword in his hand was dripping with blood. "The bastard mountain man poisoned us all!" he roared. "Look at us! We are dying!"

"What did you do to him, stranger?"

"I repaid him his treachery while still I had the strength," the man snapped angrily. "And if he was friend to you, then you will share his fate." He stumbled forward, sword raised, clearly still very drunk.

I was quite furious. I leaned over and took the sword of the nearest prone man and met the charging warrior's clumsy assault with an overhand parry and a swift kick in the balls.

"Fool," I spat as he fell to his knees. "You met an old man's hospitality with treachery."

"He poisoned us!" he declared again.

"You'd have been better by midday. Did he not drink with you?"

He tried climbing to his feet.

"He did."

"Then what poison do you suppose he could have used, that would not have felled him as well?"

He had no answer for this and I was in no particular mood to wait for him to think of one. I cleaved his head from his shoulders.

I stormed into the hut to see for myself the fate of my friend. True to his word, the barbarian had slain Karyos rather effectively; he'd been chopped up so thoroughly I hardly recognized him.

I ... did not react well to this.

I have had my moments of poor anger management through history, and this was maybe one of those times when I should have taken a few breaths and counted to ten or something. Instead, I went back outside and killed each of the five prone men one at a time, slowly and with more relish than I should admit to.

By the time I was done, I was covered in blood and not feeling much better about things. I considered moving on to the horses, but they took one look at me and ran off on their own. My first opportunity to learn how to ride a horse would have to wait.

I buried what remained of Karyos in an unmarked grave at the edge of the campsite where, for all I know, he still lies. (The soldiers I left for the wolves.) It was an inadequate memorial, but we didn't have headstones then, because unless you're talking about merchant accounting, we barely had a written language.

What we had was oral history, which was why, for centuries afterwards, I shared the story of Karyos's death with everyone who got my wine recipe.

Chapter Three

"Better the stranger with wits than a witless friend."

—From the archives of Silenus the Elder.
Text corrected and translated by Ariadne

A long life and a good memory sometimes just means any creature comfort you want to name has a maudlin story to go with it. It's gotten so I can hardly enjoy anything anymore. And I can still hear Karyos's voice recommending moderation whenever I have a hangover.

It took only an hour to polish off the Greek wine-and-water combo that Ariadne—I was assuming it was her—was good enough to set me up with, and when I was done I called room service and got some more. The next thing I knew, two days had passed and I hadn't left my room except to put my empties down in the hallway. Management had to send someone up to make sure I wasn't suicidal, and also to point out that the cash deposit I'd put down on the room was no longer adequate to cover my stay. So I threw the guy another grand and sent him off.

Eventually, I passed out.

* * *

"Good to see you're still alive," said a man at the foot of the bed. It was late at night and I'd been asleep for either two hours or twenty-six, and

I was banking on the latter. The room was pitch black, the shades drawn and the lights switched off. I couldn't recall if I'd left it like that.

I looked toward the sound of the voice, but I had no hope of seeing who had spoken. Maybe I was imagining things.

I rolled into a sitting position. "I hope you're right. If not, the afterlife has hangovers."

"There's a bottle of water on the table to your right," my visitor helpfully informed me. He had a low, gruff, but non-threatening voice that sounded not at all familiar. As dark as it was, I couldn't tell whether he had a gun on me or not, so I assumed he did. If you ever find yourself in this situation, you should absolutely assume a gun is involved.

"Thanks."

I reached out in that direction until I came upon the bottle.

"How long have you been sitting there?" I knew he was sitting because of the direction of his voice. A standing midget seemed like a bad bet.

"I dunno. A few hours."

I uncapped the water and took a deep swig.

"Guess you're not here to kill me or rob me."

"What makes you say that?"

"I'd be dead already. Unless you're looking for a fight." That would, incidentally, be incredibly stupid. I may not look like much, but you don't want to deal with me in hand-to-hand. Just trust me; you pick up a lot of things when you live this long.

"Maybe I need you to tell me where the money is."

"It's under the bed."

"Okay."

A match flame erupted from his corner of the room, which ruined what meager night vision I had been working on. He lit a cigarette.

"How much do you have?"

Well this was just silly. I put the water down and threw on the light switch next to the bed.

"Don't really know," I admitted, in regards to the money. I blinked my vision clear.

My visitor was a man of medium height and medium build, who had long, curly black hair that ran down the back of his neck and a scruffy, unshaven face with a prominent chin and a pug nose. Not what I'd call handsome. He had on black jeans and a deep blue collared shirt that was unbuttoned at the neck, with black combat boots. A tweed sports jacket was draped over the chair and I was guessing there was a tie he was supposed to be wearing in the pocket of it. Oh, and he did have a gun, but it was in a shoulder holster.

I'd been holding out hope that he was just an over- enthusiastic employee taking the presumptive suicide watch on me a bit too seriously, but he didn't look like someone who worked for a hotel; he looked like an undercover cop from a seventies TV series.

"Is that better?"

"A little," I said, still squinting. "Can I have one of those?"

"Sure." He tossed me the pack and the book of matches.

"Thanks."

I lit up.

I'm not a big smoker. Not sure why, since cancer has never been an issue for me. I think it's how it makes my lungs feel. Granted, the odds of my needing to employ any long-distance running skills in this day and age are pretty slim, but still.

"How'd you get in here?" I asked.

"Let myself in."

"I gathered that. I'm ..." I struggled for a minute to remember which name I should be giving him. I know I said I practice that sort of thing, but I'm not generally pressed to come up with it before a shower. "Jason. Jason Stargill."

"Mike Lycos."

He stepped across the room to offer his hand, which I took. Big hands, hairy knuckles. I could have probably done something about the gun once he strayed close enough to touch, but I held back. Might have been because he hadn't actually threatened me yet.

"So who do you work for, Mike?"

"Oh, I didn't say?" He pulled out a wallet from his pants and held up an identification card. "I'm FBI."

"Can I see that?"

He handed it to me. It looked legit, but since it was only the second one I'd ever seen, I couldn't be sure. The picture matched, except in the photo he was wearing a suit.

I gave it back to him and returned to my water. "What does the FBI want with me?"

"We're not sure yet," he admitted. He returned to the chair, reached down under it, and pulled out a file folder. "Let's start with this."

He stepped over and handed it to me.

"Does this person look familiar?" he asked.

Inside was a collection of photographs, the very first of which was a woman I did indeed know.

"She introduced herself as Ariadne ... terrible photo."

"It's from her ID badge. Her government badge."

"She works for you guys?"

He didn't answer. I continued through the photographs and found various action shots of her, including one taken when she leaned in to whisper in my ear.

"You look good in profile," he said. "That's definitely your best side there."

"So who were you following that night? Me or her?"

I didn't get an answer for that either. He took back the portfolio.

"Her name is Ariadne Papos. Up until about six months ago she was a systems analyst for the Bureau."

"Was?"

"She walked off the job." He dropped his cigarette butt into the bowl I'd been drinking from not so long ago.

"Uh-huh," I said, rubbing my eyes and trying to figure out just where the hell this was going. "And systems analyst means what exactly?"

He smiled. "It doesn't mean anything, Jason. That's the point. If we called her a homeland security information gatherer, that would just be awkward."

"*Spy* is pretty succinct."

"It is. But it's not accurate. Ms. Papos wasn't a field operative. She was just, well, a systems analyst, like I said. Besides, we're the FBI. You're thinking of a different agency."

"Right." I got up and disposed of my own cigarette. "Well this has been fun. Now I think I need a shower, maybe a shave. It was nice talking to you."

"You never met her before?" he asked.

"Not before that night, no. Now unless you want to tell me why the FBI is so interested in the movements of a retired analyst that breaking and entering is considered a viable option, I think we're done. Don't you?"

"What if I told you the last file she accessed from her workstation was yours, Adam?"

That caught me a little short.

"My name is Jason."

"Sure, right now. You've had a whole bevy of names, haven't you?"

Hard to argue with anybody willing to use *bevy* in a sentence.

"What do you mean, 'my file'?"

We were standing nose-to-nose now, or more precisely, my nose to his forehead. He wasn't all that tall.

"Just what I said. Now you can blow me off if you want, but I'll have to keep following until I've found out everything I need to know."

I looked down at him. "What makes you think I can't shake you?"

He just grinned. "C'mon. We can compare dick size all night."

"Yeah, all right."

I was beginning to like Mike, which is a difficult thing to admit, given he was armed and had camped out in my bedroom for goodness knows how many hours. Not to mention the fact he'd been following me before that. But he didn't remind me of the Romans like most lawmen nowadays do, and I appreciated that.

I didn't much care for the Romans, if you hadn't guessed. And I *was* one.

I paced around to stretch my legs and tried to remind my muscles how to work properly just in case this assessment of Mike was suddenly proven very wrong. "So tell me about my supposed file."

"What do you want to know?"

"How about what am I doing with a file in the first place?"

"Are you kidding? Your kind of money doesn't just spring up out of nowhere. Attention-wise, you're a very popular man."

"That makes me feel a whole lot better."

"It's not supposed to. Let me explain how the world works nowadays. Thanks to 9/11, there are whole sections of the U.S. government that do nothing but follow money. And there is a lot to follow. If you've got more than $500,000 in your account somebody somewhere has a file on you."

That made some sense. And I should have thought of it myself.

"Okay, so, it's not a big deal, this file?"

"Oh no, it's a very big deal. Especially now."

Mike was giving me a headache on top of my hangover. "Why now?" I asked, rubbing my temple.

"Ariadne," he stated, as if this had some special meaning. "Once she walked off her job, I was called in to figure out exactly what she'd been up to before she decided to disappear. Based on what we were able to reconstruct from her home hard drive, she's associated with an organization we believe has terrorist intentions."

"Guess you don't vet your employees all that well."

I walked over to the sink, which was actually outside of the bathroom, and splashed some water onto my face. The guy in the mirror looked like hell.

"Yeah, someone dropped the ball on that one. Anyway, near as we can tell, she's trying to contact you."

"She already did," I pointed out, using the hand towel to dry my face.

"But she didn't say anything. Right?"

"No, but she did send some wine up."

"Some of the guys think that was a signal. What do you think?"

I dropped the towel on the counter and sat back down on the bed. "I think she wanted me to have a bottle of wine. Why's she trying to contact me?"

"That's what we'd like to know. Based on what I've seen, she appears to have developed a profound interest in you. The running theory in the Bureau is that she wants to approach you for financing, which makes some sense."

"Because I'm rich?" I offered.

"Aren't you?"

"The hotel is full of rich people. Why me?"

"That's the question, isn't it?"

"Not exactly an answer there, Mike."

"Yeah, well I don't know the answer. Hence the problem. You traveled here on cash?"

"I did."

"And what was your thinking there? It's harder to get things done without plastic. You must know that."

"Maybe I didn't want any government agency sticking its nose into my business by tracking my credit card activity."

He grinned. "Yeah. Saw that in a movie, did you? Look, you've got about $87,000 in that suitcase under the bed."

"I thought you didn't know where the money was hidden."

He shrugged. "I lied. And I had some time to kill while waiting for you to wake up. Let me explain how folks in my line of work think. There are only three types of people who travel with that much cash specifically because they think it can't be tracked: crooks, tax evaders, and terrorists or financiers of terrorist activities."

"Gamblers?" I offered.

"Card-counters, maybe. You count cards?"

I shook my head. "How about people who just like looking at big piles of money?"

"Statistically, very unlikely," he said. "Right now, the house money is on terrorism. And you meeting up with Ariadne Papos just about sealed it."

"So supposedly I'm already financing her, is that what you're saying?"

"That's what the thinking is. Not that it makes a ton of sense. She knows you're under surveillance, or she should, so the way you two made contact doesn't fit. Too clumsy. But nobody seems to be listening when I point that out."

Now I was pacing. It's a little tough discovering exactly how transparent your activities have been when you spend so much time trying to prevent exactly that.

"I'm confused. Are FBI agents in the practice of waking up suspected terrorists in their hotel rooms and telling them they think they're a terrorist?"

"Habitually no, not unless there's torture involved, and again, that's usually not in our charter. We have the CIA for that."

"That's a joke, right?"

"Sort of. I'm not here in an entirely official capacity."

"You want to translate that for me?"

"They don't know we're talking," he clarified.

"That's fantastic."

Mike lit another cigarette, and continued. "We've had someone on you since you left the Queen Charlottes. The idea was to monitor your activities and see who you contacted, that sort of thing. None of which I was a part of. Ariadne is my problem. But when she turned up next to you on a barstool, the cases dovetailed. Since they think you're the bigger fish, their investigation ate mine and I ended up part of a team. I'm not fond of teams."

"You picked a funny profession then."

"I guess. But every pack can tolerate one or two lone wolves."

With all the talk of wolves, fish, and investigations being eaten, I suddenly realized how hungry I was.

"Anyway," he said, "I am of the minority opinion that Ariadne is the one we should be worrying about, not you. So rather than bang my head against a wall, I handed over my case files and took a vacation. They think I'm in Maui."

"Maybe you should be. It's nice there."

I picked up the phone to order some food.

"I'm more of a hiker type. Who are you calling?"

"Room service. I'm starved."

"Please don't."

"Why not?" I asked, half-expecting him to put his hand on his gun.

"Because the guy who delivers it will be an agent. Probably Ralph, unless his shift is over. And it'll be Linda who takes the order."

"No shit?"

"I told you; you're under constant surveillance."

"How long has this been going on?"

"Since you got into town, except for maybe a few hours there when you switched hotels. Right now they're trying to figure out how come none of the bugs they planted in here work anymore."

"You removed them?"

"Yeah, while you were asleep."

"I suppose there's a camera in the hallway too?"

Mike blew out a puff of smoke. "There's always a camera in the hallway. They just jacked into hotel surveillance. Cheaper. And good news for us; casinos can't put cameras in the rooms."

"Okay. So how'd you get in here without being seen?"

"Balcony."

I stared at him for a long time because that was just about impossible. The room did have a small balcony, but it was separated from the balcony for the next room by about fifteen feet of air, and from the ground by three stories. Hard to believe he made either jump.

"You seem to have gone through a whole lot of trouble just to find out I don't know anything about Ariadne Papos."

He smiled. "I already knew that."

I fell back onto the bed and surrendered to the notion that none of this was going to be making any sense anytime soon.

"You risked your job to enter the room of a guy who your bosses think is a terrorist to ask him a question you already knew the answer to? Tell you what; how about I go back to sleep, you jump out the window, and we'll pretend this never happened, okay?"

"I think we can help each other," he said.

"Really? What sort of help did you have in mind?"

"I'm guessing you don't much care to be under a government eyeball. I know the protocols; I can help you disappear."

"I can disappear on my own just fine."

"Bet that's what you thought when you left the island with all that cash," he said, flicking his cigarette and letting the ashes fall on the floor.

He had a point. "What can I do for you?"

"Ariadne is interested in you, so I am too. I think you can help me find her."

This had to be one of the more preposterous conversations I'd had in my very, very long life. Mike was either completely lying to me, or he was keeping significant portions of the story to himself, and I wasn't sure which. All I knew for certain was that the man standing in my bedroom was willing to risk a great deal to find a woman I'd spent all of two minutes with. I mean okay, she was pretty, but really. It just didn't add up.

I got up from the bed. "I'm going to take a shower. Then I'm going to order some room service and have a nice, big meal. After that, I'm going to check myself out of this hotel and go on a long vacation somewhere. You can do whatever you want."

He stood up as well. "I think you're underestimating the persistence of a coordinated FBI surveillance team."

"And I think they're underestimating me ... as are you."

"Maybe so. You're still making a mistake."

He tilted his head at me in a way not dissimilar to that of a dog who thinks he might have heard his master's voice but isn't entirely sure. "What *did* Ariadne say to you? Aside from her name."

"She told me I was being followed."

"Why do you think she warned you?"

"I don't know. Why did you?"

"To gain your confidence."

"There you go."

I offered him my hand, which he took.

"It's been weird," I said. "Call ahead next time."

"Can't guarantee that." He smiled. He obviously thought there was going to be a next time.

"Guess not. I take it you can show yourself out?"

He glanced over to the balcony. "Sure. Not a problem."

* * *

In the shower, I reflected on the foolishness of what I'd just done, meaning specifically that I had left an armed man in my hotel room with

47

a large supply of cash while I stood naked with nothing to protect me other than a flimsy—and certainly not bullet-proof—shower curtain. Either this meant that something about Mike made me want to trust him, or my low blood-sugar level was affecting my judgment.

Anyway, it was a pretty quick shower. And when I emerged from the bathroom, I found Mike had indeed let himself out. My money was exactly where it was supposed to be. And on the bed was a small pile of silver disks; he'd left the electronic bugs.

The balcony door was open. I stuck my head outside and looked around, but there was nothing to see except a parking lot.

Of course he couldn't have actually left that way. It wasn't possible.

Chapter Four

Dion.

Truly, I have had many things. But possessions only bring happiness if employed correctly. To have is not a reason unto itself.

—From the dialogues of Silenus the Younger.
Text corrected and translated by Ariadne

The funny thing about knowing you're being followed because someone thinks you're suspicious, is that once you know that, you really can't help but act suspicious.

I spent the next few days taking little trips out of the hotel, and since I hadn't been doing that before, it had to have gotten some attention. Likewise, my tendency to break into an occasional sprint probably raised a few eyebrows.

I know a little bit about surveillance. In the mid-seventeen hundreds, a French duke hired me to find out which of his friends was plotting to kill him. Since he was a high functioning paranoid with a lot of friends and an impressive imagination, this took a long time and plenty of extra staff, and was helped along by the fact that none of his friends were actually plotting anything against him. I think I could have held the position for a few decades had he not been poisoned by his own wife. We never checked her. I almost feel bad about this.

Anyway, I left the casino because then the people following my movements couldn't use casino cameras and had to actually walk around with me, and that made my prior experience mildly useful.

With a little effort, I was able to identify between three and four agents rotating on me. I could shake three or four people if this were still the mid-seventeen hundreds. It wasn't, so I couldn't be positive I was accounting for everything.

Fortunately, I know a better class of criminal than myself.

* * *

"Please say that again," Tchekhy said.

The discontent in his voice was palpable. I could have opened with telling him I was on a prepaid cell phone I just bought and was standing outside the casino, before telling him about the whole government-watching-everything-I-do thing, but I wanted to make him a little nervous because it was his own fault I was in Las Vegas in the first place. An immortal man who hates official attention shouldn't be anywhere near this many private surveillance cameras, FBI or no. I expected better from him.

For the record, I have nothing against governments as such. If countries are a logical progression from tribes, government is the tribal council, and I get that. The problem is that while it was much harder to insinuate myself into a tribe—which I had to do quite a lot—once I was in, I was in. Governments tend to require proof of who you are on a regular basis, and they don't really like it when your reason for not having proof is that you're older than their country.

I can get away with a lot, thanks to Tchekhy's exceptional forgery skills, but I haven't invested in the kind of detailed identities that could survive extensive scrutiny. And since governments tend to institutionalize paranoia (this happens with every government once it gets large enough) it wouldn't take much to get me locked up.

"The FBI thinks I'm a person of interest," I explained. "And now I've got a surveillance team on me. I could use some advice. I'm using a cell phone I just bought, by the way, so don't hang up."

"And are you ..."

"I'm on the strip watching one of my tails have an animated argument with his own ear. It's sort of funny. But I think they've already replaced the bugs in my room, and I'm afraid if I go to sleep tonight I'll wake up with one of those trackers they put on wildlife to follow migratory patterns attached to me."

"This is a valid concern."

"Is it really?" I asked, surprised. I was kidding.

"Microdot technology, yes. Probably not legal yet."

Somehow, any long conversation with Tchekhy ends with me being more terrified than when I started.

"You will need to blow up their surveillance entirely for at least one hour to allow time for the trail to disappear. As soon as you have a window, you must put as much distance between yourself and Las Vegas as possible. Do you have a car?"

"I don't. And buying one won't work, will it?"

"No. And a taxi means a driver. You would have to kill the driver."

"Yeah, I'm not going to do that." I would love to tell you I didn't consider taking this suggestion seriously.

"No. Likewise airplanes leave trails."

Standing on the corner, I was still scoping the people on the strip, passively looking for anyone showing interest in me. I saw Mike. He was in a coffee shop, pretending not to look my way.

"Let's say I've got that covered," I said. "Tell me how to open that window."

* * *

"Good coffee," I said, taking a seat at a table adjacent to Mike, who was attempting to disappear into his newspaper. It was a few minutes after I'd gotten off the phone, and Mike had no doubt spent those few minutes muttering, *Don't come in here, don't come in here* under his breath as I walked over.

"Don't talk to me," he muttered, snapping his newspaper. "Get out of here before they put us together."

"Maybe you had too much," I said cheerily. "It makes you jittery." This caused Mike to stand, or attempt to, until I put my hand on his wrist. "That will draw even more attention to you. Stay behind the paper."

Urgently, he growled, "I can't help you if I'm locked up."

I had positioned myself so that I could look straight out onto the street. None of the people who could have made our conversation extra awkward were in the shop.

"What do you want?" Mike asked.

"Well, I was thinking the best way to get you to stop following me was to prove you aren't in Maui. What do you think?"

Mike glared over the paper. I wasn't looking right at him, but it felt like a pretty violent stare.

"I'm kidding. I want your help. But you do need to relax."

"I'm pretty damn far from relaxed here."

"Look, they have a four-man team on rotation, I've made all of them, and the one with eyes on me right now is busy looking through the trashcan across the street. With the sun glare off the window, he can see me, but not you. Although I might be wrong about that last part, so keep the paper up."

"Why is he looking through the trash?"

"I tossed a prepaid cell phone in there a minute ago," I said, taking a quick sip of coffee. "I think he thinks I made an important call on it."

"Did you? They'll trace the call."

"Not on that phone. I bought two."

The paper crumpled, which may have signified either surprise or consternation. "I would hate running surveillance on you, wouldn't I?"

"I actually know what I'm doing when I'm sober."

I leaned over to pretend to tie my shoe. This put me just below his table. The coffee shop was agent-free, but it was also busy, and I didn't care to have a lot of people hearing us.

"I'm going to make some time alone for myself this evening. Do you have a car?"

"Yeah. Nice one. You can't borrow it."

"I'm a lousy driver anyway. Wait for me around the corner from here, and be ready to drive extremely fast."

"I can do that," he said. "How're you planning to get to me without an entourage?"

I sat up, because there's only so many times one can tie one's shoes before someone asks if you're not feeling well.

Glancing across the street, I saw the lead tail had found the phone and was talking to his ear again. He was looking my way. In another few seconds, the person on the other end of his earphone would be telling him to check on me from inside the shop. Incidentally, when I did this sort of thing, we had to rely on line-of-sight and hand-signals. Kids these days.

"Give me an idea, at least," Mike said.

I stood up and edged away from the window seat, right past Mike's chair.

"I think I might start a riot."

On my way out of the shop, I got to hold open the door for my FBI tail. I smiled and wished him a nice day, and he did the same for me. It's the little things.

* * *

When I reached the casino floor that night, I was extremely un-comfortable. For starters, it was a Saturday night, so it was the absolute worst place to be if one still wasn't entirely comfortable with crowds. That it was also full of attractive women practically bursting out of their evening gowns mitigated this complaint, but only slightly. I did make a point to check out many of them, and told myself it was because one might be Ariadne.

Also, I itched. I wouldn't be returning to the room unless something unfortunate happened, and there was the matter of all the cash I had in the suitcase under the bed, which I needed to keep some of in order to travel.

To that end, Mike had a marvelous point, as plastic was really the way to go. In the future, I expected I would have to accustom myself to the concept. But for now, all of that money was on my person, stuffed into two money belts and duct taped to my torso. (I did the tape in my room, which was a tremendous pain since I knew people were listening. To cover some of the noise, I turned the TV on and found a movie with lots of explosions in it. Fortunately, that defines nearly every movie nowadays.) A T-shirt went on over the money and then, in order to disguise the added bulk—I didn't know how observant the FBI was, but I had to think someone would notice if I'd suddenly gained twenty pounds—I was wearing an exceptionally large, baggy, and loud Hawaiian shirt. This also made me much easier to spot in the crowd, which was actually the idea.

My shoes were another problem. They were brand-new to go along with the new black slacks I was wearing. I hate breaking in shoes, but I always thought shoes were a stupid invention anyway. If I could go barefoot everywhere, I probably would.

All the new clothing was partly because Tchekhy had convinced himself the FBI was using trackers in my clothes. Given the way they tag-teamed me when I left the casino earlier, I thought this unlikely, but I wasn't going to argue with him. Besides, I needed to look as much like a member of security as possible from the waist down, and new clothes were the best way to approximate that.

Itching all the way, I found a seat at a bar near the blackjack tables and took my time looking over the room.

The unfortunate consequence of picking a busy casino floor for this was how difficult it made spotting my fan club. Mike told me they were jacked into the surveillance feed which was fine if that was all I had to worry about, but given my excursion earlier in the day, I was pretty positive they had at least a couple of agents on the floor in case I ran for the exit. They would be stupid not to.

After an hour, I had identified ten possible agents, and about thirty women I would have dropped the entire escape attempt for if they agreed to come back to my room. I wasn't sure whether to blame the alcohol or Clara for this.

What sobered me a little was the notion that all ten of the possibles were agents. If I really warranted that much manpower, Mike had underplayed the degree of danger I was in significantly.

At a table about fifty feet away, a man in a blue blazer removed his jacket, placed it on the back of his chair, and sat down. The jacket wasn't quite right, but it would do for the few seconds I needed it. I put down my drink and started heading his way.

* * *

I am incredibly indifferent about money. I know that as a person who has a tremendous amount of it, I can afford to be indifferent—and really, most of the people I've met who claim not to care about money already have more than they could ever need—but I have been poor many, many different times and really don't have a problem with it.

What I think people forget is that money isn't a real thing. It has value only in relation to other things—like how many actual real things it allows you to acquire. We got along fine without anything like money for a long time, is what I'm saying. Influence, for example, worked just as well for titled lords in the feudal system. And fifteen hundred years ago, you could live a fine life with a fortune made up entirely of bolts of silk.

One of the good things about money—and why I'm glad not everyone shares my perspective—is that people act predictably when in the presence of it. For instance, from the moment I left the bar to the time I reached the table with the blazer, I had been pulling cash out of my money belts and dropping it onto the floor.

* * *

The place was elbow-to-elbow when I began dropping cash on the floor, which was fantastic because nobody identified me as the source, and I was a good distance away before anyone saw the money.

What happened next was pretty close to that riot I told Mike I was hoping to start. Surprisingly, it took a little longer to catch on than I had anticipated.

Crowds can be odd. I've seen plenty of crowd-panic and mob-rule moments—the French Revolution comes to mind—and it's very difficult to anticipate when and how things will turn from order to chaos. In this case, everyone around me was dressed in their finest Saturday night clothing and there were loose piles of large bills at their feet. To pick them up, someone was going to have to make the decision to forego propriety, surrender to the possibility that their nice clothes were going to end up looking not-so-nice, and get down on that floor.

I expected it to happen all at once, but instead the half-dozen people aware they were standing on money had to first look around and see if anyone else was going after it. Nobody was. And then, all at once, everyone was.

Five or six people dropped down at the same time. The people around them looked down to figure out what they were doing, saw the money, and dropped down as well. The effect cascaded.

Since I'd left a trail that circled around the table with the blue blazer, the mayhem that followed cascaded in my direction.

These sorts of things grow exponentially. The floor, already packed to begin with, got denser and tighter as more people pushed in. It drew the attention of casino security and—I assumed although I couldn't see most of them anymore—my many FBI friends.

I had dropped a particularly large supply of one hundred dollar bills on the floor next to the gentleman in possession of the blazer, and stood to one side of the table until he noticed. It didn't take long. Then I snagged the jacket, dropped to the floor, and crawled until I was under the lip of another of the blackjack tables. This was the best I could hope to do when it came to avoiding the cameras for the few seconds it took to remove the loud Hawaiian shirt and slip on the blazer.

This is an old trick. I think the first time I saw it was onstage in Athens. I loved going to the theater then, much as I enjoy movies now despite all of the explosions. The story required that the main character vanish at the end of the play, so at the critical moment the entire chorus surrounded him until he was obscured from view, and when they parted he had disappeared.

Of course he hadn't actually disappeared. What he'd done was put on a long robe and a mask and joined the chorus, but the effect was still breathtaking.

Similarly, if one knows one is being followed, the adornment of a loud Hawaiian shirt is not only done to make oneself easier to spot; it's to train the people following you to look for the shirt.

After ditching said shirt, I crawled a few yards—half the people were on their hands and knees by then—and stood. Looking around, I spotted several members of the casino security pulling guests away from the piles of money, with some guests acting extremely unhappy about this. In the black pants and the jacket and the uncomfortable shoes, I could pass as one of them.

I grabbed the lightest person I could find—an elderly woman who was holding eight hundred dollars in her teeth and another grand in her hands— and pulled her off the floor. She grunted in disapproval, but as she was unwilling to speak and risk losing the cash in her mouth, I was spared any expletives she might have otherwise shared. I dragged her to the entrance, which was what all of the real security guards were doing.

When I turned around, I found myself somewhat face-to-face with one of the FBI tails. There was twenty feet between us, and a complicated ocean of humanity in that twenty feet, but for a few seconds I was certain he knew exactly who he was looking at.

Then he looked away, put his finger to his ear, and started shaking his head, which is something people still do when they're talking to someone who can't see them because the telephonic age hasn't quite drummed out eons of non-verbal behavior. Seeing people gesture while on the phone is almost as entertaining.

I really wanted that earpiece thing he was listening to, but it didn't seem like it was worth the risk to get it. To do it right, I'd have to get behind him, and then I'd feel a little silly since he was standing in front of one of the exits.

Getting around him would be the difficult part; taking the earpiece was easy, but once I was there, what would be the point?

I pushed toward his exit, looking for signs that he was tracking me, but he was still looking for someone in a loud Hawaiian shirt, so I didn't register.

I ended up brushing right past him. If there were cameras recording this, he was going to be getting hell from someone once they'd sorted it all out.

Outside, I didn't waste any time. The blazer I traded with a kid who looked to be about my height and who, more importantly, was heading in the opposite direction and was wearing an oversized Hard Rock Café shirt that covered up the bulk of the money on my torso. Then I walked as quickly as I could without drawing any undue attention.

Ten minutes and several blocks later, I found Mike leaning against the rear fender of his car in the alley next to the coffee shop, holding a walkie-talkie.

Mike was shaking his head.

"Jesus. You sure know how to make an exit."

"Have they figured out I left yet?" I asked, more urgently than I'd intended. It was a terrifyingly long walk to the car.

"They got no clue; they're checking the room now. It'll take 'em hours to dissect the footage and figure out what happened."

I opened the car door. "Let's assume they're more competent than that and get the hell out of here."

* * *

From the archives of Silenus the Elder. Text corrected and translated by Ariadne

And so it came about that Silenus the Elder *did first encounter* the god *upon a perilous seaward journey of many leagues and great dangers.*

The mighty Silenus, *beauteous and proud, envy of all men and beasts and advisor to kings, counsel to the greatest of warriors and to the meanest of common men, was in flight. As ordained by the gods themselves, the great wisdoms which did pour from the nimble tongue of* Silenus *one day greatly offended the sluggish ears of the Pergamon king.*

Silenus *booked hasty passage aboard the first seagoing vessel whose departure was immediate, concerned less with any particular destination than with what might happen should he remain ashore to be recovered by the doddering king's very large army. It was* not a flight of fear, *for* Silenus *the magnificent was not a cowardly man.*

And so it happened, the vessel on which Silenus *took charter was beset by* **pirates** *on the open sea. The foul brigands took only that which could be sold or ransomed and all else was offered to* Poseidon. *As a man of great importance* Silenus *the wise was spared, to be bartered back to the very king from whom he fled.*

So, too, was a second man. *He carried little but wore the finery of a noble and spoke the language of the gods. He claimed no birthright or title, and when a name was demanded of him he provided several. Tall and graceful, he wore his raven hair long and curly, and spun into a braid between his shoulders in the manner of an* Ethiopian prince. *But that his skin was too fair, he could have been mistaken as such. Likewise, with his locks and carriage and raiment the man could have been taken for a woman, on a cloudy day at dusk.*

The pirates shackled together Silenus *and the* strange man, *and fixed their chains to a bolt on the aft of the deck. There were they left to the elements until such a time as ransom could be negotiated.*

"What manner of being are you?" the strange man *asked of* Silenus, *"that walks and talks as a man but with the ears of a draught horse and the smell of a camel?"*

"I am Silenus *and I am the only,"* Silenus *said proudly, for it was* <u>true</u>. *"And what manner of man might you be, that glides through this sphere so gently and without affect? That shines of nobility but accepts the ignobility of fate without protest?"*

"I am but a man," he declared simply, to Silenus's *dissatisfaction. "But you are not. I believe I have heard tell of beings such as you in my travels."*

"You err, my lord," Silenus *declared, "for there is only* Silenus *and none other than he.* Silenus *is unlike any."*

The strange man *laughed heartily, but not so broadly as to alarm their captors. "Is it truly thus? You sprang upon the earth fully assembled? That is not so; no being that strides the dirt did so without first knowing the warmth of a mother's womb."*

"What of the gods?" Silenus *countered, taken aback by the shrewdness of his companion. "Do they not create themselves?"*

"That is not so; even the gods *have mothers. Now what is there to you aside from your peculiar ears? Do you have a talent that would help*

resolve our present concerns?"

"I have <u>a great many talents,</u>" Silenus *boasted. "I can transform myself into a goat and step free of these chains. I can call down the wrath of* Aeolus *himself to visit a great storm upon this vessel. I can summon* Proteus *from below to visit watery violence upon our captors. The* winged gorgon *does answer my ..."*

"So you have no talents, then," the stranger *interrupted. "Aside from a vast capacity for <u>exaggeration.</u>"*

"I am <u>the greatest storyteller</u> the world has ever known," Silenus *spoke angrily. "Kings weep, maidens spread their thighs, and the gods themselves ..."*

But the stranger *interrupted* Silenus *yet again.*

"You must stop," he declared, "for I have met the greatest storyteller the world has ever known and you are not he. What I require of you is a talent that will help us at this very moment. Unless you can spin a tale that convinces these **pirates** *to murder themselves, I do not find your legend-making prowess an effective survival skill. And should you try, I fear they may slay us before proceeding to themselves, as I have considered murdering you twice since we have begun speaking."*

"And what talents have you, stranger," Silenus *demanded, "that would be of use to any, aside from your skillfully insulting tone?"*

"Freed of these shackles, I can best any aboard this vessel," the strange man *said calmly, and although he was slight of build and their captors sturdy, rough and large,* Silenus *did not doubt him.*

"What of those ears?" the stranger *asked. "Do they enable you to hear better than a man might?"*

"I can hear the bristle of a fly's wing as he takes flight a league away. I can overhear the stratagems of enemy armies while safely behind my own force. I have ..."

"Then, yes?"

"You have a <u>capacity for interruption</u> that qualifies as a talent unto itself."

The strange man *smiled. "My forgiveness, storyteller; I feared if I did not intercede we would have been ransomed before you had completed your tale-telling. Now tell me, with your magnificent ears, can you ascertain the location of the keys to these manacles?"*

"I can! The large one carries them," Silenus *said with pride.*

"An overly general description. Which large one?"

"The one with the scar above his right eye and the ringlet carving on his neck, with hoop rings in his lobe and shaved head. His grin's third tooth on his eastern side is blacked. He is also quite ugly; would you like for me to quantify his ugliness in an historical context?"

Laughing now, the strange man *said, "Should you ever find the mean distance between too many words and too few, you might just succeed in being a tolerable companion. Where on his person are the keys?"*

"It is a small metal ring tied by a cord to his rope belt. Now, what magic will you be employing to obtain these keys?"

"He will require a reason to come to us, and another reason still to use the keys," the strange man *said. "I expect to give him reason enough, but if he disagrees with my logic I will be forced to remove the keys myself, and so it is a great help to know exactly where they are. I thank you."*

"And what reason will you give him to use the keys?" Silenus *asked.*

"You shall provide him with one yourself, great Silenus.*"*

And with tremendous swiftness, the stranger <u>flung</u> Silenus *<u>overboard</u>.*

The mighty Silenus *did flail and fumble in the sea, for swimming was not a skill at which he excelled. His wrists still chained, he could do little but keep his face above water as the slow boat dragged him along.*

An eternity transpired ere the stranger *appeared at the aft of the boat and implored* Silenus *to flounder himself toward the deck as he pulled the chain to guide* Silenus's *passage until, with great effort, he managed to extricate him from the deep.*

"Do you know how to sail?" the strange man *asked as he unlatched the manacles that had served as both* Silenus's *burden and salvation.*

Silenus *was struck dumb by the sight of a vacant ship, save for the two ransoms and cargo.*

"How can this be?" he asked.

"The bolt on the deck was loose, and would have soon torn free and taken me into the water, and then we would have both joined the embrace of your friend Proteus. *When your departure caught the attention of our jailor, I convinced him it would be easier to unlock my chain and remove the bolt than to pull you aboard as clearly you wished to drown."*

"I did not wish to drown!" Silenus *protested.*

"But surely you must have, as you had leapt overboard so stridently. You even told me before your departure how content you were to drag the vessel down into the depths with you."

Silenus *climbed to his feet and reappraised the ship.*

"But where did they all go?" he asked the man.

The stranger *stretched his hand over the waters.*

"A being of such <u>vast imagination</u> as yourself can surely conspire an explanation."

And Silenus *did look out upon the sea. In the distance a fleet of* **dolphins** *berthed, and an explanation did come upon him.*

"What shall I call you, my lord?" he asked the stranger.

"You hail from the court of Pergamon, do you not?"

"I call no kingdom home, and all kingdoms home," Silenus *said. "But that is where I last paused."*

"In those parts, the name I am known by is Dionysos," *the stranger said.*

"You may call me that if you wish. Now answer. Do you sail? For I fear I cannot guide this ship alone and do not wish to guess where we will settle if left to the whims of the sea."

Chapter Five

Sil.

I know this to be true as surely as the stars are fixed, and all men must eventually perish unto Hades.

Dion.

This is a poor choice, as not all men perish, nor are the stars truly fixed in the heavens.

—From the dialogues of Silenus the Younger.
Text corrected and translated by Ariadne

About two hours passed before I felt like it was okay to exhale. I spent that time in the back of Mike's Chevy convertible partly covered by an afghan that smelled like someone's basement, and working on half a bottle of scotch I found rolling along on the floor.

I was lucky the FBI only used humans when tracking me, because that casino trick would have never worked otherwise. It was modestly clever, sure, but I could think of a bunch of non-human species that wouldn't have lost me. Granted, there would have been other issues hiring, say, a demon or a vampire, and pixies and iffrits don't have much use for steady employment (or money in general, or clothing). But there are plenty of species left that could have blended in, would have been happy with the job, and would never have been fooled by a clothing change.

A goblin, for instance. Most of them look nearly human, and a healthy one could keep track of a housefly in a snowstorm. They prefer swords and knives to guns, but I always thought of that as a personal preference, not a racial mandate.

A goblin would have caught me.

Mike Lycos could be a goblin. It wasn't a perfect fit, but if he came in through the balcony of my room, he was less human than I am, and *goblin* was a decent enough guess. Except goblins aren't tremendous leapers, per se. And I know enough about both the Northern and Southern breed to recognize one; he didn't look like either type. No, he was something else.

We hadn't really talked much, Mike and I. He had yet to tell me where we were going, but I figured once I was out of the city I'd take my chances. I was nearly ready to trust him. It helped that if we were caught, he'd be in as much trouble as me, and probably more. Trust built on mutually assured destruction may sound risky (especially in the nuclear age) but it's got a solid pedigree historically.

I could have probably climbed into the front seat if I wanted, but I was actually pretty comfortable lying there and looking up at the stars. It had been a while.

* * *

Looking at the night sky is one of the first things I can remember doing, and I used to do it a lot. We all did. Granted, before television and books it was all we *had* to do, but the sky is sometimes more interesting than television or books.

For a fair number of early cultures, the night sky was more real than anything that was happening beneath it. That might be a perspective that's difficult to get your mind around, but look at it this way—on earth things are born, live, and die in a state of pretty constant change. But the heavens are static and evidently eternal. It's why so many cultures thought the stars were gods. I'd felt that way myself for a time, although I was careful about attaching names to any of them since culturally, the gods were different depending on whom I hung out with. I adhered to a sort of amorphous polytheism that worked pretty well.

I don't know when I decided there were no gods, but I can definitely identify the moment when the concept first occurred to me. It followed a somewhat extraordinary event.

This was during the ascendancy of the Sumerian empire, which is to say very long ago, even by my somewhat unique standards.

The Sumerians have been lauded in recent history books as the earliest culture worthy of the term *empire*, which is just flat-out untrue. I will grant they are the oldest civilization to leave behind a decent historical record that doesn't also involve cave drawings, but there were others who came before them. Also, it's a stretch to call what the Sumerians slapped together an empire or even a civilization with a culture.

What they did have was a talent for building things out of stone, a basic written language, and a sincere interest in eradicating all evidence of every other culture they came into contact with. The reason archaeologists haven't discovered earlier mid-East examples of civilized man—yet—has more to do with Sumerian vindictiveness than that no such prior cultures existed.

Actually, calling them vindictive isn't entirely fair, because in most ways they were typical for the time. The Sumerian religion was extremely rudimentary, and followed a common assumption that their lives were manipulated by fickle and ill-tempered gods whose displeasure could be determined through any *post hoc* analysis of major and minor natural disasters. To ward off these disasters, they spent a whole lot of time trying to keep their gods happy via a number of complex rituals, many involving copious amounts of sex ("the gods wish us to have sex" is the oldest pickup line in the world) and human sacrifice. And whoever happened to be their king was also a god, which simplified the political process quite a lot.

This wasn't an unusual way of seeing things. Most of the above also works for the Egyptians, the early Greeks, the Hindus, the African Bushmen tribes and the descendant cultures of the Sumerians, i.e., the Akkadians and the pre-Mosaic Jews, and also probably the American Indian cultures and, for all I know, the prehistoric Chinese and the Australian Aborigines. It is, in short, a nearly universal perspective. Why? I don't know, but I bet all of it started when somebody looked up.

A couple of things did set the Sumerians apart. For some reason they looked at the tribes that came before them as an affront to their gods and felt morally justified in eliminating all evidence of them. Also, they retained much of the warrior past that predated their comparatively civilized present, specifically the manner in which a king was declared. They had no kings by birthright, or not at first; instead, the biggest, baddest, most fertile and strongest son of a bitch around was their king, an honor bestowed partly because he could kill anybody who suggested otherwise. The Alpha Male, in other words.

I did not ingratiate myself into the Sumerian society, for the simple and obvious reason that I'd get my head handed to me if I tried. Admittedly, I was at one time the Alpha Male in my own tribe, but we were starving African hunters. In contrast, the lands of Sumer were agriculturally rich and well farmed, and a steady supply of food will always result in a bigger and stronger warrior class, or at least bigger and stronger than me.

But I did interact with them from time to time.

* * *

Very occasionally, I will pop up in the historical record. Most of the time I'm not at all easy to spot, because most of the time I'm just a guy who does a thing and then disappears again into the background behind someone-or-other who's busy doing something much more important. But there are a couple of rare occasions when I get a starring role. *The Epic of Gilgamesh* is one of those occasions.

Don't go pulling out a copy to see if you can spot me because for one thing, it's a really dull read. It made for a fantastic tale in spoken form—provided one knew the language—but whoever chiseled it down for posterity on those clay tablets they found in Nineveh was a bit of a hack. For another thing, it's pretty obvious who I am if you can stay awake to the end, so I'll just tell you. In the story, King Gilgamesh decided upon discovering he was a mortal man and was going to die someday, to go on a great quest to seek out the legendary Ut-Naphishtim, the immortal man. Hello, me.

As with most stories retold successively for hundreds of years before being recorded for posterity, much of the epic is just flat-out bunk, with gods coming down and exacting their wrath directly—rather than through a nice, indirect pestilence—and heroes who are capable of unfathomable physical acts. My favorite part of the story is when the wild, god-created animal-man, Enkidu, is tamed by a prostitute. As soon as he has sex with her, all his body hair falls off, making the creatures of the forest fear him because suddenly he looks more human than animal.

Whenever I think about the Enkidu story, I think Kipling really missed out on a much better ending for *The Jungle Book*.

Nobody who looks closely at *The Epic of Gilgamesh* could mistake it for a historical text, but in a way it is. It's a collection of several tales told about different people—all exaggerated beyond recognition— throughout early Sumerian history, most predating Gilgamesh.

And there really was a Gilgamesh. He was a king in pre-Akkadian Sumeria. (The Akkadians, a Semitic people, conquered the Sumerians— who were more white-skinned and from the North—and took over their empire in such a way that many consider Sumerian and Akkadian to be synonymous. I never stopped calling them Sumerians because truthfully, they didn't act all that different.) And Gilgamesh really did come to seek out my advice one day.

The event that set things in motion was something we would now consider mundane, or failing that, something we would have a ready explanation for. It happened while I was sitting alone outside the small shelter I'd made for myself in a stretch of woods I'd called home for roughly a century.

I was in one of my back-to-nature phases. Not in the man-animal sense of the warrior Enkidu, more in a crazy hermit on the hill way. With a civilization only few days' walk, I could have been more sociable, but as I said the Sumerians were quite nuts. I did stop by for the fertility rites in springtime, but that was just to enjoy (and participate in) the spectacle of a thousand temple prostitutes copulating in the name of the gods. Great fun, that.

It was a clear, warm evening during a new moon, and I had decided to forego a fire in order to spend the night studying the stars, something I did a lot. (And which came in handy later when I became a vizier in Egypt. The Egyptian kings were crazy for astronomy.) At sometime well past the point when the moon reached its zenith, an amazing thing happened. A part of the sky fell.

I first spotted it low on the horizon—a flash of something I didn't think had been there a second before. It flared brighter and brighter, this point in the sky. It appeared to grow larger, but in fact it was simply getting closer. And then it disappeared from view. About ten rapid heartbeats later, a tremendous bang rang out, similar to the sound of a thousand whips cracked against a thousand backs at the same time.

I had already been on the planet for a good long while by then, and had of course heard stories about parts of the sky falling. But this was the first time I'd seen it with my own eyes. I had no idea what it meant. For me, and everybody else in this time, the sky simply *was*. It didn't change. Sure, over the course of a year—and even a night—elements of the sky moved in a predictable pattern, but pieces of it weren't supposed to just drop off like that.

I re-examined the portion of the firmament the piece hailed from, but it didn't look as if any of the stars were missing. It was as if it hadn't happened at all.

By morning, I decided I had imagined it. This seemed like a much safer conclusion than any other option such as, say, one of the gods had slipped on something. A day later, I'd forgotten the whole event.

But I wasn't the only one who'd seen it, as I discovered when Gilgamesh arrived at my door three days later, looking scared.

All legendary exaggeration aside, Gilgamesh really was a pretty huge guy, a full head and shoulders taller than me. He was also profoundly hairy, more than a little ugly, and fond of going about without clothes on. This last part was just to make things easier on him when it came to passing on his seed, something he did at least three or four times daily because basically the guy always had an erection and always knew what to do with it; clothes just slowed him down. Seeing him afraid was quite a surprise.

"Ut-Naphishtim," he boomed, "you must tell me what I have done to anger the gods!"

This may have sounded like an order, but it really wasn't. More like a plea. I got some decent respect from Gilgamesh, who believed that my apparently eternal good health meant the very gods who suddenly had it out for him, had smiled on me for some reason. (It should be said that even though I'd never conversed with any god at anytime, I assumed much the same.)

"Why do you suppose you have?" I asked, showing him in.

I lived alone in an extremely modest dwelling. *The Epic of Gilgamesh* had me ensconced with a bunch of nubile women, but consider the source. Whereas the great men of the Old Testament were recognized as great by their uncommonly long life spans, the Sumerians equated greatness with sexual prowess. Both were meant to be taken metaphorically. Well, except in the case of Gilgamesh the Virile.

"You did not see the heavens fall?" he asked. "You did not hear their displeasure?"

"I did," I admitted. "But perhaps you are being hasty. Come sit."

We sat on the floor, atop some animal hides I used for just such a purpose. We wouldn't get around to inventing decent furniture for a while. "Tell me, what do the people think?"

"They only know fear now," he said. "But this will change. For if I have insulted a god, the people will do me harm to save themselves. Already the muttering has begun."

This is something that's never really changed, by the way. Look at how random fluctuations in economic indicators affect a U.S. presidential election.

"The crops?"

"Robust. The cattle as well. It cannot last. Ut-Naphishtim, you must help me."

"I do not know how."

"Can you not speak to the gods? Discover how I have stirred them?"

I think of this conversation whenever I encounter a priest or, well, any holy man. (Like popes. I've met a couple.) Gilgamesh—and everyone else in the land of Sumer—just assumed I had a direct line to the gods, and I never did anything to disabuse them of the notion because it was one of the things that kept me alive. But I didn't have a direct line, and sometimes pretending you do can put you in uncomfortable situations like this one.

It's ten times worse when people think you *are* a god, incidentally. I've had a little experience with that too.

"I fear my pleas will be met with silence," I said, "as I have been seeking audience with the gods since the night in which their ire was demonstrated."

This was sort of true, if you can call sleeping a bunch and basically pretending nothing happened seeking audience.

"And?"

"I have no answer for you. I am sorry."

His face fell. "Then I am lost," he cried.

I pondered his dilemma. "Perhaps you are thinking of this incorrectly."

"How do you mean?"

"Consider that it was not displeasure at all, but a gift." In today's lingo this is called spin.

"A gift?"

"Something fell from the heavens to the earth."

"T'was a thunderbolt out of the clear night sky!"

"It did arrive as if borne on lightning," I agreed. "But something struck the land that night. I heard it. It was an object, a solid thing. Possibly a godly object presented in a spectacular way? A thing that the gods wish upon you?"

He ruminated on this line of reasoning for a few minutes.

Although barbaric and quick to violence, rapacious and voracious, Gilgamesh was not stupid. He actually had a keen political mind when one got right down to it. Not quite Solomonic, but good enough to out-maneuver lesser tacticians in most fields of life. One might think a lengthy pause like this meant he couldn't figure something out, when in fact he was running through a decent number of implications.

Finally, he nodded. "Then we must go."

"I am coming?" I asked.

He looked surprised, as if we'd already had this part of the conversation.

"Of course you are."

It wasn't a question.

* * *

Traveling the Fertile Crescent in those days was often a treacherous endeavor, but one could hardly ask for a better companion than the mightiest warrior in all the land. Gilgamesh strode the earth like the king he was, and sometimes it seemed as if even the animals acknowledged his sovereignty, practically volunteering their lives for the honor of being eaten by him. Or maybe it just seemed that way when he casually walked up behind a stag and crushed its head with a large rock.

"How did you do that?" I asked later, as we sat beside a fire on the first night of our journey, feasting on the stag's meaty remains. "You are hardly a difficult man to notice."

"You know how to hunt."

"I do. But I might spend days hunting. You appear to hunt almost by accident."

He grinned, his bloody teeth dripping with his conquest. (We didn't cook the stag; the fire was for warmth.) "Then you are doing it wrong. Approach silently from behind the beast's head and downwind, and you will be close enough to braid its tail hair before it notices you."

"I suppose it depends on what it is you are hunting."

"That it does."

"You know, there was a time when we worshipped the stag and the hart as gods themselves."

He laughed. "Nonsense. They are but creatures."

I leaned back, forsaking the remainder of the leg I'd been gnawing on. Raw meat always fills me up more quickly for some reason. "True. And yet, if these creatures had not presented themselves to us, we would have died. Is it so strange to pray to a stag in the hopes that it would arrive and rescue us from our hunger?"

He tossed aside the shoulder he'd managed to denude and moved on to another body part. "The creatures of this wood are plentiful. You saw yourself how we chanced upon this one."

"It was not always so. In another time and place, beasts such as this were rare and wondrous. Do you not offer appeasement to the gods for plentiful crops? It is the same thing."

"No. It is different. The gods control the rains, and the rains feed the plants. One does not pray to a god that the animals will fuck more often so as to provide man with a larger supply of meat. And prayer to the animal itself? Madness. It is but a thing."

"Perhaps. And perhaps in a land where the rain is more frequent and the crops grow with unchecked regularity, a man there might think it madness to ask the gods for help growing things."

He nodded.

"I accept that you have great wisdom in these matters. But I ask that you step away from me a few paces. When the gods strike you down, they might hit me as well."

* * *

Searching for the landfall of an unknown object that struck the earth an undetermined distance away isn't an easy thing. When we initially set out, we made a beeline for where I had heard the strange impact, which presupposed I wasn't hearing an echo of a sound made from a different location.

We assumed it landed somewhere within the cup of the valley, as it seemed improbable the sound would travel over a steep hill, which did put an outside limit on our search parameters, but we were still talking about a vast terrain. And from a geometric standpoint, if the initial path we set off on was incorrect by even a half a degree, by the time we reached a parallel with the impact crater we could have been—depending on how long we'd walked to get to that point—a league or two off.

The details of this semi-mathematical analysis (it could hardly be called math when math beyond very basic arithmetic hadn't been invented yet) was an ongoing concern in my discussions with Gilgamesh over the following month. He thought the object must be massive and therefore not difficult to locate. So when we didn't come upon it immediately, he became quite frustrated.

"You have made me a fool, Ut-Naphishtim," he growled after another day passed without success.

"Oh, I have not, you big baby." We'd become familiar enough with one another that our discourses had begun to resemble the bickering of an old married couple.

"A full cycle!" he blasted.

He was referring to the fact that a couple of days ago we'd seen the coming of a new moon, meaning it had been a complete lunar cycle since the sky fell. "Soon the harvest will be upon us, and if I am not present ..."

Well, we didn't know what would happen then. The king is supposed to be present for the Day of Harvest because technically, without the gods smiling favor upon the king there *is* no harvest. So he kind of had to be there. (Not surprisingly in a drought the first head on the chopping block is invariably the king's. It's a perilous existence.)

From a scientific standpoint, I was curious to see if his not being there really resulted in a bad harvest, but Gilgamesh would have none of it. If he wasn't there, his people would starve, period. For him, there really wasn't any other way to see things.

Meanwhile, neither of us knew how his prolonged absence was playing back at home. It would have been easy, in light of the circumstances of his disappearance, to postulate that he'd slinked away in fear. So the political damage our journey was taking could not be calculated, but the odds were it wasn't good.

All this put him in a consistently foul mood.

"Foolishness!" he said, continuing his rant. "I should never have listened to you!"

It was getting dark and we were, again, wandering about at random through the deep woods. Needless to say, we wouldn't be sneaking up on any food on this night.

"Nobody told you to seek me out," I said. "So don't blame me for this."

"Ahhh! I do not think *anything* landed on that night. Why did the gods see fit to grant you immortality when you are clearly too much of an idiot to warrant such grace!" He bulled his way through a heavy set of branches and stormed temporarily out of sight, which was not a terribly challenging thing to do even when you were the size of Gilgamesh—not in these woods.

"You're just envious," I declared, following after him. And he was. One of our recurring conversations revolved around his interest in becoming an immortal and my inability to provide him with a successful formula to do so.

I pushed past the trees and promptly fell about five feet into a small crater, landing next to an astonished Gilgamesh, he having already fallen and not thought to warn me.

"Hey!" I exclaimed, pulling myself off him. By the gods, he smelled bad.

He looked bewildered. "Is this the thing?" he asked quietly.

I climbed to my feet and took in the view in the gentle moonlight. To my left, a straight line had been drawn in the forest floor at an upward slant pointing to the heavens. Several trees along the path showed signs of recent wounding, and one tree that fell dead center had been nearly halved. This, I reflected, was the sound I heard.

To my right, the piece of the sky had burrowed a wide swath into the ground. And resting at the bottom was ... a rock.

Gilgamesh knelt before the rock with a sense of reverence priests would later reserve for a chalice of Christ's transubstantiated blood.

I stood next to him. "Well?"

"It is beautiful," he whispered.

"It is a rock. We already have plenty of those. I was expecting something more from the gods."

"You blaspheme," he said, almost as an afterthought because he wasn't really listening to me. He reached down and picked it up.

"It is cool to the touch," he noted. "And heavy."

Reluctantly, he handed the rock over so I could examine it for myself. It was a bit bigger than my hand, and was very dense and much heavier than it looked. A better examination would have to come in the daylight, but it seemed to be composed of a mixture of metal and stone. Appearance-wise, it looked somewhat like a pineapple (which I had not ever seen up to that time) or a large pinecone (which I had), encircled with an irregular series of jagged protrusions. It was also riddled with smallish holes, and one larger one at the base. Had I not seen for myself that it had once been a portion of the sky, I would have inferred a volcanic origin.

The most remarkable thing about it was that it was not at all remarkable. Although opinions differed.

"It is beautiful," Gilgamesh repeated.

I handed his rock back and held my tongue, as he was clearly having a religious moment that my sarcasm wouldn't have helped. "But what is it, do you suppose?"

"I do not know," he said. "I will think on it."

The next morning, Gilgamesh awoke me with a triumphant declaration. "It is a weapon!"

"What is?" I yawned, not quite awake.

"This gift from Enlil himself!" He held the rock up over his head, as if a higher elevation would somehow transform it into something more extraordinary.

"So, you have decided which god shows you favor. That is good. Have we any food?"

"You should rejoice with me, Ut-Naphishtim! This is a great day!"

"I would, but I cannot rejoice properly on an empty stomach."

"When we return triumphant, I will treat you to the finest banquet man has ever seen! For the gods have indeed shown favor."

"Super," I muttered. We were at least five days from any banquets. "So how do you see this … rock … as a weapon? It appears no less rock-like in the sunlight than it did by moon. Will you be sneaking up behind your foes and caving in their heads as you did the stag?"

"Aha!" He dropped his god-given rock on the ground and produced a staff. I gathered—insofar as staffs do not transform themselves whole from the trees—that he spent much of the evening finding and crafting it for just this moment.

"A stick?"

He reared back, and with a precisely aimed strike, thrust the tip of the staff into the opening at the base of the rock. When he pulled the staff up again, it had the rock stuck on the end of it. "Behold the Hammer of Gilgamesh!"

"Um, okay." I probably should have applauded, but I was too busy trying not to laugh.

He looked disappointed. "It is temporary. I will make a finer staff of bronze once I return. It will be the greatest weapon ever wielded!"

"A rock stuck on the end of a stick?"

"A heavenly gift bestowed upon the mightiest of warriors!"

I admit his angle was better than mine.

"I don't mean to be negative," I said, running right past several danger signs in my head, "but have you considered the possibility that sometimes a rock is just a rock?"

He looked perplexed. "I am not sure I understand."

I sat up and tried to organize the thoughts that had been buzzing around in my head since we'd discovered the object. "The heavens are unchanging, are they not?"

"Of course," he agreed. "A child knows this."

"Did I ever tell you of a time, very long ago, when I witnessed the death of a star?"

We didn't call them stars, but there's no exact modern version for the word we did use. It was a little more than "star" and a little less than "god".

"Blasphemy!" he declared angrily.

"No. I wasn't the only witness, either. It flared brightly for six days and then disappeared. I can show you where it used to reside in the night sky if you wish."

"Then it was a war! A war in the heavens!"

"But if we presuppose the heavens are unchanging, this would contradict such a thing. And I have seen other oddities as well, such as bright streaks of light across the sky, one every hundred or so years. These are things that most mortal men would never live long enough to see repeated, but which I have witnessed many times over."

"I see." He sat at the edge of the crater, not much looking like someone who believed what he was hearing. "And what did you make of these strange events?"

"I did not know what to conclude. The people of those times took them to be portents of doom, just as you and your people took this heavenly rock to mean the displeasure of the gods. As did I."

I stood and picked up his makeshift hammer. The rock was heavy and cold, and no more remarkable than it had been the night before.

"Then came this thing. You call it a weapon. I say it is just a rock. And by that I mean it is not a gift from the gods, or a punishment, or a message. A rock fell from the sky and that is all that has happened. Do you understand?"

"You mean it fell to earth by accident?" he asked. He was trying.

"No. I mean that in the sky there are rocks. The rocks float and glow and sometimes, one of them falls. And that is all that is up there."

"Then where are the gods if not in the sky?" he asked.

"Exactly."

He stared at me, as only a man who thinks himself a god on earth can stare at a man who just wondered aloud if there might not be any gods.

Not to say I'd come to any conclusions one way or another; it was just something that had been gestating for a while and would continue to gestate for a while longer. In hindsight, it probably wasn't a notion I should have shared with Gilgamesh. But I was hungry, and people sometimes make bad decisions when they're hungry.

"I should strike you dead right now," he said, snatching the Hammer of Gilgamesh out of my hands. "But I expect mighty Enlil will do that himself. Leave me, Ut-Naphishtim. Go home, and do not speak of this again."

* * *

It was the last time I saw Gilgamesh, but that was as much a result of circumstance as anything. He was dead barely a year later. From what I was able to gather, he spent much of the last few months of his life making a series of wild, reputedly prophetic statements that he claimed were given to him directly from Enlil. This didn't sit well with the general population—the prophesies were almost never good—and eventually someone decided to challenge him in combat, possibly just to shut him the hell up. Unfortunately, Gilgamesh had been fasting a lot, and wasn't up to strength. He didn't do so well.

I received this news by messenger, who also carried with him a gift from the legendary king.

"He commanded that you have this."

The messenger unwrapped the cloth package he carried over his shoulder and revealed the Hammer of Gilgamesh. As he'd promised, it had been fixed upon a bronze haft. It also had dried blood on it, indicating he had indeed tried using it as a weapon, probably in his final battle.

"I thank you," I said to the messenger.

"There is more, great Ut-Naphishtim."

"Yes?"

"His final words. He asked that I tell you 'I see.' "

"He said 'I see?' "

"Do you know what this might mean?"

The messenger looked eager, as I'm sure he'd spent the last three days puzzling it over.

"It is private," I replied, and his face fell with disappointment. So I decided to throw him something. "Gilgamesh the mighty wished to become immortal, as I am. I told him he should spend less time worrying about death and more time living his life. His final words indicate he understood this lesson."

He nodded slowly and bowed deeply.

"I thank you, great Ut- Naphishtim."

Since my words to the messenger appear more or less exactly as I spoke them in *The Epic of Gilgamesh*, I imagine he repeated it a few dozen times when he got back.

Chapter Six

Silenus:

You have handed out pieces of your life to me, and I am their keeper.
But the answer you seek is not among them.

—From the Tragedy of Silenus,
text corrected and translated by Ariadne

"Are you going to tell me where we're going?" I asked, as we watched the sunrise from a truck stop somewhere along Interstate 58.

We'd driven straight through the evening in a non-direct path that had us leaving the highway several times to meander along random tributaries that appeared to serve no purpose other than to confuse me as to our eventual destination. Mike claimed these side jaunts were to make sure we weren't being followed, which seemed a mildly paranoid thing for an FBI agent to worry about, except that this agent was transporting a fugitive. Now we were somewhere in Northern California enjoying the Northern California sunrise.

Mike sipped his coffee and failed to respond, or at least not to the question I asked.

"So where'd your money come from?" he asked instead.

"Smart investing."

I drank my own cup of coffee with earnest. I've had worse coffee, about three hundred years ago. But it served the minimum requirement of being black in color and caffeinated in substance, and that's all I really ask of my coffee.

Mike gave me the evil eye. "You're what? Thirty-two? C'mon. I put money away in my 401K every month and net fifteen percent in a really good year, and I'll be lucky if I can buy a decent condo when I retire. You bought an island. What's the real story, hombre?"

"Maybe I'm older than I look."

Neither of us was feeling particularly chipper. Morning conversations should be between very close friends or lovers, and otherwise avoided entirely, I've learned.

He leaned back and stole a glance at the waitress, who was busy smoking a Pall Mall all the way down to the filter and most definitely not bringing us our food.

"You're a tough nut," Mike said.

"Is that a compliment?"

"Take it however you want to." Mike grunted as he lit up his own cigarette and went back to staring at me.

I wasn't about to confide in him about anything. I learned the hard way—somewhat recently—that it was no longer safe to tell anybody about my curiously long life, and that meant anybody. Plus there was the whole problem of him having ulterior motives in this extracurricular trip of ours.

"All right." I sighed. "Take your best shot. I'll tell you if you get close."

He took a couple of puffs of the cigarette and then started spit-balling.

"You're American by birth. You were an athlete when you were younger and you still keep in shape. You ... jog. Maybe yoga, or some other Vedic shit. I know you're not a vegetarian."

"I ordered bacon," I confirmed.

"You like the outdoors. You'd probably be pretty good in a fight."

"Did you want to fight me?"

"I'm just saying what comes to mind. You may be an alcoholic."

"That's a little judgmental."

"There are people who like to drink and people who *have* to drink. You've been slipping scotch into your coffee since we sat down."

"It's your bottle."

"Yeah, it's been under the seat of my car for a year or two. And it was left there by a friend who has bad taste in scotch."

"I've had better," I agreed.

"Yet you're still drinking it."

"I'm still on vacation."

He grabbed my hand and flipped it palm-up. "Soft hands; you don't do a lot of hard labor." He sniffed. "And you washed them when you went to the john a few minutes back."

"Good sense of smell," I noted.

"I have an above-average nose. All your clothing is new, right? But you never changed your socks."

"A surprising observation."

"Am I right?"

"Yes. That's pretty good; you could do parties with that nose."

"It's not helping much now."

He leaned back, as if getting a view of me from a distance would improve the analysis. "You're pretty sharp, I know that."

"Thank you."

"Seriously, that was a hell of a stunt you pulled with the money." He thought about it for a second. "You don't care all that much about money, even though you have a ton of it."

"This is true," I agreed.

"But not always true. Everyone cares about money."

I smiled. "No comment."

He tamped out his cigarette and lit another one. I really thought smoking wasn't allowed in public places anymore, but that did not appear to be the case unless Mike's car also took us back to the mid-90's.

"Tell me about the girl," he said.

"Ariadne?"

"Clara Wasserman."

"Nothing to talk about there." It was an unconvincing response.

"I disagree; there's plenty to talk about. Like, she got paid $5 million by a guy named Robert Grindel, a guy that's conveniently dead now, the same guy who also used to own that island you bought."

"Well, I wouldn't say anything about Bob Grindel was convenient."

"But you knew he was dead."

"Of course I did. That's why people have estate sales. Listen, Clara isn't anybody. She's a girl I got to know, that's all."

"What did she do to earn $5 million?"

"You'd have to ask her."

"Which you suggest I not do, because she isn't anybody."

"Now you're catching on."

"Left you, huh?"

"I really don't want to talk about it."

"It was the age thing, right? I mean I know you look thirty-something, but you've gotta be older. And she's, what, in her twenties?"

Part of me wanted to tell him that yes, that was exactly the problem, that although Clara and I are both going to live a very long time, her childhood memories included music television, the Internet, and rock music from Seattle while mine involved goring a wild animal and wearing its lower intestines as a trophy. Instead, I changed the subject. "So what's your verdict? Have you figured me out?"

"I figure you stole your money and killed the guy who had it last."

"Like Bob Grindel?"

"Like him. Course you have more money than he did. And I wouldn't wanna jump to any premature conclusions here. Am I close?"

"No, but points for creativity."

"Yeah ... it's too much money anyway." He fixed me with another one of his stares. "Mug a guy, get his wallet that's one thing. But this is royalty money. People notice when royalty get mugged."

I smiled as he continued.

"Just the same, I think killing someone is well within the scope of your abilities."

"Isn't that true for everybody?"

"No. Only certain people." He sniffed the air. "The food's ready."

* * *

I haven't spent much of my life in cars, as you can imagine. Being in one is still something I have to consciously accustom myself to. It's not the same as with airplanes, which are totally divorced from any prior experience. But cars go on the ground just like horses and carriages, and the only real difference is the traveling speed. Well, that and the comparative comforts of a pair of shock absorbers and wheels covered in vulcanized rubber, which is a nice step up from wooden wagon wheels on an unpaved road.

It's the velocity that gives me trouble, basically. I spend most short car trips feeling anxious, and long car trips—especially at highway speeds—can reduce me to a puddle of nervous twitches. This does not make me the best traveling companion in the world.

"Oh my God, will you lie down in the back again or something?" Mike complained. I was sitting in the passenger seat, and my knee was bouncing up and down at a rate that may have equaled the car's pistons.

"That won't help," I said. "Are you going to tell me where we're going so at least I can look forward to an upcoming exit?"

"You're like a child, I swear. Just outside of Sacramento, okay?"

"See, that's helpful. Now what's just outside of Sacramento?"

"Something I want you to see."

"Useful."

"It isn't meant to be."

We were going eighty-seven miles per hour. I was thoroughly amazed, both that anything could go that fast and not crumble to dust for violating some basic physical laws, and that we hadn't been pulled over by anybody. Mike said we were off the grid, but I bet we'd pop right back up on the grid—and damned if I knew what the grid was—if he were stopped for speeding.

"I'm not trying to be cryptic," Mike said. "I just don't want to bias your impression by telling you too much beforehand."

"And does this thing have to do with Ariadne Papos?" I asked.

"It does," he said reluctantly. "And that's all I'm saying."

This didn't help at all because I already knew it, but we had struck a deal. In exchange for helping me get out of Vegas, I'd look at his thing, whatever it was. I am not exactly legendary when it comes to keeping my word, but in this case I was planning to, because it was entirely possible I wasn't done needing Mike's help.

When you find out the government of a particular nation is actively searching for you, it's almost always in your best interest to get out of that nation as quickly as possible; anything less than an immediate departure just increases the chances that you never get to leave. So I probably should have headed for the airport. On the other hand, that's undoubtedly what they expected me to do, and did I want to be somewhere over the Midwest when they figured out I was on a particular flight? I did not. It isn't like I could get off in the middle somewhere.

There were too many variables. How fast was their response time? Was I "wanted" in the sense of my face being plastered all over the place, or did they still have laws in this country that required them to actually pin a crime on me first? And was what I did in the casino a big enough crime to qualify?

A guy could go crazy thinking about it. I much preferred going crazy watching the speedometer.

"Do you have to use the bathroom or something?" Mike asked. My knee must have been quite the distraction.

"I don't travel by car much."

"You spent too much time on that island," he said.

I think Mike took it personally, like I was criticizing his driving. I wasn't; just the speed at which he was accomplishing it. But then our exit was coming up and Mike slowed down, as did my knee. A few minutes later we were taking an off-ramp to a place called Rancho Cordova.

A wave of relief flooded through me.

"Is this it?"

"Almost. Jesus, a pretty day like this, and you spend it watching the car gauges."

"One of us has to," I muttered. "Besides, the day was moving past too quickly to enjoy."

He rolled us into a nice suburban neighborhood, and after a few more twists and turns, we came to a stop in front of a modest one story ranch home. It had yellow siding, red shingles, and a covered patio, small in the sense that the garage was nearly as large as the living space portion.

It was such a mundane terminus I didn't know what to think.

"Are we meeting your mom?"

"No," he said, shutting the car's engine down.

"You're a realtor on the side?"

"No. Shut up."

"Okay."

I stepped out of the car. Mike was right; it was a beautiful day. And I'd stepped right into an episode of *Leave It To Beaver*. I could hear neighborhood kids playing in the not-too-great distance and closer, the sound of somebody mowing their lawn. A few houses down, an elderly couple was drinking—I swear—lemonade on their front porch. Under the circumstances (rogue FBI agent and all that) this was surreal.

Mike led me up to the front door, which was crossed with yellow police tape reading DO NOT CROSS.

"That's more like it."

Mike peered through the window beside the door, looking for goodness-knows-what.

"Do police really expect the yellow tape to keep people out?" I asked, just trying to make conversation.

"Yeah. It's a psychological deterrent."

"But does it work?"

"Who knows? Anyway, she's not coming back here. They yanked my surveillance team almost a week ago, after a month. The tape is new."

"This is Ariadne's place?"

"Yeah."

He pulled a key out of his pocket and opened the front door.

We were greeted by a central air-conditioning system that had clearly been working much too hard, perhaps out of boredom. The front entrance gave way to a moderately appointed living room with matching couch and chair, a couple of end tables, and a TV. Certainly, nothing to warrant the yellow tape warning like severed human heads or body parts, whose presence would certainly explain the cold air.

"It's this way."

He led me past the living room and to a corridor on the right.

I peeked through the first doorway I came to. "Oh, a bedroom." Again, no severed human heads there. Next came a bathroom, and then a third door, which was closed. Mike stopped at it.

"This is it," he said. "You ready?"

"I guess."

He turned the knob and pushed open the door.

I stepped into a darkened room, and until Mike hit the light switch, I was wondering if I was about to get jumped. But then, I saw what the room looked like, and finally I understood why I was there, and why Mike went through so much trouble.

To call it a shrine would be a gross over-simplification. It was more like a series of small, interconnected shrines devoted to a variety of arcana, the most prominent of which appeared to be dedicated to me personally. In fact, I took up one whole wall, right over the computer.

"I thought you said she just had me on her computer."

"That was her work console. We didn't find this until later. Actually—and I feel stupid even mentioning this—while I was here looking at this wall wondering who the fuck you were, someone else was looking at the photo in your FBI file. It was a good week before we put the two pieces together."

"Efficient."

"That's why I like to work alone. We're usually fifty left hands not knowing what the fifty right hands are doing."

I stepped up to the wall and took a closer look at myself. Most of the photos were current.

"She's been following you around for a while," he commented, noting my interest specifically in a photograph taken outside of Central Park in New York City. It was over two years old. I knew that both because I was sporting the bald look at the time, and because I more or less commissioned the photo.

"No," I said. "She got these from the Internet."

"Really?"

"It's a long story. Thing is, I know for a fact the site is shut down."

"That doesn't mean it's gone. A lot of sites are archived on the server level."

"No kidding?" I actually had no idea what he just said, but it didn't sound like something I needed more details on. I know enough about computers to use the Internet competently, but that's about it.

"Yeah. Wanna know how I know that?"

"Ariadne."

"Accessing non-public archived web pages was one of her functions."

"For my FBI file?"

"For terrorist activity. My point is, if these pictures were once in the public domain, she knew how to find them. But why did she?"

I didn't answer that, because I didn't know. My eyes drifted to the bottom of the pictures, where there were a variety of words tacked on the wall. None were in English.

"We know what most of those say, but there are still a couple we're not sure of."

"This one is Lazarus," I said. "It's in Greek. This here ... it's Aramaic. It means *Wandering Jew*."

"Very good." Mike sounded impressed. "How about that one on the side there?"

"Sumerian. Not surprised you're having trouble finding someone who can identify that."

"What's it say?"

"Ut-Naphishtim. It's a name, just like the others."

"Okay, so how'd you know that?"

"I'm something of a collector of dead languages."

I pulled myself away from the Giant Wall of Me and moved to the wall opposite the door and next to the only window in the room, which was shuttered closed. The wall was papered with pages of highlighted text of all shapes and sizes, along with a small poster of what looked to me like a comic book character of some sort. I based that on the nature of the artwork, not because the man depicted had a big S on his chest or anything similarly archetypal. It was of a thin, pale man with spiky black hair and black eyes and a long, flowing robe. He actually looked like a vampire I knew once. Especially the eyes. Vampires all have black eyes.

"This I'm clueless about."

"That's a comic book character called Sandman," Mike said. "In the stories, he's one of the Eternals, a living incarnation of Dream. Or something. Got a comic book geek in the Sacramento office who identified it for me."

"And the text?"

"Pages from novels. Heinlein, Neil Stephenson, Bova, Grimwood, and a couple others."

I leaned forward to read some highlighted text: a quotation from a character named Lazarus Long.

She sure knew how to hammer home a theme.

I moved to the third wall. A small table had been set up against the center of the wall, and in the center of the table was a scale model of a Greek temple I recognized as belonging to Dionysos.

More pictures took up the wall-space, mostly consisting of Greek statuettes and photos of artifacts. At the top of the wall was a banner, also in the Greek language.

"Dionysos," Mike interpreted for me, possibly aware that he didn't have to. "God of wine," he added.

I leaned forward to focus on a small Polaroid just above the temple model.

"God of the theater too," I said. "And madness."

"Didn't know that."

"Every Greek god took on extra duties. It was easier than inventing new gods all the time."

The photo was of a simple metal box. There was nothing else in the picture for scale, but I knew from the last time I was near it that it was roughly the size of a steamer trunk. I also knew that, like the copy of the ancient ritual that was still in my pocket, this box was supposed to have disappeared about two thousand years ago.

I'd clearly underestimated the persistence of devotion.

With Mike preoccupied with another section of the room, I took the photo down and slipped it into my pocket.

"So what else?"

I stepped away from the wall.

"There were papers on the desk," Mike said. "The originals are getting the full treatment right now, but I got copies in the car. I'll show 'em to you if you think it'll help."

"It should."

"You wanna share anything with me now?"

"Like what?"

"How about telling me what the hell you're doing all over her wall?" Mike was obviously hoping for a stronger reaction.

"I don't know."

"Sure you do."

I stared at him. "Maybe you have something you'd like to share with me, then."

"Yeah. Let's play that game again from the truck stop. For real this time." He pointed to the poster depicting the Sandman character. "An Eternal, right? Lives forever?"

"That's certainly implicit in the name."

"Lazarus, the Wandering Jew, both from the Bible, one risen from the dead, one reputed to walk the earth until Judgment Day. And here ..." He pointed emphatically as he went, like a lawyer running through evidence. "References from novels with immortal characters in them. And I don't know who the hell Ut-Nap-whatever is, but I bet if I went down to the library, I'd find out he was a guy with a pretty big lifespan."

"You'd be right."

"Thought so. Now I look at all of this shit, and I look at those photos of you—a guy who dropped in from nowhere with more money than a third world nation—and I think there's a connection. So why don't we start with you telling me how old you are?"

Well. That was a pretty impressive leap of understanding for Mike.

I mean, those of us who are aware of the possibility of immortality would probably view the steps required to reach that conclusion as somewhat logical. But most people don't have an immortality wrench in their mental toolbox, just like they don't have one for demons, vampires, pixies, and the like. Many others, when faced with a similar aggregation of facts, have managed to come up with a number of preposterous options specifically to avoid the obvious.

"How long have you been working on that speech?" I asked.

"A little while. How'd I do?"

"Pretty good."

"So?"

"So, I don't really know how old I am."

"Ballpark figure."

I sighed.

"Hypothetically, let's say I told you I was older than recorded history. What difference would that make? What haven't you told me about Ariadne Papos? Why the hell do you care so much about her?"

Honestly, when I threw out the older than history line, he didn't blink.

"I'm just doing my job," he said, which came off as a bit silly from an agent who had already admitted he'd wandered off the proverbial ranch.

Mike pulled back the shutters on the windows and looked out over the back yard. I realized this was the edge of a new development; the whole back of the house fronted a deep copse of trees.

"You ever heard the name Peter Arnheit?" he asked.

I chewed on that for a second while Mike tried to open the window. He was planning to smoke a cigarette, and amusingly—given the lady of the house was probably never going to be coming back home—was doing what every conscientious smoker does in someone else's house.

I *did* recognize the name, but only barely. I seemed to recall a number of news stories about a year earlier where the name figured prominently.

"Something about a murder?" I guessed. But I didn't get a chance to consider it more carefully, because then Mike was shouting at me.

"Get down!"

Now, I was standing a good five or six feet away from him in roughly the middle of the room. I'm telling you this so you can understand that what he did next was basically impossible. He spun around, took one step, sprang across the room, hit me square in the chest, and brought me down to the floor, all in less than a full second. I know this because I tried to speak and never got the opportunity.

And it was a good thing Mike could move that quickly, because I scarcely had time to register that I was on Ariadne Papos's hardwood floor before bullets tore through the window, past the open space I'd been occupying rather calmly a moment before, and into the hallway, where they struck and killed a portion of faux wood paneling.

It was over in a couple of seconds.

"What?" I finally managed to say.

Mike rolled off and dragged me away from the window while my nervous system tried to catch up.

"Are you hit?" he asked, drawing his own weapon and keeping an eye on the window.

I checked. No apparent bullet holes. "No."

"Good."

Still not looking at me, he pulled the car keys out of his jacket pocket and dropped them on my stomach. "We have more to talk about, but not now. Take the car. There's a diner we passed on the highway about ten miles back. Randy's. Do you remember it?"

"I think so."

"Fine. I'll meet you there."

"I'm really not a good driver," I insisted.

"Learn fast. Look, somebody heard that, and that somebody is calling the police right now. You can't be here when they are."

"I see your point."

"Good. Go to the diner."

"What are you going to do?"

"Figure out who wants one of us dead, and then clean things up with the cops."

"How are you going to ..." But I didn't get a chance to finish that question. Mike jumped up, and in one fluid motion broke right through the already half-shattered window and into the back yard. Surprisingly, whoever was out there with the semi-automatic weapon (it sounded like a TEC-9) didn't open up on him. Either Mike was really lucky, or he already knew the shooter was fleeing the scene. I suspected the latter.

Any doubts I still might have had about Mike were gone. He definitely wasn't fully human.

Chapter Seven

The god berated Silenus. "Your stories do not enrich the world for any who listen."

"But men do weep, and clamor for more tales," Silenus protested. "Would you starve them of these things?"

"Stories have a place in the breast of all men, but only when not supposed true. There are many enough real perils in this life for men to fear; birthing imagined horrors serves no purpose, and is a danger to any who cannot parse the difference."

"You speak of gods as imagined horrors?"

"I do exactly."

—From the archives of Silenus the Elder.
Text corrected and translated by Ariadne

The first time I saw an automobile, it nearly ran me over, and that's pretty much colored how I've felt about them since.

Granted, it was easier to show disdain in the early days when they were only occasionally capable of outstripping a horse in full gallop, made a profound stink, and broke down every few miles. And that was just what you had to deal with when sharing the road with them; riding inside of one was infinitely worse. Imagine letting all the air out of your tires, removing your windshield, your shock absorbers, and the cushions in your car seats, and then driving on a dirt road. You'd start pricing horses pretty fast.

Mike's convertible was a standard transmission, which was okay since I learned how to drive a car with a stick. That was in 1942, back when cars still traveled at a moderately acceptable speed and a stick was all you got.

It still took five minutes to start his car. First, I had to crawl to the front door of the house and duck and bob my way to the driver's seat, not entirely certain the gunman from the back yard hadn't simply relocated to the front under the reasonable assumption that we might wish to drive the hell away once we found out somebody was trying to kill us. I even entertained the notion that Mike had sent me out the front on purpose. Seemed out of character for him but hey, he's not human, and since I didn't know for sure exactly what he was, being a good liar might have been part of the package. (Goblin was definitely out; they can't move that fast.) Once in the seat, I relaxed a little, but then there was the matter of remembering how cars work.

I stuck the key into the ignition and turned it, and nothing happened. I tried turning it a half-dozen more times to the same effect, feeling more and more like a caveman with a cell phone, until it occurred to me to step on some pedals. Through trial and error, I discovered that in order to fire up the internal combustion engine, I had to stomp on both the clutch and the brake first.

The next few minutes were spent reviewing the steps necessary to propel the car in some sort of direction, and discovering how easy it was to stall with very little provocation on my part. I eventually discovered reverse, and even better, first gear. Then I tried second gear, and that was so wonderful, I stuck with it for several blocks, until a burning smell suggested that it might be time to try third gear.

By the time I reached Randy's Diner, a couple of hours had passed and I hadn't killed myself or anybody else, but Mike's car wasn't sounding too hot. As I locked it and went in, I reminded myself that the next time I took a car onto the highway, I was going to have to use a higher gear than third.

* * *

"More coffee, hon?" Linda the waitress asked. She was a cheerful older woman with a vague trace of a mustache and teeth the color of tea. Since my arrival, she'd been offering me refills on a highly regular basis.

"Sure," I agreed absently. My head was stuck in the files Mike left in the car. He probably hadn't meant to, but his bag of interesting FBI case files had been left under the passenger seat when we'd gone into Ariadne's home and I certainly wasn't going to leave it there unread. Not with all this time to kill.

Linda splashed another load of the brackish, coffee-like substance I'd been drinking for the past two hours into the cup and toddled off again. Preoccupied as I was with Mike's files, my devotion to the coffee had become nearly Pavlovian; I didn't want any more, but I couldn't stop drinking the refills.

The first file I turned to was my own, and I found it satisfying to discover that Mike hadn't held anything back in that regard. Except there had to be a much larger version of it elsewhere, given how slight it was and the fact that there was nothing inside that justified the full-on 24-hour observation I'd gotten. Maybe, I reflected, Mike didn't have access to the rest. More likely he anticipated handing over the file at some point, and had deliberately omitted documents.

The folder on Ariadne was considerably larger and more involved. I found photos of her house, her apartment in Sacramento, and her workstation at the office. None of that was particularly intriguing; I'd seen the most important stuff in person already. What I hadn't seen before was the notes and documents she left behind in Rancho Cordova. The originals were probably being dusted, treated, and fingerprinted within an inch of their lives in some sort of underground lab somewhere, but Mike had copies of everything.

The first item of note was a lengthy treatise on the Dionysian Mysteries. It was a ten-page thing she probably pulled off some university site somewhere and about half of it was wrong, through no fault of anybody, since the original participants had sworn to keep everything that went on in the mystery cults a secret. Considering what I already knew about her, it was a curious find. Between the note she left in my room, and what I'd seen in her house, she already knew more about the Mysteries than anybody who isn't me should expect to. So what was she doing with this essay on her desk?

There were a half-dozen other articles that pretty much parroted the same stuff the first article had said. I'd find an occasional note in a margin, but there was nothing to further illuminate the open question. Still, just seeing the Mysteries brought up in print made a few things come together for me.

Mike said she was connected to a terrorist organization. If this was it, either Mike was horribly misinformed, or I was, since the Cult I knew ceased to exist long ago. And when it did exist, it certainly didn't commit acts of terrorism, or whatever the ancient Greek version of a terrorist act might be.

Then came the articles on Peter Arnheit. I was right; it was a name I'd seen before, and it did involve a murder case.

I spent a good half an hour reading through all the material she'd pulled down from various news sites until I realized that Peter Arnheit was the subject of the third file folder in Mike's bag.

All I knew about him was what I'd read in the news, and I'm not much for keeping up with current events so that wasn't a lot. And a quick review of Mike's file showed me that the papers knew far less than they realized.

* * *

Peter was one of the lucky ones in this life, insofar as he was fortunate enough to have a mother who attracted rich men on a semi-regular basis. She'd been married four times to four men who'd each made at least one appearance on the Fortune 500 list in their lifetime.

Although it wasn't clearly stated in any of Mike's documents, Peter had obviously fallen into the trap of the uncommonly privileged and became very bored with himself. I've seen this a lot, as you can probably imagine.

Bored wealthy people can be dangerous, like when they decide to start a war just because it's something to do. In Peter's case, he reached a certain level of ennui sometime in college—UCLA—and decided to take a year off to hike through the rainforest with his roommate, a kid named Lonnie Wicks.

That was a mistake. I've been to my share of tropical rainforests, and they tend to be the sort of thing one tries very hard to get the hell out of, not actively hike into. Especially now. Back in the early days, we understood that damn near everything on the planet wanted to kill us for one reason or another and we were prepared for that, because it was the only way we knew. But in the twenty-first century, one can walk for weeks without coming across something that wants to eat you and has the means to do so. A city kid like Peter Arnheit should have known better. (As an aside, this is why I don't understand most anybody involved in the environmental movement. These people probably think we used to pet panthers and sing to rhinos or something. It's all Walt Disney's fault.)

Peter and Lonnie were both well trained in survival techniques, as apparently it was a hobby of theirs. They also had access to the best gear money could buy, including a couple of satellite phones, something called a GPS, plenty of cash, and their health, which is always important.

And then they disappeared into a South American rainforest.

Four months later, nobody had heard from them, and their families were worried. Peter's mother had died of leukemia during his freshman year in college, but his biological father, a former senator from the state of New Mexico, was still very much alive. And Lonnie's parents were the owners of the largest retail chain of women's footwear in the Western

United States. With that kind of clout, it's not surprising that the government was soon politely requesting assistance from four different South American countries in locating them.

Unfortunately—and I could have told them this—political pressure doesn't make a huge difference if someone is lost in a rainforest. Just about the only thing they could confirm was that the kids hadn't been kidnapped. Or if they had, it was by some incredibly stupid kidnappers who didn't understand that demanding a ransom is kind of important.

So everyone in the Arnheit and Wick households sort of just freaked out for a little while, up until one afternoon when, seven months after he'd last been heard from, Peter called home.

"I made it, Dad," he had told the stunned Senator Arnheit, "but it got Lonnie."

What followed was something of a minor scandal. The Wicks family had lost their only child, and the one person who knew exactly how and why, wasn't making any sense at all.

Peter was half-starved and badly dehydrated when he emerged from the woods, and the last lucid thing he did for a good three months was place that call to his father. Hospitalized first in Colombia, before being flown *gratis* by the American government to a more up-to-date medical facility in Los Angeles, he was never conscious for more than a half hour at a time, and had to be resuscitated twice when his heart decided to give up and stop beating.

The problem was a severe infection. He had over a dozen unexplained wounds on his body, the two deepest and oldest of which hadn't healed well at all. The locations of the cuts—Mike had pictures—implied he'd been attacked by a wild animal, and on more than one occasion. But the wounds themselves weren't consistent with any indigenous animal, so the consensus was they were knife wounds caused by another person. The possibility that this person had been Lonnie Wicks was floated.

Looking at the photos, I couldn't think of any animal that might have made the wounds, and I'm pulling from a much wider data pool than your average zoologist. A dragon, maybe, but dragon wounds were usually wider and more definitively lethal. And dragons are extinct.

When the infection was fought back and Peter's fever finally abated, the police were called in to ask him what happened to his friend.

His official response was short and not terribly illuminating, essentially saying they would never believe him if he told them. Beyond that, he wouldn't utter a word until after the arraignment.

By the time Peter was released from the hospital, the L.A. County District Attorney had put together what he thought was enough of a case to try for a murder conviction, and the grand jury agreed.

But the case had a few weaknesses. Even I could see that, and the closest I ever got to a defense attorney was turning on the television. For starters, there was no body, and the only proof that Lonnie met a tragic end was Peter's own statement to his father that *something* had gotten Lonnie (which Senator Arnheit would probably deny). There was also no discernible motive. On the other hand, Lonnie Wicks had still not emerged from the Amazon, and the day Peter walked out, he was carrying with him several of Lonnie's possessions: his bedroll, his tinderbox, and most damningly, Peter was wearing one of Lonnie's shirts.

And there were the wounds on Peter. Lonnie owned a large Bowie knife he was rather proud of, and the district attorney had an expert who was prepared to testify that the wounds were consistent with the knife. They weren't, because knife attacks don't generally result in a series of parallel slash marks, but hey, I'm not an expert.

Peter made bail. His passport was confiscated and he still wasn't very healthy, so his high-priced attorneys had no trouble convincing the judge to hand him over to his family.

Then he disappeared. That was five months ago.

I couldn't imagine why any of this mattered to Ariadne, but obviously it did. What I did understand, finally, was why Mike was so interested in finding Ariadne. It wasn't really her he was after.

It was Peter.

There were dozens of photos in the Arnheit file. The very last one was a photo of Lonnie Wicks, dated about a year before his apparent death. It looked like someone snapped it at a cookout somewhere. Captured in the shot were Lonnie, his parents, an older man I didn't recognize, and agent Mike Lycos with a big smile and a Frisbee in his mouth as a joke, and one arm around young Lonnie.

* * *

So I had the Arnheit case, a dead mystery cult, a woman who was obsessed with both (and with me), a non-human FBI agent possibly with vengeance on his mind, and an unknown gunman. None of it was coming close to adding up, which was downright annoying as I am generally pretty good at this sort of puzzle.

I sipped on the stale coffee that was now eating a large hole through the lower portion of my stomach, and tried flipping through the pages one more time to see if an inspirational thunderbolt was hiding in there anywhere.

I ended up on a scratch page. Ariadne had kept a blank sheet of paper on her desk for jotting down random notes, the occasional phone number, and doodles that all looked a bit like the creature from the Black Lagoon.

None of the notes made much sense out of context, and I was ready to move on to the next page when I realized I was looking at a name, and that I recognized the name.

"More coffee, dearie?" Linda asked, as I jumped several inches off the bench. I didn't realize she was there.

"Actually, no. Do you have a payphone?"

"Near the john," she said, pointing with the half empty urn.

"Thanks." I scooped up the pages and shoved them back into the bag in case Linda was the curious sort. There wasn't anything in there that was particularly damning, but still, they were confidential files. Not that I had any more clearance than Linda did.

I reached the phone and dialed up the operator, which naturally didn't work. Back when phones were just becoming regular things, you could actually pick one up and get connected to someone, and you could ask that someone to connect you to another someone, and then they went and did it. It was an amazing thing. Now you have to pay to get the phone company on the line, pay again to get the number, and pay a third time so they can dial it for you. You would think I'd be used to this sort of thing by now.

"City and state," asked a very congested woman after I pumped some change into the phone.

"Um, Berkeley, California," I said haltingly.

I at first thought she meant what city and state I was calling from, and I couldn't imagine why it would matter. Again, technologically speaking, I'm still a caveman.

"Number for?" she asked.

"Cassandra Jones," I answered. And if Cassandra had moved from the Berkeley area this was going to take a very long time.

The pause on the other end of the line was quite dramatic. "Hold please for your number." And then a computer read the number to me. Because apparently it's too much work to have the operator read off ten digits.

I jotted the number down on my hand, hung up, and then dialed it. The machine on the other end of the line—a different machine than the one that had given me the number in the first place—listed an exorbitant sum necessary to complete a call of this magnitude. You would think they were laying the phone wires one call at a time. I put in the change, nearly including Ariadne's drachma, which I can't imagine the phone would have taken kindly to.

The phone rang, and a familiar voice answered.

"Cass, it's an old friend," I said.

"Spencer!" she exclaimed. I did figured she'd remember me. "I knew I'd be hearing from you soon."

"Did you?"

"Of course, darling. It's what I do. When can you be here?"

Chapter Eight

Oracle:
When serving one to find the other,
Lies will trap you 'twixt the two.
For the other will not greet the one you serve
And all will be lost e'er the shadows dance.

Silenus:
What?
Your speech is woefully unclear.

Oracle:
Such is the way of prophecy.

—From The Tragedy of Silenus,
text corrected and translated by Ariadne

This wasn't my first time in California, although aside from the occasional connecting flight, I hadn't spent any real time in the state since 1967, and that time was spent on the campus of UC Berkeley.

As I may have mentioned before, there are two kinds of people who are great to be around if you feel like confessing your immortality, and not get a lot of blank stares in return—bar drunks and college students. In the case of the former, that's sort of easy to understand because many bar drunks are also semi-crazy people, and semi-crazy people are having their sense of reality mucked up on such a regular basis that one more muck-up isn't really that much of a big deal for them. With college students, it's hard to say exactly what it is.

In the sixties, it helped immensely that so many of the very best—or at least the most entertaining—students were also stoned a great deal of the time. It was the same in the seventies, but the drugs of choice—and the overall philosophy of the students—had changed a lot by then, so it was more difficult to find an entertaining student population that wasn't also seriously considering taking hostages for some cause or another. And the eighties and nineties were the absolute worst, up until the latter stages of the nineties, when cultural relativism and deconstructionism started to become vogue. This worked for me because to a cultural relativist, it makes perfect sense that in My Culture immortality was a fact, and they felt compelled to accept it at face value, which led to some mind-blowing discussions. At least for them. Inevitably, the deconstructionists brought up their ongoing problems with certain dead white men, which got sort of uncomfortable given how many of those dead white men I happened to know. But they were still pretty fun.

Amazingly, deconstructionists and cultural relativists were almost never stoned, which meant the crap they were spouting came to them when they were in a non-altered state, so they were invariably fairly stupid, or at least not nearly as smart as they thought they were. They also never passed out, which was unfortunate. The upside was that I never felt left out of the fun, insofar as I can't get stoned.

I don't know why this is, but I'll wager it has a lot to do with why I can't be poisoned or get sick, so it's not a bad tradeoff. Still, it looks like fun.

Anyway, I met Cassandra Jones on the UC Berkeley campus at a party. Well, no, a party implies a cause for celebration of some kind, and we weren't celebrating something. Really, from a definition standpoint, nobody can fairly describe an event that occurs nightly a party at all.

I digress.

Cassandra was a student, and a part of the counter-cultural flower child phenomenon that seemed so much fun back then but nowadays looks silly. For my part, I always thought it was silly, but as I was a raging drunk at the time, I didn't do much complaining about it.

I remember very clearly when things went weird for her. We were sitting around a tree on a hill somewhere, and she was mad stoned on some hashish that a guy named Goofy had scored in Mexico. (Goofy was not his real name. His real name was Lawrence and he is now a prosperous estate attorney in Butte, Montana. It's sort of a hobby of mine to look up people I knew as total nut jobs to see what happened to them.)

Cassandra was sitting cross-legged, and had adopted a Buddha-like pose—although she was not in the least bit fat or bald—and hadn't spoken for several minutes, despite a rousing discussion the other five of us were having on the merits of Paul McCartney's bangs and what they said about the geopolitical status of third world nations *vis-a-vis* colonialist America and the socio-economic pressures of hair products in general, and more specifically, how napalm and hair spray are really pretty much the same thing when you look at it a certain way.

See, you don't get that kind of conversation just anywhere.

Quite suddenly Cassandra opened her eyes, and with a strange expression on her face, declared loudly, "Ask!"

My four stoned friends found this exceptionally funny. Me, I sobered up, because I'd seen this act before.

"Ask what?"

"Ask," she repeated. Her eyes were unfocused, like ... well, yes, like she was stoned, but more than that. Like she was staring intently at something that was actually on the inside of her eyeballs.

"What is her trip?" asked Chandra, a lovely girl to my right whom I fully intended to bed later in the evening. (I didn't.)

"Ask her something," I suggested. "A decision. Do you have a decision you need to make soon? An important one?"

"You serious?" Chandra laughed.

"Completely."

The others quieted down, as this had ceased being something to giggle over. Chandra looked furtively at the others.

"I can't," she muttered, suddenly very nervous. "C'mon, someone else."

"Okay," Kenneth piped in. When he wasn't stoned, Kenneth was an extraordinarily shallow person, which was why he was always stoned. He had a great future ahead of him that probably would consist of robbing somebody's pension fund.

"Should I go skiing over the break?" he asked.

Kenneth was from a rich family; it was his money Goofy used in Mexico.

Cassandra sat quietly for about thirty seconds, which seemed like approximately two days to us.

"Dude, I think she's asleep," Goofy said.

"Naw, her eyes are open," Kenneth argued rightly.

"Why doesn't she blink?" Chandra asked.

Suddenly, Cassandra boomed, "You will soar 'ere the pines do walk. Beware the straightest path."

And then she closed her eyes.

"What?" Kenneth was confused. "What the hell did she just say?"

"You're going to have to figure that out," I said.

I crawled to Cassandra's side and put my arm around her. If this was what I thought, she was about to lose some motor coordination.

"Figure what out?" Kenneth shouted.

"Soaring through the walking pines or something," Goofy said.

"No, she was asking about the sidewalk," Chandra said.

Dear Baal, these people were stoned.

"Kenneth," I began, as Cassandra predictably slumped into my lap, "what she said to you was important. You need to figure out what it means and act accordingly."

"Man, you're stoned," Kenneth laughed.

"No, I'm drunk. There's a difference."

"Yeah, whatever."

"What ..." Cassandra asked, her eyes opening again and looking surprised to be in my lap. "Spencer? What happened?"

"You'll be all right," I said.

"Did I ... was I talking? What was I saying?"

"Your first prophecy," I said.

"My what?"

"Cassandra, did your mother ever tell you why she gave you that name?"

"No," she said, trying to sit up and ultimately failing. "Just liked the sound of it, I think."

"Ask her sometime. I'm betting it's an old family name."

"What are you talking about?"

"You're an oracle, Cassandra."

* * *

In truth, the original Cassandra wasn't an oracle at all.

As Homer told it, she was given the gift of future-sight and the concomitant curse of having nobody believe her when she foretold the future. But she was just the stuff of legend, whereas the Delphic oracles were very real. And like the Cassandra of Berkeley, the oracles of the temple of Delphi were stoned when they gave their prophecies. The temple itself was built over a fissure, and rising from that fissure was a gas that had a psychotropic effect. I know this not because I ever went to them for advice, but because I used to hang in the temple after hours with a couple of the girls. (The gas made them almost perpetually horny, which was quite a conundrum for a group that was both highly respected and deeply feared by everybody in Greece: everyone was afraid to touch them. Worse, seventy percent of the male population was devotedly homosexual, whereas I was perfectly happy with either sex at the time.)

As I have said before, and will say again, as far as I can tell there is no such thing as real magic. But oracles don't perform magic. They aren't fortune-tellers either, not in the sense that most of us understand the term to mean. They can't find lost children, divine the identity of a murderer, or tell you much at all about what your future holds.

It's very strict. You ask them a question, they give you an answer, and that's it. They can see major events but they're brief, episodic flashes, often without context, and always presented cryptically.

There's no point asking for clarification. I brought that up once to a Delphic oracle who informed me she described what she saw—nothing more, nothing less. The real problem is figuring out what to make of the answer you get.

That was Kenneth's problem. He didn't put much thought into it, or he would have realized Cassandra told him not to go skiing. He went, and found his favorite trail was temporarily closed. But at the end of what was described to me as a glorious day on the mountain, Kenneth challenged his buddy to a race to the bottom of the hill. He decided to win that race by taking the most direct route, i.e., the closed trail. The problem was the trail was being widened at the time, and right as Kenneth soared down the slope, a crew was busy removing a large pine tree. They had felled it and dragged it right into the middle of the slope. It was twilight by then, and Kenneth didn't see the felled tree until it took out his ankles. He slid head first into another tree. Miraculously, he didn't die. But he never walked again, and took five years to get back onto solid foods.

I never formally sought an oracle's advice. The whole idea was just too much of a head-trip. I did spend a couple of years helping out Cassandra, however, who needed all the assistance she could get and was extremely fortunate to know a guy who had kept the company of the original oracles. The sex was pretty good, too.

* * *

I was a little hung up on what Cassandra said on the phone, shortly before giving me directions.

She had been expecting me.

The claim that she knew because that was her job was more than a little disingenuous because she can't give herself a prophecy. In order for her to know I was coming, she had to see me in someone else's future. So whom had she been sitting for?

This thought was what occupied my time as I made the two-hour trip from the diner to her home in Berkeley. Well, that and the constant recitation of the proper steps necessary to operate a motorized vehicle. (It would have been an even longer trip were it not for the miraculous discovery of fifth gear I made about midway through the drive.) The most obvious candidate was Ariadne, and that brought up another, much more interesting question. Did Ariadne intend for me to follow her all along?

The drachma, the note in my hotel room, and the orgy of information on the walls of her study—which more and more seemed like a place she tacitly expected me to see—all suggested I was following a deliberate trail of bread crumbs. If she had also gone to Cassandra, the possibility existed that she not only knew much more about me than anyone living should have; she might know more than I do: she might know my future.

I was probably missing some information. It would have been nice to ask Mike about it, except I never waited long enough at the diner for him to show. He probably assumed I headed straight for Canada. And really, I should have.

It was dark by the time I reached Cassandra's house, a nice Victorian-style place within spitting distance of the campus. She'd done well for herself. Not spectacularly well, but well enough. I wondered if oracle duty was her sole source of income.

She was waiting on the porch when I pulled up.

"Spencer!" she called out. "You haven't changed at all, damn you!"

"You know how it is."

I shut down Mike's car and stepped out for a good stretch.

"Yes, I do," she answered. "Come on in, I've already brewed some tea."

* * *

We met one another inside the foyer with the embrace of a pair of old lovers, something I have a great deal of experience in and typically don't look forward to at all.

Nothing quite reminds one of the transitory nature of youth and beauty as seeing someone remembered as a buxom twenty year old after forty or fifty years have passed. In most cases, time is extremely unkind, even though I generally say just the opposite to be polite.

It can be pretty alarming. I remember running into a former lover I'd known as a slight, exciting, moderately creative seventeen year old when she was a 240 pound grandmother of twelve. And I could have sworn I'd just left her.

But Cass hadn't changed as much as she probably thought. She was still rail-thin and seemed as full of youthful vitality as ever. Her frantic auburn hair had gotten thinner and grayer, and her skin had loosened up, but she still could have passed for someone ten or fifteen years younger than the mid-sixties she had to be. She still smelled the same. I wondered if she was as limber as before, but that struck me as too much to expect.

We separated, and she gave me a long stare with those cobalt blue eyes. "To think, I used to think of you as an older man."

"I am."

She slapped me on the arm.

"You could pass for my son! Come, to the kitchen!"

I followed her theatrical gesture beckoning me through the front sitting room—tastefully appointed and hardly used, from the looks of it—and into a very lived-in kitchen. On the counter were two steeping cups of tea, causing me to wonder if perhaps Cassandra had picked up additional soothsaying tricks since I'd last seen her. How would she know when to have the tea ready?

"I took a guess on your arrival time," she said, and for just a second I thought she'd been reading my mind. But nobody can do that. "You said you were an hour away, so I doubled the time and here you are."

"Why double it?" I asked, although it was hard to argue the point given how right she was.

"You said once that the day you get behind the wheel of a car is the day you give up hope on surviving another century. I took that to mean you're not a good driver, and the roads between hither and yon are littered with the remains of not-so-good drivers."

It shouldn't surprise you to know Cassandra majored in English.

"So, have you?"

"Have I what?" I was fiddling with my tea bag. Not a big fan of the bags, but I understand their practicality. Still, brewed tea is always the best way to do things, and don't let anybody tell you otherwise.

"Given up hope?"

"Not as far as I know. Just seemed like too long of a walk. And I had a car already."

"Sure, sweetie. Not yours?"

"No," I smiled. "Not mine."

She nodded and expertly extracted her own teabag, squeezed the last remnants from it by pressing it against the concavity of the spoon, and flung it into an open trashcan that was sitting beside the counter.

I sipped from my cup. Darjeeling.

"So how have you been, Cass?"

"I have been aging," she said. "But not so badly."

"No, you've done a very good job of it." I meant it as a compliment even though it probably didn't sound like one. Yes, there is a reason I don't speak to old lovers very often. I suck at it.

"I teach," she continued. "The classics, of course."

"Of course. No problems with dead white men?"

"We continue to allow dead white men to be brilliant," she smiled. She still had that smile. Honestly, I didn't know whether I should be flirting or not.

"Family?" I asked.

She took a sip of her tea. "Never married. I had offers, but I found sleeping around was much more satisfying. I am looking into a couple of decent prospects now, if only just to get someone into this house willing to mow the lawn for free."

I grinned. Cassandra never had much use for the male portion of the species outside of their obvious insert-tab-A-into-slot-B qualities. It was true when we shared an apartment, and was apparently no less so now.

Then we fell into an awkward silence. Possibly, it was my turn to say something about how my life had been going, but I had a feeling that telling her *I drank and moved around a lot* wasn't going to make for a terribly engaging tale. Instead I asked, "Are you still an oracle?"

"Of course I am. Isn't that why you came?"

"That's the short version."

"I imagine the long version is a hell of a lot more interesting," she remarked, still daintily sipping her tea. Something brushed up against my leg.

"Ahh!" I cried out, somewhat less manly than was really warranted. It was a cat.

"That's Wally. Hello, Wally!" She chirped a couple of times and up jumped Wally, right onto the counter and yes, this bugged me. "You don't like cats," she said matter-of-factly, rubbing the beast gently behind its ear.

"I used to hunt them, when they weren't hunting me," I said. "It's not something you get over. Wasn't Wally the name of ..."

"Yes."

Cassandra "left" me for a guy named Wally. I put that in scare quotes because it's not entirely fair to classify what Cass and I shared as a full-time monogamous relationship.

One might be of a mind to assume that, no, of course it wasn't because we were in Berkeley, it was the sixties, and we were all into this free love thing. Except free love was pretty much a bunch of crap. It was an ideal, but it only worked out in the sense that everybody assumed everybody else was doing the multiple-partner-no-attachments sex-with-whomever thing, somewhere, even if they themselves couldn't quite get the hang of it. It's a lot like cannibalism in that sense. It was always the other tribe that practiced cannibalism, while that other tribe was saying the same thing about your tribe, and really, hardly anybody was actually doing it.

The unavoidable reality is, people who have sex with other people develop attachments, and from that springs all that is good and bad about romance. So while we may have declared free love all we wanted, most of us were still looking for one person to spend time with in a relatively monogamous sense. The only difference was that when we became jealous due to some perceived infidelity, we blamed ourselves instead of the person who made us feel that way. It wasn't healthy.

Or maybe that was just me.

"I give up; why Wally?"

By all accounts, after I left and she moved in with Wally—who was an asshole, and I can produce independent confirmation of that—he didn't treat her particularly well.

"It gave me great satisfaction to have him neutered," she said. "Isn't that right, Wally?"

I winced. "You don't have a dog named Spencer, do you?"

She laughed, and touched my arm affectionately. "No, darling. I never felt that way about you." She shooed Wally away. "So let's get down to it. I assume you are here on business?"

"How'd you know I was coming?" I asked, happily getting back on-topic.

"Ah. An excellent question."

"Are you going to answer it?"

"No, I don't think so. Come."

She took my hand and led me from the kitchen, through a short hall, and to a set of steps.

"It's down here," she said, flipping on a light.

The basement was... well, there's no subtle way to describe it. It was an opium den. There was a huge couch with big, cushy pillows, heavy shag carpeting, a velvet-covered coffee table and, the *pièce de résistance*, a gigantic hookah.

"Wow! Bet that would have come in handy back in the day."

"Ugh," she sighed, plopping down on the couch. "*Please* don't use that phrase. My students are constantly saying it." She adopted a singsongy high-pitched voice. " 'Was Shakespeare, like, rich, you know, back in the day an' all?' God! It's horrible."

"You weren't that different."

"Don't you dare repeat that outside of this room," she snapped, possibly unaware that she sounded exactly like all the teachers she mocked when she was a student herself.

She reached around the couch and emerged with a full bottle of tequila. "It was the best bottle I could find. I hope it's okay. I know you can't do much with what I plan to be using."

She tossed it to me.

"Um, okay. I really just wanted information is all."

"Don't be such a woman, Spencer." A lighter emerged from somewhere in her loose-fitting dress. "It's time."

"Time for what?" I asked, as my hands unscrewed the bottle, although I didn't tell them to do that.

"Your first prophecy. Don't make that face. You knew how this little visit was going to end up."

"No," I insisted, "I'm just trying to make sense of a few things."

Cassandra looked up at me.

"You're scared!"

She laughed while I sat down and took a very generous swig of the tequila. "All this time, I thought you just didn't have anything important to see me about."

"If you knew half of what I know about oracles you'd be scared, too."

She gave a reassuring smile. "One mustn't fear one's future, darling."

"Do you tell that to everybody?"

"Yes."

She sparked the lighter to life and got the pre-loaded hookah going. "This is the finest Turkish hashish I can get my hands on. Over time, the cheap stuff stopped working. And if you're wondering how I can afford it, you should see my rates. But don't worry; I'm doing this one as a favor. Drink."

I complied, although again, I didn't tell my body to do anything of the kind. This is what happens when you put alcohol in my hand.

"You've gotten good at this then," I remarked.

When I was helping her she was very hit-or-miss about the whole process. Sometimes it worked; sometimes she just giggled for a while and then passed out.

"You have no idea," she said calmly before taking several quick drags off the hookah hose to clear out the air trapped within.

"I am entirely opposed to this," I said. "For the record."

"I know." Another sharp intake and this time she exhaled smoke. "But if you must know, I found out you were coming when I discovered your future intertwined with another client. I expected I would see you myself soon enough."

"Can't you just tell me what you told her?"

She smiled at the choice of pronouns. Or, she was smiling because the drag she'd just taken was particularly good. It was difficult to tell. She exhaled.

"That's confidential. You didn't think I'd break my rules just for you, did you?"

"Guess not."

"I will tell you that I first sat with her over a year ago. Now shut up."

I drank, and tried not to look surprised.

If Ariadne had sat with Cassandra over a year ago, this must have been the *first* place she'd gone, not the last, which meant a lot of things now made sense.

Depending on what the prophecy had been, how long it was, and how clearly it had been interpreted, it was possible Ariadne set all of this up knowing exactly how it would play out. She could have known that Mike would lead me to her home, that I'd be in Vegas, and that I'd come to see the oracle myself.

With that, I felt as if I'd gotten all I needed to get from Cassandra, and nearly convinced myself to get up and leave the room. Instead, I watched the very familiar ceremony of an oracle getting into character.

* * *

When Cassandra first began seeing other peoples' futures, it was my job to keep her grounded and help her understand there wasn't anything odd about what she was doing.

I mean, it *is* odd in the sense that maybe a dozen people in the world at any given time are capable of doing it—and more than half of them will never know insofar as a minimum requirement is the attainment of an altered state—but it's not really a mystical event. The Ancients believed the Delphic oracles were tapping into a direct channel to the gods, because that was what they were conditioned to believe and because it just made a whole lot of sense. (And when there was a particularly tough customer I would, at times, pop in to play the part of a god in order to get them out. The Delphics worked on commission, and since some people were not all that happy with their readings, having a god turn up to scare them off helped. It was fun.)

There wasn't any higher power involved, but for a long time I couldn't explain what it *was* either. I still can't. But I do understand a little more about time as a concept, and that it's possible to view time as something more than a straight-line narrative event.

As I look at it, the oracle has the ability to break free, temporarily, of the constraints of time as we all perceive it, and catch glimpses of other points along the line.

Cassandra took a while to get past the notion there was a sort of mental lens she could focus to get a clearer picture. I had to keep reminding her this was as good as it got, and it was up to the person she was sitting for to interpret. I'm well aware that this is the cop-out of all cop-outs when it comes to your standard fortune-telling charlatan, astrologer, and what-have-you, but in the case of an oracle, it's perfectly true.

And given how very many oracular declarations I've been privy to, I've gotten pretty good at helping people interpret them.

Eventually, Cassandra got better at it and I had outlived my usefulness. This coincided neatly with the gradual reduction in the regularity and boisterousness of our sex life, and led to the insertion of Wally.

* * *

I'd nearly reached the halfway point on the bottle of tequila when Cassandra stopped puffing and entered a familiar calm state. She was sitting cross-legged in the center of her couch, immobile, the tip of the hookah pipe tube hanging loosely off the edge of the table. Her breathing was minimal and her eyes were closed.

The hookah suddenly made a whole lot of sense. Any hand-held device—a pipe or a joint—might at this point cause a fire, as Cass was no longer home. I found I was unconsciously holding my own breath.

A few minutes later her eyes snapped open, her pupils clouded over, not appearing to focus on anything in the room.

"*Ask!*" she commanded.

When seeking an oracle, it's always a good idea to have a question in mind ahead of time. I had nothing, because I didn't really want to do this.

Truthfully, the question has only a minor connection to the answer because she was looking at the future in general terms. Thus, a question wondering if you should marry your girlfriend gets roughly the same answer as wondering if you needed to pull all of your IBM stock because in both cases, she's checking in on you at some distant future point.

That's what I mean when I say it's up to the questioner to figure out how the answer pertains to them. If you're told that you will be fruitful and you take it as a green light to get married, okay. But it could also mean you should get your money out of the stock because it's about to plummet. Or it could mean neither, and she saw you working in an orange grove for minimum wage to support your many children after you moved your money into a different stock and lost all of it on an even worse investment. The future is tricky like that.

So I went for the simplest question I could think of.

"What will happen when I catch up with Ariadne Papos?"

Cassandra rocked back and forth like a machine churning out a solution. Finally, she spoke.

"The tree of life will strike, red on white, red on white! Godhood reclaimed marks the sojourner's end and the pretender's fall. Seek the source!"

And then she was done. She closed her eyes again, shuddered, and toppled over onto her side.

It would be a few minutes before she came around, which was okay; I needed time to figure out what I'd just heard, and maybe to hope desperately I'd heard it wrong.

Because as near as I could tell, Cassandra Jones had just predicted my death.

PART TWO

Toys in the Attic

Chapter Nine

Dion.
The only madness greater than challenging fate is accepting it.

> —From the dialogues of Silenus the Younger.
> Text corrected and translated by Ariadne

I needed some air, so I extricated myself from Cassandra's basement and found my way to the kitchen. With the tequila bottle running on low, I went through the cupboard until I found a backup bottle of cheap coffee liqueur. From there, I discovered the rear patio, which overlooked a modest but tasteful garden, just about right for somebody like Cass. I sat down on a lawn chair, took another large swig of the tequila bottle, and pondered things while every mosquito on the west coast slowly found its way to me.

I was mulling over the *sojourner's end* Cassandra mentioned. In several of the old cultures, that was my nickname—the sojourner.

The Greeks loved that about me. I used to carry messages from place to place, just because everyone knew me, or knew *of* me, and figured I'd be heading in the right direction eventually. And I usually was. I couldn't imagine the sojourner in the prophesy being anyone but me.

The rest of it I couldn't figure out. The part about the tree of life striking, and the red on white was entirely open to interpretation. Maybe it meant the Red Sox were going to win the World Series. I likewise had no idea who the pretender was, although I seemed to recall a rock band by that name. Godhood reclaimed? That could also mean anything. It could mean that only God could help me—and since I had not once gotten help from any god, up to this point, I wasn't expecting any in my future—or it could mean the tree of life was also a god. Either way, there were a lot more gods kicking around in the prophecy than I was entirely comfortable with.

Inevitably, I would figure these things out only when it was entirely too late to be of use. That's how it usually works. It wasn't the sort of thing I could run away from either, which was the really bad part.

I'm not a huge fan of fate as a concept. In the old days, people were so hung up on fate they didn't do anything at all; they just mucked about resignedly and figured they couldn't change what was in store. Not so different from people who obsessively play the lottery, hoping luck will drop a crap-load of money on them so they can live comfortably, when it would probably be a better idea if they just got a good job and stuck with it for a while.

And knowing one's fate never made a whit of difference, except it made the fated a tad more anxious. Often, attempting to evade the future brought it about, which was the point of *Oedipus Rex*. (Sophocles loved this stuff.)

Anyway, I was stuck. Also, I was incredibly drunk, which just amplified my tremendous sense of helplessness regarding the entire matter, while at the same time reducing my observational abilities considerably. I didn't even notice Mike until he was right next to me.

"Evening," he said, as if we were neighbors chatting over a fence somewhere. Provided neighbors actually did that sort of thing anymore.

I jumped several inches off the chair and spilled a minor portion of the remaining tequila.

"Hi."

Mike stepped past me and sat in the other lawn chair, lighting up a cigarette. I drank some more and wondered if I'd had so much I had forgotten Mike made the trip with me.

After a lengthy silence, he said, "GPS."

"What?"

"Global Positioning System. I have a GPS in the car. That's how I found you."

"Ah," I replied meaningfully.

"A buddy on the force gave me a lift."

"Ah."

"Just in case you were wondering."

I drank, he puffed, and we sat. The mosquitoes feasted.

"Sorry I didn't wait," I decided to say. Seemed like a good thing to bring up given I'd sort of stolen his car.

"S'okay. Although I'm surprised you didn't make for the airport."

"Thought about driving to Canada."

"Probably a better idea. Why didn't you?"

"Decided to see an old friend instead."

"Cassandra Jones?"

"That's her. She's inside, but I don't think she'd be a very good host right now."

Mike sniffed. "I can tell."

Somewhere in the dark recesses of my brain the words *marijuana* and *law enforcement representative* danced around each other. I suspected they did not belong together. "Glaucoma," I explained.

"Hmm?"

"She has glaucoma."

"Okay."

"It helps with ..."

"Don't worry about it," he said. "I've been known to partake myself. This is California; we don't give a shit here. So she's just an old friend?"

"Knew her when she went to college here. I figured it wasn't far."

"And you saw her name in Ariadne's notes."

"That too," I admitted.

"Can I get a sip of that?"

I handed him the tequila bottle and then opened up the coffee liqueur for myself.

He took a short pull. "Thing is," he went on, "we were never sure which Cassandra Jones the note referred to. There are about fifteen on this coast. None of them really had the connections we were looking for, so we dropped it. I figured it'd turn up again eventually."

"I only know one. Guess I'm just lucky it was the right one."

I was trying to sober up, but that's thoroughly impossible when you've drunk most of a bottle of tequila, so I went with faking it instead. Generally that involves making the other guy do all the talking. "Tell me about Peter Arnheit."

He looked at me for a few seconds, and then took a longer drink from the bottle. "You read that file, too."

"I did."

"The Wicks are family friends. Lonnie was my godson."

"You don't strike me as the religious type."

"I'm not."

"Okay."

"I find Ariadne, I think I'll find Peter, too."

I nodded. "Find me to find her, find her to find him. This is quite an entertaining chain you've worked up."

"I know. I'm a little desperate, if that wasn't already obvious."

It looked like Mike had finally decided to level with me. I went for it. "So what connects a very tired immortal man, an AWOL FBI analyst, and a bail-skipping possible murderer?"

"He *is* a murderer," Mike said fiercely. Apparently, he had held the trial already all by himself.

"Fine. What's the connection, other than you?"

"The Mystery Cult."

There it was again. "There is no such thing," I said, somewhat unconvincingly. "Not anymore."

"You better re-check that. And by the way, I'm having a little trouble with the whole immortal thing. I've been thinking about it all day and I'm not so sure I can allow myself to believe it."

"That's a common reaction. Let it simmer for a while."

"I'm trying."

"So are you telling me there's a mystery cult out there that I don't know about?"

"There are several, and they all call themselves a Dionysian Mystery Cult. Most look like pretty harmless Internet groups; more a social deal than a religious one. Seems to be an excellent excuse to party. But there's one that's a problem. There's almost no documentation, but we've found adherent records going back at least eighty years. The Eleusinians is what they call themselves; right now that group appears to be exceptionally dangerous."

The true Eleusinians—the name came from Eleusis, where the annual major ceremony took place—ceased to exist a long time ago, and they weren't dangerous. But I saw no advantage in bringing that up. "Like hiding in the woods with a TEC-9 dangerous?"

"The same."

"Did you catch the shooter?"

"Nope. Hopped in a car a couple of blocks over. Got the plates, but it came up stolen. We might still get lucky, but ..." He trailed off, either deep in thought or starting to feel the effects of the tequila.

I took a sip of the liqueur and made a note to never follow up tequila with coffee liqueur ever again. "What's so dangerous about this particular cult?"

"You first," he said. "Why did Ariadne come here?"

"Cassandra is an oracle."

"A what?"

"She can deliver prophecies," I elaborated. "It's all very complicated."

"She gets stoned to do that?"

I nodded. "Only way to get it to work."

"Sounds like a crock."

"So does an immortal man."

"True."

"I don't know why Ariadne came here," I said, which was half-true. "But she's not here now."

"And this Cassandra person doesn't have anything to do with her?"

"Ariadne was just one of her clients," I said.

"And the fact that you also happen to know Cassandra Jones? Is that a coincidence?"

"I don't think so, no."

"Me neither," he agreed. "I'm gonna have to question her."

I looked back towards the house. "She's kind of out of it right now.

Maybe later."

He looked hard at me. "She give you a ... what did you call it? A prophecy?"

"Mystery Cults," I said, changing the subject.

"Right. Eco-terrorism."

"What?"

"The Eleusinian Mystery Cult is run by a guy named Gordon Alecto."

"Like the Fury?"

"Um ..."

"The three Furies in Greek mythology. Megaera, Tisiphone, and Alecto. Alecto the Unceasing."

"Yeah, fine. Let me finish. Gordon Alecto is an eco-terrorist."

"I have no idea what that means."

"They like to commit crimes in the name of nature."

"You're not helping."

"Like blowing up a logging company's headquarters to save some trees."

"Ah," I said. "Sounds vaguely moronic."

"It is. But also very dangerous. Some of these groups don't mind all that much if the headquarters is staffed when the bomb goes off. Gordon's cult is one of those groups. And I've got good information that Ariadne Papos has been involved with the same group at least as far back as two years ago."

"And Peter Arnheit?"

"Peter was a part of the organization back before Lonnie was killed. We didn't know this until about a month ago when we raided Gordon's last known base of operations and found some of Peter's belongings there. Had we known, and had it been brought up in court, it probably would have been enough to keep him in jail. Problem is, nobody knows where they are now. Any of them. The cult has about thirty known members in the state of California, and they've all disappeared in the past month."

"Except for when they pop up to shoot at us."

"Except then. So my thinking is, Ariadne figured out the same thing I did, that you're the only living member of the original Cult. The reason she came out of hiding was to recruit you—and your money—to the cause. And since that's the last time anybody's seen her, it's a fairly big deal."

"But your superiors think they're not something to worry about?"

"They don't know. Everybody figures we'll know what the Eleusinians have been up to once they're done doing it."

"I feel so safe."

"Sometimes that's the way it is," he said. "It's the same with serial killers; you have to wait for the next victim to turn up. Besides, domestic terror groups aren't in vogue right now at the Bureau."

"So where does that leave me?"

"Dunno. It seems like the Cult has given up trying to recruit you. And you don't strike me as the type to get involved in something like that."

"The original Mystery Cult was a celebration of springtime and a good harvest. We didn't blow up things."

"Like I said."

He lit another cigarette, putting down the bottle he'd successfully finished off.

I'd finally met someone who could go drink-to-drink with me and still form complete sentences.

"I got you into this mess because I knew they were looking for you," Mike continued. "But that was before the shooting started."

"You think I was the target?"

"Pretty sure, yeah. And now I think maybe the best course is for you to get the hell out of here before I manage to get you killed. I'd feel pretty bad about that."

"Me too," I said. "So that's all this ever was? Keep me around because she's interested in me?"

"Pretty much. And I wanted to see if you could look at the same stuff I had and see something I'd missed. Like I said, I'm kind of desperate."

"How much of this do your superiors even know?" I asked, thinking specifically of Peter Arnheit and Mike's connection to Lonnie Wicks.

"Not much," he admitted. "If they knew it all, I'd be off the case. And I don't wanna be off the case. Anyway." He pulled himself up. "Unless you have some revelation to share with me, I'll be taking my leave."

"None that I can think of," I said. "But I am pretty drunk."

"Me too," he admitted. "Not so bad I can't drive, though. How's the car?"

"It'll work."

"You didn't fuck with it too much?"

"Not at all." I carefully omitted the fact he'd probably need a new clutch soon. I handed him the keys and he handed me a business card.

"This is my private line. Reaches me and only me. You call if anything comes up. I mean anything."

"I will." I stood, and we shook hands.

"Oh, and don't worry about the FBI. Right now about a dozen people are on the verge of losing their jobs thanks to what happened in

Vegas. Nobody's looking for you right now."

"Airports?" I asked.

"You're clear."

"I'll take your word on that."

"You should. You get caught and tell someone how you left town and I'm in trouble. So I've got something invested in you getting out untouched, don't I?"

"True enough."

He took a step to leave, then turned back with a thought.

"Tell me one more thing. What's in the box?"

"Pardon?"

"The box. I did some reading on the historical Eleusinian Cult. Every year, there'd be a festival, and this box would show up at the festival and somebody would open it up and show off the contents, but in everything I've read nobody can say what the contents were. So what was it?"

"I can't tell you," I said. "I took an oath."

"Seriously."

"I am being serious."

He looked at me funny for a few seconds, and then shrugged. "Guess you have a lot of secrets, don't you?"

"Only a few, but they're important ones."

"Box is long gone by now, anyway. Oh well. Until next time."

I nodded, and off he went. What I didn't tell him was that the box he was referring to was the same one in the photo on the wall of Ariadne's study. It wasn't nearly as long gone as anyone thought.

Chapter Ten

The beast stomped its hooves angrily and snorted rage and fire. In its hands it held a staff of wood as it were a feather, though it was wide as a tree base. And mighty Silenus did know fear.

"Do not be affrighted," the god said to Silenus. "Like all of the beasts of this world, this satyr is my brother."

—From the archives of Silenus the Elder.
Text corrected and translated by Ariadne

I didn't start to relax until after I'd made the connecting flight in Seattle that took me out of the country. Before I was out of reach of the FBI, I couldn't be completely positive Mike was right, and it was really okay to travel.

Logically, it made perfect sense. Emotionally, I was less sure, and sometimes emotions can do funny things to the logic centers of one's brain. For instance, most of my trip from Sacramento to Seattle was taken up concocting an involved fantasy about how Mike could *think* things were all clear for me, but was being misled in that regard by people who suspected that he himself was untrustworthy.

(To that end, he *was* untrustworthy. But if they already knew that, it made no sense to set up some kind of sting operation to catch me, in order to catch him, if they already had him. Better to catch him and find out how to subsequently catch me. This didn't occur to me at all until later.)

This fantasy scenario became a matter of near-certainty by the time I was on the ground, and didn't truly dissolve until I got off the flight and did not end up surrounded by gun-wielding government operatives.

So I was on my way to Amsterdam. If I had one ounce of sense in my head, I'd be stopping there and maybe hanging out for a century or two. But that was just where I was meeting up with a second connecting flight to Athens.

This was maybe not one of my better ideas.

* * *

After Mike left Cassandra's patio, I'd made my way back inside to see how she was doing and found her still on her couch, eyes open, enjoying the kind of relaxation I haven't achieved since I was a practicing Buddhist, which was a very long time ago.

"So?" she asked. "What do you think?"

I stood in the doorway and sipped at her liqueur bottle. "Do you remember it?"

"I do."

In the beginning, she not only couldn't remember her own prophecies, she couldn't even recall having been in a trance. Which fit; the older oracles of history could recall their prophecies exactly, but the younger ones had trouble with it. It was something I assumed one got better at with time.

"What do *you* think?"

"It's not for me to say," she'd said, dodging, which I hated.

"C'mon, it's me. I know the rules, and how I'm supposed to be the one to figure it out, so you can skip that. You heard what I heard. I'm asking what you thought about it."

Sitting up unsteadily, she gave it her best shot. "You're in danger."

"Yeah, I thought so, too. Of the end-of-the-road variety."

"There were two paths. One led directly to this woman. The other..."

" ... probably leads indirectly to her. Can't escape one's destiny, right?"

She waved her hands dismissively. "Of course you can. Don't be ridiculous. I gave you what might happen."

I took another sip. "You don't really believe that, do you?"

"I do! There is no such thing as predestination."

I skipped the irony inherent in such a proclamation coming from an actual oracle and went on to a better point.

"Have you ever given a prophecy that did not turn out to come true?"

"No, but I refuse to accept that they are all inescapable. And if there is any man who can escape his, it's the one man who has also managed to cheat death for a thousand lifetimes. You, my dear Spencer, are the exception to every other rule. Why not this one as well?"

"You mentioned two paths."

She took a casual puff of the hookah and said, "*Seek the source.* The first part of the prophecy is one path. That's the second. That's how I see it."

"Unless they're different bends on the same path."

"You know how it goes. I don't know if I'm looking at anything in any particular order. But that part felt different."

"Source of what?"

"I've no idea, darling."

By the time I found my way to her guest bedroom (she made no attempt to invite me into her bed, and I made no effort to work myself into it) and slept off the magnificent quantity of alcohol I'd downed, I realized what the source was. And that was what got me on the plane to Athens.

* * *

By the time of the birth of Christ, there were hundreds of different mystery cults in Greece, but the one I was interested in—the most famous one—took place in the Attic region: The Eleusinian Mystery. (*Mystery* in this context means something slightly different now than it did then. The root word is *mysterion*, which in Greek just meant rite or ceremony.) Each year at harvest, the Eleusinians held their celebratory rites, thanking Demeter, goddess of the harvest for the blessings she'd bestowed that year on their crops. The conclusion of the ceremony was the formal initiation of new supplicants. It was a little like the Christian baptism, but with less water and more drinking.

The new adherents were brought before a large iron box—called the kiste—and then the box was opened and the sacred items were revealed to them. Only those who were properly sworn in knew how to open the box, as the process was fairly involved and entirely counter-intuitive. I knew how to do it, but I doubted anybody else alive did, and I further doubted anybody else would be able to figure out how, even today. That might just be pride talking; I'd designed it myself.

But all of that was only for the boring part of the ceremony. The much more entertaining part—the private part, the part nobody knows about because the participants were sworn to secrecy—went to Dionysos, god of wine, dance, orgies, theater and, well, everything that makes life on this planet fun, plus death and madness, the two more obvious consequences of having too much fun for too long.

This is how all religions should work, incidentally; after a nice big sacred ceremony, a nice big party should always follow. The Greeks found a way to do that and still claim the Bacchanal was a religious rite, which is another reason I miss old Athens.

In the third century A.D., when the Romans broke up the party once and for all, the kiste was presumed lost. But if it wasn't, the place to begin looking for it was Eleusis—the source.

Assuming there were still satyrs living in Athens, I knew exactly where to start.

* * *

My first encounters with satyrs date back to before the death of Karyos, but after the destruction of Minos, in that hazy century or so in which I wandered the woods of the southern Greek peninsula. I'd heard rumors from as early as the days of the Sumerian empire, of wild men in the woods who stood upright but hunted like pack animals. I didn't put too much stock in it.

Most every old civilization looks at others—members of the same species but not of the same tribe—as wild men. It's a common rationalization, because when you reduce someone else to a level of something like an animal, it makes them easier to kill. So I tended to dismiss the rumors, which worked out fine up until the day I found myself face-to-face with a wild satyr.

I don't recall specifically what I was doing on that day, but I wager it had something to do with hunting or eating, as that was the extent of my activities during that time. Whatever I was doing, it was interrupted by a noise. It wasn't a large noise—a faint rustling is all—and it was the sort of sound most people would have dismissed as being part of the natural background of a growing forest. I knew better, because I'd been in the forest for quite a while and could make the distinction.

"Is someone there?" I asked, in the Minoan tongue. As a rule, game runs away and predators attack, and whatever had made this noise had done neither. I was presuming something sentient and probably human.

I pushed back a few branches and found myself staring down at something I'd never seen before.

He seemed human from the waist up, but his entire lower section was covered in hair. Unshod, it appeared his feet had only three toes. He was naked, and from the expression on his face, he was nervous.

Were he human, I'd take him to be no more than seven years of age.

I tried to put on a nonthreatening smile.

"Hello. What might you be?"

Then his father stepped out of the brush behind him. He was much more impressive.

Like the child, he was covered in a thick layer of dark brown hair from his waist down. His chest was bare, but his shoulders were covered with wispy hair that was a bit lighter than the rest. Likewise, the knuckles on his hand were hairy, as was almost his entire face. A thick beard ran up his protruded jaw, nearly obscuring his ears and meeting up with a fantastically unkempt mane of hair atop his head. His eyebrows were like things unto themselves, tapering upward and outward so dramatically that they appeared to be horns.

He put a protective hand on the boy's shoulder and drew him slowly away, never taking his brown eyes off me.

He spoke, but I couldn't understand what he was saying as it was no tongue I'd ever heard before. His voice had a low, growling canine sort of timbre.

"I don't understand," I said, making an effort to show the palms of both hands so it was clear I had no weapons.

"You speak island words," he growled.

It was difficult to understand—he was putting the emphases in the wrong places—but I got it okay.

"Yes. I came from there. How did you learn it?"

He looked me up and down, a little unsure.

"My son," he said finally. "Too young to ... be quietly."

"He will learn."

I offered my hand, and my strange new friend studied it carefully, but did not take it. Handshakes were not common with his people, apparently. So when that failed, I pointed to my own chest instead.

"Human," I said. Then I pointed to him.

"Gylin," he responded. At first I thought I was dealing with a race of Gylins, up until he pointed to his son and said, "Liakhil."

He didn't give me a chance to explain that I was trading species names and not surnames.

He pointed to the west and said, "Come, Hu-man, we eat. Okay?"

* * *

As we trudged through the forest, a remarkable thing happened—other satyrs began popping up out of nowhere.

I thought I knew how to disappear when it came to hiding in woods; I clearly had no idea what I was doing. One of them stepped out right next to me. Had he chosen to stay hidden, I wouldn't have known he was there, and he was barely an arm's-length away. I wondered how long they'd been watching me, given that detecting them when they didn't want to be detected was clearly not within my abilities.

We ended up with a dozen others of roughly the same size and build of Gylin. Liakhil was the only child among the group. I gathered that this was Liakhil's first foray away from their home. He had probably disappointed his father by getting caught by the likes of me.

Another thing I noticed as we walked silently through the underbrush, was that the legs of my new friends were somewhat more distinctive than I'd first realized. Their ankles were higher than they are on humans, by about a hand's-width. I wondered what sort of advantages this physical difference imparted. I soon found out.

We reached the apparent end of our journey when we came upon a particularly thick patch of plant life. From a distance it didn't look any different than any other portion of the forest, but once we got up close, I saw that the tangle of vines, moss, and low-branching trees was all but impassable. Had I come there alone, I'd have probably thought nothing of it and simply been shunted sideways until a clearer path was discovered. That, I reflected, was exactly the point.

Gylin spoke in his own tongue to a couple of his fellow adults, who nodded. Then they walked to one side and jumped more or less straight up.

I believe my jaw dropped at approximately the same speed at which they ascended, as the height they attained far exceeded anything I could ever hope to pull off myself. Both were soon out of view and somewhere within the forest ceiling. Gylin then instructed Liakhil to follow. The stripling's jump wasn't quite as impressive—better still than anything I could do—and he ended up dangling from the side of the wall of vines. He climbed from there and disappeared from view as well.

Gylin looked at me.

"Jump?"

"I can't," I said. "Climb?"

He smiled. Or I think it was a smile. If he were an animal, I'd take it as a teeth-baring threat. Then he gestured to two of the others, who stepped beside me. I wrapped my arms around their respective shoulders, they wrapped their arms around my torso, and I said a quiet prayer to the Minoan god of accidental death and dismemberment. Then we all bent our knees and pushed off.

The degree of force I applied personally to the jump didn't make a good deal of difference, but my two new friends didn't need my help. We rocketed through the upper canopy of the forest almost as quickly as if we were falling from the trees and to the ground. When we reached the acme of our ascent, they grabbed onto a series of vines that were possibly there for just this purpose. And with their help, I reached up and did the same.

Directly ahead was open space. With one of them first showing me how it was done, I worked hand-over-hand through the opening and crossed over, past what was now very clearly a deliberate wall of plants, and onto the other side. Then I was dangling over open space and an apparently fatal drop to the ground below. I saw that the two adults who'd gone before us were standing on the forest floor with Liakhil, watching expectantly. I didn't think they were there to catch me, but it was nice to imagine they might try, should I lose my grip.

I didn't have to worry about that, though, as I was rejoined by the two who had helped me up there in the first place. They flanked me once more, grabbed my torso, and instructed me through head gestures to let go of the ceiling and take hold of their shoulders. I did, with some trepidation, as I knew what was coming next.

I'd been wrong. The jump up wasn't nearly the same thing as falling down. Falling down was a good deal faster and decidedly more frightening.

Picturing my legs snapping in two, I tucked them under me and hoped that the others were capable of cushioning our landing sufficiently, as I didn't care to weather the rest of eternity with a pronounced limp. I needn't have worried; the landing was unexpectedly gentle.

Once the rest of the group made it over the wall, we walked a little further until coming upon their settlement.

It was a small village. I counted about fifty or sixty inhabitants and more than two dozen dwellings that amounted to little more than three-sided lean-tos somewhat similar to the tepees later used by Native Americans. All of the men in the village were as naked as the bunch that had taken me there, but all of the women were clothed. I found this odd until I realized that the women were all human. That was odd, too, but in an entirely different way.

Gylin slowly led me through the settlement. Everyone there had been in the midst of doing something—chatting, carrying water, tending a fire, cleaning—up until they spotted me. Apparently, my being there was a big deal.

By the time we reached the main building, nearly everybody in the village had come out to see, albeit at a safe distance just in case I was rabid. The children looked scared, the adults mostly curious. They talked to one another in Gylin's strange guttural language.

Presently, an older version of Gylin stepped out of the building, said building only differing from the others in size. Next to him was a human woman who looked at least fifty years of age. (I had no way of telling how old the men were.)

"Welcome," the elder male said, as Gylin stepped away from me.

I was now totally surrounded and standing alone. Possibly, I was about to be eaten.

"Thank you for your welcome."

I offered my hand.

The elder stared at the open palm, confused. The woman beside him whispered something in his ear. He nodded slowly, then stepped forward and extended his own hand. We shook.

The woman spoke to me in the Minoan tongue. "You'll have to excuse them. They don't have handshakes. And none have ever quite mastered the language you and I speak."

We ended our handshake, and I focused my attention to the woman who'd addressed me, the only person in the camp who seemed capable of conversation.

"If you don't mind my asking, what manner of beings are these?"

"They are the satyros," she explained. "But the much more interesting question is, what manner of being are you?"

* * *

It turned out the satyros had been watching me for over thirty years and were aware that I did not age. So while I looked like a man and acted like a man—albeit one with better survival skills than most of those who fled Minos after the great eruption—clearly I was not.

The consensus was that I was a god of men. It was also not

particularly satisfying as I didn't act very godlike, but it was the best anybody could come up with.

One thing they were certain of was that I was reasonably harmless, and so I became a living training exercise for their young. Whenever a male child was of age, they'd send a scout team to find me and then the youngster was told to get as close as he could without being detected. Poor Liakhil was the first to fail.

The women were indeed human; for some reason there were no actual female satyrs. The mating of a human female and a satyr male could either produce a human female or (much more commonly) a satyr male. At the time, this made no more sense to me than anything else. Now I have biology textbooks that tell me this is impossible, which is why I don't read biology textbooks.

The female elder of the village was named Mara, wife of Poleyt. Along with most of the women there, she'd come from Minoan stock. Her family had survived the blast and made it to the mainland, and managed to eke out an adequate existence in the wild for a few years before tragedy struck.

When I asked her over dinner one evening what that tragedy was, she asked, "In your time on Minos, did you ever hear of the Toah-Har?"

I had. When parents needed to quiet a child, they would threaten him or her with a visit from the Toah-Har. The approximate modern equivalent would be the bogeyman.

"The creature that would come in the night," I offered, "and eat bad children."

"Essentially, yes."

"You're saying your family was slain by the Toah-Har?"

She smiled. "No, wanderer. I am saying I don't know what else to call it; the only thing I can compare it to is the nightmare creature of a child. We numbered fifty people or more before that night, and scarcely eight remained by sunrise the following day. And we would have all been lost to the elements if the satyros hadn't come for us."

In this time, I could think of a half-dozen large creatures that possessed the malevolence and facility to kill forty-odd people, but so far as I was aware none of those creatures lived in these woods.

"Do the satyrs know what it was?" I asked.

Mara glanced at her husband, who either looked her off, or had indigestion. I was not good at reading their expressions at this time.

"The Toah-Har of Minos is what they call it as well," she said, with just enough peculiarity to give the impression she wasn't telling me the truth.

"Poleyt, I've lived in the forest for many moons and never have I seen a thing that could do this."

My tact was a bit rusty, but I knew enough not to openly state that I was thinking the most likely suspect was a band of satyrs. Knowing their need for women to maintain their race, it would make sense for them to attack the adults in the night and then "save" the rest and blame the deaths on some indefinable primitive force. If I were a tribal leader facing this kind of gender inequity, I might do the same thing. In fact, I did just that more than once.

Poleyt stared me down, something satyrs are naturally good at. "I know you have not, because you are still alive."

Most of the conversations I had with Mara and the rest of the village's inhabitants were decidedly more cheerful, and I enjoyed my time with the satyrs. I stayed for about a month, learned to master the basics of their tongue, and picked up a few hunting tips.

For my part, I shared some of the more interesting stories of my life up to that point—they were particularly amused by the story of the Hammer of Gilgamesh—and I convinced them pretty soundly that I really was just a guy who didn't happen to get any older.

* * *

The satyros population in the woods of Greece was a good deal greater than just that one small village, although I doubt they were ever as populous as man later became in those same lands. Learning their tongue served me very well in the subsequent years, because although there were many different satyr tribes—most considerably less efficient and peaceful as Poleyt's—they all spoke the same language. Knowing that language marked me as a friend to an otherwise violent race of beings.

In addition to their marvelous leaping ability, satyrs hunt and kill with the effectiveness of a pack of wolves, only with opposable thumbs. It's a bit trite to claim they are half-animal and therefore more prone to violence, but in some ways that was true.

Pity the army of men that sought to do away with the satyrs of the wood. I witnessed that once: a Greek general with a number of bad habits—one being a powerful hatred of the satyros—decided to send half a regiment into the northern woods. His soldiers were armed with swords and the satyrs with wood staffs and their fists. Despite that, no man walked out of the woods alive. (Coincidentally, the general's name was Kuster.)

When the Greeks settled down into the more civilized pre-Socratic culture, I was instrumental in introducing the wayward satyrs to the men of Athens less likely to have genocide on their minds. By then, whatever societal structure that once existed in the community of the satyros had broken down considerably, and they were forced to accept that mankind was a necessary evil, especially if they wanted to get their hands on womankind.

And the fact they needed human women would always be a problem. The lesson I took from Mara's tale of the Minoan Toah-Har was that satyrs in need of women are not to be taken lightly. So I'd go out of my way to bring a few satyrs along to every bacchanal I could. I would also bring women into the woods with me. This might strike you as hard to imagine, but consider that if you were a woman in Athens in those days, your prospects were really not very good at all. Just in terms of finding someone willing to have sex with you was a huge undertaking. After a while, a guy covered with hair from the navel on down started to look pretty good.

When the concept of the bacchanal became subsumed by the somewhat more religious concept of the Mystery Cult, the satyrs continued to garner invites, often at my personal insistence. One of the great things about the cults was that they were open to everybody, human or not. We even had a couple of vampires. Soon the cults were more important to the satyros than they were to the humans—perpetuation of the species and all that; a few were even run by satyrs.

So in a way, the only reason there are still some satyrs around today (assuming there are) is because I liked them and wanted to keep them around.

If anybody knew whether the old cult—the real one, the one with access to the sacred items and to the correct ceremonial procedures—was still around, it would be the satyrs, because it was the one group with an unbroken lineage to the ancient times.

The hard part would be finding them.

Chapter Eleven

Silenus:
Of all the gods that walk,
Why is it Demeter you do so ache to greet?

Dionysos:
I have met the other gods and have seen their fickle impiety.
That they would care more for the polis of mortal man
Than the wonder of all that is
Betrays them as no better and perhaps far worse.
Demeter cares for the soil and the fruit and the wood. If there is any
god worthy of your affection it is she.

Silenus:
More so even than the affection I show for you?

Dionysos:
More than that, yes; truly, I am no god for you.

—From The Tragedy of Silenus.
Text corrected and translated by Ariadne

A comparatively brief flight took me from Amsterdam to Athens. I didn't have to wait for luggage; I didn't have any. What I did have was all of my cash once again taped to my body so that I didn't have to claim it on my way out of the U.S. By the end of the twenty-hour trip, I was possibly the least comfortable person on the planet, what with the duct tape and all.

The first thing I did was buy a large satchel at one of the airport stores—conveniently, they took U.S. dollars. Then I stepped into the nearest bathroom and tore off the tape that was vying to become a permanent part of my body, trying not to scream while doing so. This required some self-control.

I exchanged some of the bills for Euros at a money counter, and then stepped out into the Athens night.

Well, not precisely. The airport was outside of Athens. Looking around, I couldn't even tell whether I was north of the city or south. My disorientation would only increase with time.

The cab ride to the city proper took about forty-five minutes, during which time I entertained myself by polishing my Greek in a conversation with George the taxi driver. George was kind enough to recommend a decent hotel that was cheap but had air conditioning, which is a very good thing to have in Greece in the summer time. Trust me, a day in the Athens heat and you're thinking those chitons and sandals were a pretty damn good idea.

The city itself was nothing like I remembered. This should come as absolutely no surprise to anybody, given I hadn't been there in almost two thousand years, but still. Moments like this remind me why I'm so fond of the United States; it's the only place I can go without becoming irredeemably confused. I'm sure if both of us are still around in another four thousand years, I'll feel the same about the States as I do about Europe.

What was immediately evident upon my re-entrance to Athens was that it had managed to catch up with the twenty-first century, even if I had not. The streets were paved, the buildings were tall, and the cars were everywhere. There wasn't a single recognizable structure in sight. George, ever helpful, was kind enough to shout out the occasional historical landmark, but whenever I turned to see, I found something that didn't look like what he'd named.

It went on that way until we spotted the Parthenon in the distance. That made me feel better until the moonlight broke from the clouds and I saw how crumbled it was.

I had outlasted stone, and if that's not a humbling discovery I don't know what is.

George dropped me off at the Hotel Attalos. After some brief dickering with the desk, I managed to secure a room that looked directly out at the Acropolis. However crumbled, it still helped me feel more at home.

* * *

I don't know what other people think of when they look at the Acropolis, if they think of anything at all. I look at it and I'm reminded of war.

The time of Socrates and Plato—the era most people associate with Greece—lasted less than two hundred years. And the seeds of philosophical thought, theater, democracy, and all the rest were planted well beforehand in the minds of obscure persons largely lost to history. But the elemental explosion of creativity that made up the Classical Period took place in a bubble of peace amidst a nearly constant state of war.

The Athenians defeated the Trojans, the Persians defeated the Athenians, the Persians defeated Spartans, the Athenians and the Spartans defeated the Persians, the Spartans defeated the Athenians, the Thebans defeated the Spartans, and the Macedonians defeated everybody. So you can understand why I didn't go out of my way to establish a firm residence anywhere in the Greek sphere; sometimes I was afraid to even sit down.

For most of the early history of Athens as a human settlement, the Acropolis was where the city's people went to hide. It was nearly siege-proof in those days due to its nearly flat hilltop surrounded by a steep climb, augmented by a wall. Before we started building castles, you couldn't do much better than that. (There was a period in there when a

Delphic oracle—clearly not one of the better ones—declared that the entire Acropolis was off-limits to everyone but the gods. Shortly thereafter, the Persians destroyed the city, which I'm sure wasn't a coincidence.)

It was Perikles who saw the hilltop for what it could be and commissioned the Parthenon—the temple of Athena Parthenos—and dammit if that wasn't one of the prettiest buildings I've ever seen.

One other thing the Acropolis—and the Parthenon specifically—reminded me of, was the gods.

* * *

The first ruler I ever met who actually had his act together was a fellow named Solon, one of the *archons eponymos* of Athens in the sixth century. *Archons* were elected into their positions somewhat like today's senators are—from members of the elite ruling class. Every year one of them was elected to fulfill the role of *eponymos*. Quite a few of the *eponymos* turned out to be complete bastards, which was bad, but since they only held the position for a year, they couldn't do too much permanent damage. And sometimes they could do some good.

Solon was one of the good ones. He established a system that could be considered the first version of democracy in history. It wasn't really a democracy in the sense that the word is now understood, but it was a big step up from anything anyone had going on before that. Basically, different classes of people were granted certain rights, and almost all of them had some say in government. As he once told me, a man will fight much harder to save his own home when it is under attack than he will to save his neighbor's home.

Solon's democracy worked extremely well for an extremely short period of time. The problem was that Athens—or rather, the people of Athens—just wasn't ready for it yet.

All of Attic (Athens and the surrounding region) was routinely plunged into intertribal warfare between the men of the hills, the men of the plains, and the men of the coast. These little mini wars were always unpleasant, very bloody, and typically instigated by events that an outside observer such as myself would laugh at. For example, the coast men and the plainsmen warred with one another for ten years after the leader of the coast men accused the leader of the plainsmen of spitting on him—during a rainstorm and twenty paces apart from one another. This crowd wouldn't have bothered to wait for Archduke Ferdinand's assassination to jump into war; they would have made something up long before it had gotten to that point.

I'm not entirely positive when or how things got as bad as they did. I only know that I left right near the end of Solon's rule and returned a few years later to find the three tribes squabbling so fiercely they'd stopped electing *archons* altogether. (Anarchy = *anarchia* = a city without *archons*.) But there was still an assembly, and there were still persons of power in those assemblies.

One such person was Pisistratus of the hill men, Solon's cousin and an exceedingly crafty son of a bitch. He staged a fake assassination attempt on himself and then used that to convince the assembly he needed a private guard to protect him. Then he used the guard to seize the Acropolis and from there declared himself tyrant.

There's only one thing coast men and plainsmen hate more than each other, and that was a hill man who wants to be king. So they got together and stormed the Acropolis and drove Pisistratus away.

And then, a year or so later, a most remarkable thing happened.

* * *

I was dining at the estate of my friend, Linnaeus, on this particular day. Linnaeus was by birth an Athenian citizen (as were all men born in the city and fathered by a resident) and by family a coast man. He was old enough to remember what peace was like and wise enough to understand that the way things were currently going in the assembly, nobody was going to be stumbling across peace anytime soon.

"You should listen to them, Epaphios," he said, using the name by which he best knew me while munching on the leg of a piglet. "These are not men of reason. There is no middle ground, no politicking, no concessions ... hatred and distrust, and that is all."

"How do they get anything done?"

I'd had my fill of roast pig and was sipping my wine appreciatively. I had been away from Athens for just long enough to miss the taste of Athenian wine, which was better than any of the wine I tried anywhere else. And half of those places learned how to make wine based on my instructions; one would think they'd be better at it. The Spartans, for example, couldn't make a decent vat if their lives hung in the balance.

"They don't!" Linnaeus spat. "We've no archons, no jurisprudence ... the tribes are making up their own rules and enforcing their own laws as they each see fit. In yesterday's assembly, the vote was passed to nullify everything we'd agreed upon in the *last* assembly. Next week I expect we'll vote to nullify the nullification. I tell you, Epaphios, you have to *do* something."

I shook my head. "No, old friend, I'm sorry; you know I don't get involved."

"By your own rule. You can break your own rule."

"You cannot believe anything I say or do will make a difference."

"Pah! Of course it will. *You* are the only one who believes otherwise." He leaned forward and put his greasy hand on my elbow. "There are many ... many, who know well the full extent of your true nature. These are people of influence, Epaphios. More influence than I can lay claim to. They will listen."

"And what would I say?" I asked. "Stop fighting because I said so?"

"Why not?"

"Linnaeus, you cannot impose reason by fiat. Is that not what Solon attempted?"

"Yes. And it worked."

"Temporarily."

"That is all I ask. A little peace before I encounter Charon." He tossed aside the meat he'd been picking at and drank deeply of his own wine.

"The thing that I fear most," he continued, once he'd drained his bowl, "is war. Real war. As we stand now, we are weak. I am afraid our differences will become too great to set aside for the sake of mutual defense."

"Such fear is misplaced. If it's peace you want between the tribes, then you should welcome an interloper. Nothing unifies a people better than war. I've known some kings who started wars specifically for that reason."

We were interrupted by a commotion from the road below us, a distraction I welcomed. Linnaeus wasn't the first person to ask me to step in and resolve a political dispute and he would hardly be the last. But I had learned from prior experience that the worst results could come from the best intentions, which was doubly true when it came to local politics. The best way to stay out of trouble was to recognize it beforehand.

This might come off as selfish, but consider it from my perspective. Either I risk my neck—and my good standing with the Athenians—to try and put to rest disputes that had been going on for centuries, or I let it run its course and hope Athens is still standing when all's done. As I seriously doubted my ability to alter the natural course of history by acting, not acting was the most prudent route.

"What in Hades' name is going on down there?"

Linnaeus's attention was drawn to the crowd that had gathered on the road.

His estate was on a small hill that overlooked the main path through the city. As it was springtime, we were seated outdoors on the terrace—on the ground, as Athenians rarely ate on tables—that circled his modest home, so viewing the road was simply a matter of standing up and looking down. And so I stood up and looked down.

Dozens of common folk had gathered on the road and were pointing excitedly in the direction of the city gates. Up the road a ways, was a chariot being drawn by a magnificent white horse. In the bright sunlight, it looked as if the chariot was gilded, which is a downright foolish thing to do. Imagine building a Chevy with solid gold trim and then imagine how long it would last parked on the streets of New York. It was that kind of dumb. Especially since we didn't have chariot alarms.

As the chariot drew closer, I noticed a larger crowd was following behind. It looked like nearly the whole city. Who in the world was riding in it?

"Can you see who it is?" Linnaeus asked, as my eyesight was better.

"Not yet, no."

There was a figure riding tall at the front of the chariot in full battle gear and wearing a white-and-gold plumed helmet. And long blonde hair.

"It's a woman."

"What sort of woman?"

"I don't think you'd believe me."

Linnaeus looked down at one of the men who gathered just beneath us.

"Ho, slave!" he shouted. "Who rides forth?"

"Athena herself, wise master!" the slave shouted back.

"Hah!" Linnaeus answered, saying to me, "I have been chastened. Never trust a Persian."

"He speaks truth," I said. "Such as it is."

"What?"

"She will be upon us presently."

Linnaeus squinted until the chariot reached a point within his vision radius.

"What sort of mad theater is this?" he exclaimed.

"Do you see the man standing beside her?"

"I cannot make him out."

"Pisistratus, my friend. The tyrant of Athens has returned."

* * *

And so he had. The crafty bastard had fashioned a solution to his popularity problem: he brought the god of Athens to personally vouch for him.

This did nothing to fool educated men such as Linnaeus, but it didn't have to. There was such a hue and cry from the masses that to not elect Pisistratus tyrant would have caused a massive riot.

I had other concerns. Which was why a few nights later—and before the formal vote in the assembly to swear in Pisistratus—I found my way to the gates of his private palace.

"I wish an audience with the goddess," I told the guard.

"She speaks to none except the lord of this house," the guard proclaimed tiredly. I gathered he'd repeated this declaration a number of times already.

"I am no Athenian; I am Epaphios. And you know who I am."

He leaned forward to examine my features in the torchlight.

"So you are. I am still bound by my lord to turn away all callers. Even you, sojourner."

I said quietly, "Phiklopanus of the hill clan, do you really wish to enjoy my wrath?"

He seemed mildly awed that I knew his name, which was little more than a lucky guess (I'd known his father, and he was a good likeness.) That, combined with what was a legitimate threat, did the trick. He stepped aside.

"My thanks. Now please tell me which chamber I am seeking."

He inclined his head. "A left, and two rights. The goddess keeps her own counsel."

"As she should. And your lord?"

"He will be away until very late," Phiklopanus said.

"Pisistratus left you alone as guard and took his entire retinue?" I asked, fairly surprised.

He nodded. "I am here to ward off the inquisitive. Not as a guard. When does a god need protection?"

"True enough," I agreed.

I made my way inside, wondering privately whether Pisistratus was really that foolish.

After a left and two rights, I came upon the closed doors of a private bedchamber. Not standing on ceremony, I pushed the doors open.

She was lying atop the bed in a simple white robe. The breastplate, leggings, and helmet she'd ridden into town in lay upon a chair beside the bed, with her sword on the floor.

At the sound of the room being breached she sat up quickly, one hand holding the robe closed.

"Who dares!" she bellowed.

"Oh, be quiet," I said, closing the doors behind me.

She leapt to her feet and reached for her sword. "You will pay for this affront!" she muttered, sounding far less impressive than I think she was hoping to.

The goddess Athena was one of the most beautiful women I'd ever seen up to that point, and possibly for several centuries thereafter. Taller than I was, she was round in all the right places and slim everywhere else. She had a long face and high cheekbones, a thin nose, and flowing locks of blonde hair that reached her navel. Through the thin white cotton of her evening robe, I could just make out the shape of her breasts, which had not yet been discovered by gravity.

"Calm down," I said, "you'll just embarrass yourself."

Too late. She popped up with her sword drawn and pointed in my general direction.

"Leave!" she commanded.

"No."

I was trying to figure out where she was from. Greek women tended to have rounder faces and darker hair. I vaguely recalled a few far northern tribes where fair features such as hers were commonplace.

She swung the sword at me, a rather ineffectual gesture given she was also trying to hold her robe closed. A real warrior would show little concern about the view afforded the person she was about to kill.

I slapped the blade aside with my staff. It clattered to the floor a few steps away.

"*I am not here to harm you,*" I said, trying one of the dialects of the north.

Obviously distressed, she looked at the weapon she didn't know how to use, then back at me. "What did you say?"

"You hail from the northern climes, do you not?"

"*I do,*" she answered, in her own tongue, before switching back to Greek. "But I prefer this language. My people are low, and so is their speech. This is the language of the gods."

"All right."

"Why are you here?" she asked, sitting on the bed.

"To save your life."

"It is *your* life that is in danger. When the lord of the house returns..."

161

"When he returns, I think it would be wise if neither of us were here any longer."

"So this is a kidnapping?"

I sighed. "The sooner you stop acting like an idiot, the sooner we can leave. Do you have anything to wear other than the armor?"

"I don't wish to leave," she said stubbornly.

For someone who was hired to play the role of a goddess before the entire city of Athens, she was remarkably guileless.

"What did he promise you?"

"Just this. I am a god to these people. I can have whatever I want."

"Then you truly *are* an idiot."

"Hey!"

"Listen to me. Pisistratus made a great show of presenting himself aligned with the god of this city, but he did it only to gain power. In a few days, he will be declared tyrant. What do you suppose will happen next?"

"I will rule at his side," she said hesitantly. She had an enormously cute pout, which I was trying very hard to ignore.

"Suppose you do. What happens in ten years, when the Athenians realize their god has aged?"

"I ... I hadn't thought that far ahead."

"I guarantee you Pisistratus has. Does he strike you as the sort of man who would willingly take that risk? No? Does he strike you as the sort of man who would willingly share his power with anyone, much less a strumpet from the north who is privately in his employ?"

"I ..."

"Keeping you even this long is a great risk. I could have been here to kill you. Can you imagine the reaction of the people of the city if they discovered their supposed god could be felled so easily?"

"You're frightening me."

"You should be frightened. Not because I intend to kill you; I don't. But Pisistratus will as soon as it's convenient. He'll do it quietly, and rid himself of your body as discreetly as possible. It will be as if Athena simply returned to her seat on Olympus, happy that her chosen one ruled her city. Do you understand now?"

"I do," she said quietly.

"Good. Again; do you have any other clothing here?"

"Yes. But before I go anywhere with you ..." She raised her perfect chin and affected her regal manner just briefly. "Who are you? And why are you doing this?"

"I am known in these lands as Epaphios. And I am doing this because you are the most beautiful woman I have ever seen."

She looked at me, and I noticed her eyes were a stormy blue. "I will go with you. But don't get your hopes up."

"I'm not lying."

"You also called me a strumpet."

"Will you get dressed?"

I heard the door swing open behind me, and knew we'd already run out of time. I spun around.

Pisistratus did not cut an imposing figure. Somewhat smallish and tubby, it was clear that the warrior blood that ran in his family had gone dry long before reaching him, possibly replaced by snake venom. But the two men behind him looked like they had plenty of warrior in them to spare.

"Epaphios Choreios!" he said, surprised. "What are you doing here?"

"Taking audience with the goddess. Perhaps you'd like to join us. In private."

He stared at me for a long second, and then waved his hand dismissively. The guards shut the doors and left us alone.

"You have something you wish to discuss?" he asked.

"A negotiation, tyrant of Athens." Incidentally, 'tyrant' was not an insult at that time. The Greek word is *tyrannos*, and it means non-hereditary king.

He didn't look very happy.

"I am listening."

I had to tread carefully. Pisistratus was a smart man. It was his only good quality. His weakness was an ego the size of the Aegean. "Let me first commend you for acquiring the services of Athena herself. Truly, a remarkable feat."

"Pah! She's a slave. I bought her from her father six months ago. Of all in Attic, you would know this. Do not patronize me."

"Fair enough. Nevertheless, well-played."

"Thank you."

"And if she is no more than a slave to you, I would look to buy her services for myself."

"Hey!" Athena piped in.

"Be quiet," I said urgently.

"Yes," Pisistratus concurred. "Silence yourself. Or I'll have you put to the sword." To me he asked, "What use has one such as you for her? You have many women, provided the tales are accurate."

"They are. But this one has caught my eye. Would you deny me?"

He rubbed his chin thoughtfully. "You would pay for her?"

"I would."

"In what form? As tyrant I have no need for any currency you might offer."

"You have already suggested the method of payment."

"Have I?"

"You are not yet tyrant, Pisistratus, and I of all people should know when I am gazing upon a false god. Do you suppose my declaring so, loudly, before the assembly itself, might sway opinion?"

"And suppose I decide not to let you leave my home alive!" he bit back.

"Don't be foolish," I said calmly. "You have no man here who can best me. Certainly *you* are no match."

Pisistratus was painfully aware that he was unguarded in a room with me, and that I'd maneuvered myself between him and the door as we talked.

"But I know you, Thyoneus," he said, using another one of my names. You would not believe how many names an immortal can pick up over time. "You do not intervene."

"I don't, but I can."

He deflated visibly. "What do you propose?"

"Just what I was planning before you interrupted. Let me leave with her. I'll keep her countenance hidden until well beyond the gates."

"That is not enough," he said firmly, but quietly.

"What else?"

"You need to swear you will not return in my lifetime. Promise that, and you both may go. I will even have a curtained chariot ride you out."

I pretended to think about it, even though this was basically the deal I was hoping for. "All right. I have been away from the satyros of the woods for too long anyway."

"Satyrs?" Athena said. "Are you kidding?"

"Shut up and get dressed," I said.

Pisistratus offered his hand, and we shook on it.

"You know," he said, "I was hoping you simply wouldn't be in Athens for this. I only needed a few days. I suppose the fates saw otherwise."

"Pray that the fates have nothing worse in mind for you. Pray also that your stewardship of Athens meets my approval. I do love this city, and only grudgingly leave it to the likes of you."

His expression grew hard. I guess he thought we were sharing a moment. "You abide by your promise."

"I will. But that doesn't mean I won't be watching."

* * *

Athena didn't speak again until we were alone in the chariot.

"I've heard three names for you so far," she said. "What sort of man goes by as many as three names?"

"I have more than three. To most of the Athenian citizens, I'm Epaphios Choreios. To the hill tribes I've also been called Thyoneus."

"And which one should I call you?"

"Whichever one sounds the best to your ears is fine."

I considered asking what her real name was, but Athena seemed so perfect, it didn't matter; I'd much rather have kept on calling her that.

The chariot tilted downward with the road I knew would be taking us out of the city. To our left would have been the home of Linnaeus, who so recently implored me to get directly involved in the affairs of the state. It was a shame I'd just brokered my way out of town without getting a chance to wish him well.

"He was afraid of you," Athena said.

"Who, Pisistratus? He's afraid of a lot of things."

"He walked in with two armored guards. You're dressed in cloth with a bag and a wood staff. Yet you threatened him into bargaining with you. Why would he be so frightened?"

I smiled. "You're trying to figure me out. Does this mean you're not going to run off as soon as we're out of sight of Athens?"

"I have nowhere particular to run," she said. "But I'd like to know why he was so afraid when he clearly had the tactical upper hand."

"And whether you should be afraid as well?"

"That, too."

"You don't need to be afraid of me," I said, peeking out the curtain for one last look at the city. "But Pisistratus did, because he believed I could have bested both his men and himself."

"Could you have?"

"Probably, yes. And the warrior goddess Athena, too, if I had to."

She reached up and pulled the curtain closed, and looked me in the eye.

"Who *are* you?" she demanded.

"All right," I nodded, softening my tone. "There are more names. The satyrs call me Philopaigmos."

"I'm not a satyr."

"Also Botryophoros to some, and Lyseus, and Iakchos, and to a few I'm Thriambos. And there are dozens more. But the name the slaves and low Athenians know me by, the one you're likely to have heard before, is Dionysos."

* * *

I should point out that pretending to be a god is almost always a really bad idea, and I absolutely do not recommend it. Eventually someone comes around asking for enemy smiting and crop growing and whatnot, and then you have a problem. But sometimes you can get away with it okay.

Dionysian mythology includes references to *the god who comes*, i.e. a guy that walks around the earth all the time instead of hanging out on Olympus. That same guy introduced wine and turned up on the final day of the Mystery Ceremonies and befriended the satyrs and so on.

That was all me.

But godhood was sort of flexible to the Greeks, who borrowed good god ideas from everybody. Their flexibility meant I could be considered only one incarnation of the god; I was never expected to do anything unequivocally supernatural.

Still, it's not something I'm all that proud of.

* * *

Athena blinked several times. "*The* Dionysos?"

I fixed my gaze on her lips. "I haven't come across anyone else using the name."

"I'm having some trouble believing that."

"I understand. But maybe now you can appreciate how Pisistratus could get away with claiming to have Athena at his disposal. In a way, the predicament I just got you out of is my fault."

Athena leaned back and mulled over the notion.

"He said you're known to have plenty of women with you."

"I've had my share. But most of them go mad eventually. I'm not sure why."

"Are you particularly maddening?"

I smiled. "Not as far as I know."

"And will I go mad?"

"Possibly. If you'd like, I can just return you to your village instead."

"No," she said, smiling. She had a brilliant smile, and I made a note to try and get her to do that more often. "I think I might enjoy risking madness to travel with an actual god. Besides, my family sold me; if you bring me back, there they'll just sell me again."

"Well, you have been warned."

"Indeed I have." She reached out to touch my knee. "My god."

* * *

I wish I could say Athena avoided the curse of madness that seemed to strike everyone who spent too much time around me in those days, but she didn't. (It would be a century before I figured out the cause.) But up until she tried to kill me with a knitting needle, we had a spectacular time together. I ended up leaving her with the satyros, who were happy to have her, madness or no.

As for Pisistratus, he and his descendants ruled Athens in my absence until his entire family was exiled by a fed-up populace. By then they were finally ready for long-dead Solon's democracy.

Chapter Twelve

Dion:

I would go to Athens. For it is only in Athens that I may spend all morn arguing real truths with a philosopher, all afternoon watching clever lies from a dramaturg, and all night drinking lies into truths with a Senator.

—From the dialogues of Silenus the Younger.
Text corrected and translated by Ariadne

My first few days in Athens were spent just trying to figure out what happened to the city. To that end, I bought a cheap tour book and an even cheaper city map and then walked around a lot, from Filopappou Hill to Likavitos, Kolonos to Syngrou Park. And then I returned to my little hotel room on Athinas Street and drank myself silly.

Coming to Athens had been a mistake. All I'd managed to accomplish was to deepen the depression I was already fighting—being a short flight away from Clara did not help this at all— while allowing the trail I was following to run cold.

There were no satyrs in sight. I'm one of the few humans on the planet who could easily identify one at a glance, and I was more than moderately certain I'd not seen one in my travails. If they were still around—and I was nearly certain they were—either they weren't common or they weren't in Athens.

With the help of the hotel desk, I secured a tour bus trip to modern Eleusis—now called Elefsina, which is a decidedly less graceful name. I spent the day there, wandering around the ruins of the Telesterion temple, and listening to a graduate student mispronounce words that used to mean a great deal to a goodly number of her ancestors. As always, the details of the sacred rites were butchered, filtered through the suppositions of modern archaeology.

It was the first time I'd been to the Telesterion without expecting a cup of kykeon at some point. Kykeon was what the adherents drank for a large portion of the nine-day ceremony. It was similar to beer, but with a few extra additives that induced hallucinations, an aspect I personally never got to experience because of my unique body chemistry.

There have been numerous concerted efforts to recreate kykeon since those days, efforts I know could not possibly have succeeded because of one particular additive that may or may not exist anymore.

My tour guide claimed it was poppy seeds. I actually bit my tongue.

The cave—the Ploutonion—was the only thing still standing. It was supposed to be the place where Demeter's daughter, Persephone, returned to Hades and as such, it served a major function in the larger Mystery Ceremonies. I couldn't imagine conducting the rites using the cave and then marching around the ruins. If the cult was indeed still active, it wasn't active in Eleusis.

As I rode the bus back into the city and prepared for another evening of blind drunkenness, I considered that I was thinking about this all wrong.

The last days of the cult were contemporaneous with the rise of the Christian faith. One thing the Christians did well—and they did a lot of things well—was create a thoroughly mobile religion. It's hard to think of them that way now with all the churches everywhere, but in the beginning they were as secretive and decentralized as anybody. Put a bunch of Jesus worshippers together, and they could make any place sacred for as long as they needed to. Whereas if you wanted to do away with the mystery cults— as the Romans did—all you had to do was bar adherents from accessing the places they considered sacred. So if the cult went underground, it had to be a version of the cult unlike anything with which I was familiar; it had to become mobile.

That meant they could be anywhere. They didn't have to be in Greece at all.

* * *

The Hotel Attalos has a good bar with a bartender named Stavros whose company I rather enjoyed, especially after three or four drinks. I don't think Stavros knew exactly what to make of me.

Since I'd arrived in Athens without any luggage, I had purchased a few sets of clothing that identified me as a local, rather than a tourist. This caused confusion everywhere I went, because when one is dressed like a native and speaking Greek, one doesn't generally ask for directions.

Likewise, in the hotel, other guests routinely kept assuming I knew where everything was.

Stavros was aware that I was a guest and that it was my first time in (modern) Athens, so he didn't know what to do with the fact that I spoke his language as well as he did, and that when I was drunk I told him details about his own city he didn't know. Consequently, we spent a lot of time talking. Stavros was determined to figure me out.

"And how was Eleusis?" he asked.

I was on my fourth glass of ouzo, which was when I usually became conversational.

"Ruins," I answered. "Terrible. Used to be a beautiful place."

"Was it?" he asked. "When was that?"

I smiled. "Thousands would come from all across Attic into the city of Athens. And on the fourteenth day of Boedromion, they would walk the Sacred Path, cross the Bridge of Rhiti, and go see the priestesses of Eleusis. The procession would last an entire day, and all who could make the walk were welcome: male and female, citizen and slave, human and ... well. All were welcome. It was beautiful. Today? I took a bus."

Stavros smiled. "Very romantic, Mr. Lenaios. You sound like you were there."

I was traveling under the name Greg Lenaios. I figured claiming Greek lineage would answer some questions regarding my fluency. "I was. Today, I mean."

"In the days of the pagans," he clarified.

"Pagans," I scoffed. "You Catholic, Stavros?"

"Greek Orthodox," he answered. "Somewhat."

I grinned. Stavros was twenty-five and thoroughly enjoyed his life as a bartender in a hotel that has an ample supply of attractive American women looking for a little action on the side during their vacation. Darkly handsome, he defined the word *swarthy*. He was probably not the most devout Christian around.

"Pagan wasn't always a bad word. It's all a matter of perspective."

"You speak with longing," he said, refilling my glass. "I think perhaps you were born in the wrong age."

"There's more truth in that than you know." I raised my glass in an exaggerated toast. "Anyway, I think I'll be leaving here soon."

"Where to?" he asked. "You fit in so nicely. I was preparing to recommend a realtor."

"I can't stay. I have some unfinished business elsewhere."

On the television in the background, the late news had come on. Stavros had the sound down because it was in Greek and he was the only person within fifty feet of it—other than me—who could understand what they were saying.

After having spent most of the twentieth century in America, I'd grown accustomed to the high-quality nature of TV broadcasts there, so it was something of a shock the first time I witnessed a European news program. It reminded me of the way the news looked in the sixties, just in terms of technological expertise.

Stavros looked curious. "Where might that be?"

"It's just business."

There was an inset behind the anchors that showed an artistic rendition of something that could have been either Bigfoot or a very hairy wrestler.

"So this is a vacation?" Stavros asked. Unlike Mike, he was never going to get enough information to figure me out.

I ignored his question and pointed to the screen. "Can you turn that up?"

He looked over his shoulder. "Ah. You want to know about the wolf-man?"

"Pardon?"

He reached up and manually adjusted the sound just in time to get the end of the report, which consisted of a phone number and a warning not to approach whatever was being depicted in the background.

"Too late."

"What's a 'wolf-man'?" I asked.

"It's nonsense. You've heard of *El Chupacabra*?"

I had. Supposedly it was a goat-man sort of monster that mauls cows and small animals in South America. I took note when I first heard of it because when you know there is such a thing as a satyr, anything described as a man looking like a goat gets your attention. Not that actual satyrs are half-goat; it's just how they've always been depicted. "Is this the same thing?"

"No... and yes. The wolf-man is supposed to be half wolf or dog, not goat. And yes, because there is no such thing. It is people getting carried away. Urban legend, as the Americans call it."

"A werewolf?"

He smiled. "Are you going to tell me now that wolf-men are real? Perhaps they, too, were at Eleusis in the old days, yes?"

"No, of course not," I lied, because they were. "But I find this interesting."

"Ah, but you have pressing business elsewhere."

"It might not be all that pressing."

I slapped the empty cup down for another refill.

* * *

The next morning, after purging a significant portion of the ouzo I'd drunk the night before in an explosive manner that I don't need to recount, I picked up a copy of the latest edition of the English language Athens News. I hunted through until I found a story about the local wolf-man, whom they were calling (appropriately enough) the Lykanthropos. It was buried near the back of the paper, which made some sense as one didn't want to alarm the tourists with local legends. And the story itself was almost entirely useless; it presented a brief recap with hardly any details, and concluded that there was nothing to it. So go out and spend money, you Americans, you.

But the gift shop had a selection of Greek language newspapers, including a few of the less reputable tabloids. I grabbed a bunch and returned to my room.

Stavros was right; it did sound like an urban legend, one that was being given far too much play by a credulous team of reporters. The roots of the story went back as far as six months, when a local woman claimed she was attacked by a wolf-man, and the reports popped up again every time there was a full moon. Of course, there was no hard information to be found. What eyewitness quotes they had, came from people who didn't want to be identified in the press. And the

175

statements from people who did want their names mentioned all heard from a so-called friend about it, and didn't witness anything personally.

Worse, the abilities of the Lykanthropos far exceeded anything moderately rational. He was supposed to be eight feet tall and capable of leaping ten stories. He had an enormous jaw and wild eyes, was covered in hair, and either scampered on all fours or walked upright depending on who was describing him. His claws were five or six centimeters long, and his howl could cause small dogs and other pets to drop dead on the spot. He was bulletproof and fireproof, and the only reason nobody had been killed yet, was either incredible good luck or the direct providence of God, depending again on who was being asked. When I compared artistic renditions from four different newspapers— all supposedly based on eyewitnesses—I got four entirely different images.

The police were doing everything they could to keep the locals from overreacting, insisting repeatedly that there was no wolf-man. This just fed into the conspiracy-minded media frenzy. One of the tabloids went so far as to conclude that the Lykanthropos was a member of the police force, or a government experiment gone wrong.

Either this was a mass panic (fairly normal) or there was an unschooled werewolf out there (extremely rare) that was very confused. If I was lucky, it was the latter.

I spent the next few hours pairing the reported sightings with my handy tourist map and came to an interesting conclusion. More than half of the sightings had taken place in or around the National Gardens.

There was only one night of full moon left. If I was going to catch up with him, it was going to have to be soon.

* * *

I arrived at the National Gardens later that afternoon on what was turning out to be an extraordinarily hot day. Mingling in with a group of tourists, I entered from Amalias Street behind the Tomb of the Unknown Soldier and followed the crowd, trying to reconcile what I was seeing with what the little park direction signs said about where I was. (Every time I look at one of those *You-Are-Here* maps, I think how many times in my life I could have used a sign like that. Like when I was avoiding the Inquisition.)

It was still a few hours before sunset, so I familiarized myself with the gardens, which didn't exist in my day. That in itself was a reassuring thing. I did come across a few ruins in my first circuit around the place, but I couldn't even tell what they were ruins of, so it didn't bother me all that much.

What did bother me was the ducks. There were hundreds of them, and they thought I was under some sort of obligation to feed them something. I also saw enough cats to make me think this was more than simply a case of somebody letting a house cat run free. It looked like the cats lived in the park along with the ducks. Maybe they even ate the ducks. If so, they weren't doing a very good job of it.

I had to decide where I would go if I were a confused kid who thought he was turning into a monster. After much consideration, I settled on the zoo. Specifically—the wolf paddock.

According to the placard, the wolves were Bulgarian, which would have had an added appeal to the Lykanthropos if he was a student of his own myth history, since werewolves, like vampires, purportedly hailed from Eastern Europe. Bulgaria would do nicely in that regard. (In truth, werewolves aren't anything like vampires. They're far less common and the condition is hereditary, not acquired.)

I bought a soft drink and settled down on a bench across from the wolves, and spent the afternoon trying to remember what it was that had stood on that spot. This was a daily ritual, and not at all healthy; it typically led me to drink, which only made the nostalgia worse. Hence, the soda. My other option was a lemonade-type beverage whose principle ingredient was ouzo. It looked tempting, but I had to stay sharp.

I people-watched. When the objects of my attention are female I call it voyeurism, or if I'm drunk, ogling. On this day, I was checking out everybody, so it was just people-watching. With a little voyeurism mixed in, but not much. All the pretty tourists were probably at the Parthenon.

After a couple of hours, with the sun starting to set and my deciding the spot upon which I sat used to be a farm, I spied a likely suspect. He looked about fourteen years old, very muscular and pretty hairy.

In Greece, this is not at all unusual, as body hair was always commonplace. What was unusual was that he was alone, he was definitely not a tourist, and he stared at the wolves for a quarter of an hour without moving. I got up and stepped beside him.

"Nice afternoon," I said, in Greek.

He looked surprised to have been addressed, and I realized he hadn't just been staring at the wolves; he'd been speaking to them.

"Yes."

He edged away slightly.

"I don't think they can hear you from here," I said. The wolves didn't give a damn that either one of us were there. They were too busy sleeping in the shade, which is what sane animals do when it's very hot. Unlike people.

"They know I am here."

I smiled. "Come here a lot?"

He stared hard at me, and the hairs on the back of my neck decided to do a little dance. "You should leave me alone."

"Okay," I replied pleasantly, trying very hard to pretend he didn't scare me. "Just making conversation. I don't find many other people here who think the wolves are as fascinating as I do. You seem to like them a lot."

"I hate them," he grunted.

"Oh. My mistake."

My new friend stared at the sky with significant trepidation; the sun had just set.

"You have someplace to be?" I asked.

"Yes."

He stepped away and started down the path, trying to get some distance between us, which wouldn't do. I caught up with him and put my hand on his shoulder. He reacted as someone might if touched by a hot pan.

"What is the matter with you? Leave me alone!"

I offered him a handshake. "Take my hand. My name is Greg."

"I am not your friend! Now get away from me!"

"I think you should shake my hand," I repeated. "It will help you get the scent."

"What?"

"For later. When the moon comes up, you'll want to look for me."

"You are insane."

"One of us is. Might be me. We'll find out in an hour, won't we?"

He stared at me, and for a change he looked more frightened than intimidating. Then he turned and ran.

I watched him up until he hit the trees and disappeared into the brush and the twilight. Definitely much faster than he should have been. And he never shook my hand. That was okay, though; that's why I'd touched his shoulder. In a little while, he'd realize I knew he was the legendary Lykanthropos and decide he had to protect himself.

* * *

I drifted through the gardens as dusk begat nighttime and the attendant darkness that wasn't really all that dark. There were streetlights, of course, but there was also the full moon to contend with.

Moonlight used to be considered a source of madness. I remember not so long ago seeing grown women walk around with parasols at night to prevent moonlight from striking them on the head. People are weird. But it's easy to see how the werewolf mythos ended up conflated with the supposed power of moonlight. (That and the whole howling at the moon thing, which real wolves don't actually do.)

I always thought it was terribly inconvenient. I mean, if you're going to be a monster, wouldn't you rather be one during the new moon? It's a whole lot easier to sneak up on somebody without the gigantic source of illumination in the sky. What a hassle.

Anyway, real werewolves don't transform by the light of the full moon. They simply are. It's a genetic condition.

For the first hour, I made a point of sticking close to the zoo, but it was so well lit, I decided I'd make much better bait somewhere more secluded. So I wandered down the path until I found a nice clearing a decent enough distance from the streetlamps to allow my night vision to return, and also so I could be overwhelmed by a large community of aggressive ducks near a small pond. Never mind that I was there waiting for a werewolf; the ducks were frightening enough.

Soon, I heard a growl coming from the trees about twenty feet away.

"There you are," I said. "Thank goodness; maybe you can help me with these ducks."

He didn't answer, but it would have gone a lot easier for everybody if he had. Instead, he charged forward, scampering at me on all fours. I didn't have much time to register anything about him other than that he was the same kid I'd spoken to in the zoo, and that he'd managed to tear off all of his clothing. The ducks scattered before him, which I appreciated.

At the last second he leapt at me, arms outstretched and mouth open intending to rip out my throat. If I were too afraid to move, or perhaps were I some sort of exotic statue, he would have succeeded. But it was a simple attack to counter.

I don't care how big and strong and fast you are; unless you're a bird, the minute you leave the ground you're vulnerable. Your nastier creatures— like, say, real wolves—don't do it until they're right in front of you, when their large teeth can latch on before you have an opportunity to evade them. But this boy had a normal-sized mouth and it was a few feet behind his outstretched arms. I swatted the arms aside with a sweep of my own right arm, punched him in the exposed kidneys with my left fist, and let his momentum do the business of carrying him away from me. He landed clumsily on his side with a couple of the slower ducks trapped beneath him.

"There, see what a bad idea that was?" I said.

He rolled to his feet and howled, while the injured ducks limped off and quacked angrily.

"C'mon, cut that out."

He wasn't listening. He lunged forward again, and I reminded myself that even though this was just a kid, he was still faster and stronger than a normal human and I should maybe take him a little seriously.

He swung hard with his left arm, showing off a nasty set of claws. (Or rather, unreasonably long fingernails.) Instead of jumping away— which would have put me off balance and made me a nice target for the right arm—I stepped forward, blocked him with my elbow, and punched him as hard as I could in the nose.

The boy staggered backward, covering his face and emitting a little whimper.

I kept my fist up, ready to hit him again.

"Are you ready to talk yet? Because I could beat you up all night."

But no; we weren't in our reasoning place yet.

He pounced. The move was so surprising I had time only to catch his arms with my hands. His superior strength propelled us backward so I went with it, falling onto the ground and in one neat move flipping him over my head. I was up again before he even hit the ground.

"Okay, that does it. You want me to beat the crap out of you? Fine. I'll beat the crap out of you. Just remember; this wasn't my idea."

He clambered to his feet as I took off the light jacket I was wearing in anticipation of the cool evening that never arrived. Holding it by the sleeves, I stood still and waited for the new attack.

It came in the form of a half-crazed charge, both arms reaching out in just about the stupidest attack he could have possibly devised.

I waited until he was close enough, flipped the jacket up and around, and before he realized exactly what was happening, I had his arms tied up in a nice little knot.

I jerked the arms up over his head and punched him in the stomach with my free hand. When he crumpled forward, I elbowed him in the back of the head.

He tried to fall down, but I was still holding him securely by his bound wrists, so he just sort of sagged to the side, trying hard to keep his feet under him.

"Tell me to stop," I said, slapping him in his already broken nose.

The trick was to keep him staggering. If he got his feet under him properly, he'd be able to overpower me pretty quickly.

He made a muffled noise, but didn't offer anything else. So I kicked a particular part of his leg in such a way that it probably felt like I'd broken it.

"A naked man has an awful lot of good targets to hit," I said. "Tell me to stop."

Still nothing. I stabbed two fingers into a tender spot between his ribs. Hurts like hell. He howled.

"Tell me to stop," I repeated.

I was about to do something really terrible to his free-hanging testicles when he finally spoke.

"S-stop ..."

"What?"

"Stop!"

I did. With a quick yank, his arms were free of the jacket, and he was sagging to the ground. I slipped the jacket back on and sat down beside him.

After a time, he asked, "Have you cured me?"

"There was nothing wrong with you to cure."

He sat up, and I saw how badly I screwed up his nose. I'd have felt bad about it, but he was trying to kill me at the time.

"Then how?"

"How come you can sit here and talk to me under the light of a full moon when you should be peeing on a tree or something?"

"Y-yes."

"What's your name, son?"

"Piotr."

"Piotr, do you know what you are?"

"I am a monster." He looked at the ground in shame. "Lykanthropos."

"Very true. And do you know what that is?"

"I am cursed. A tool of the devil."

I laughed. "Tell me, since you started having these little moonlight jaunts, did you ever look in a mirror?"

"No, I was ..."

"... too busy wreaking havoc on the countryside, I know. Well, Piotr, I looked at you a few hours ago, and aside from the broken nose, you look about the same. Except for the nudity. Speaking of which, I hope you didn't rip your clothes apart."

"I removed them before the moon rose," he explained. "I've learned this much."

"Good. Otherwise, the bus ride home is going to be pretty awkward."

He managed a smile. "Why are you not afraid of me?"

"You're just a scared kid, Piotr. And there are people other than myself who can help you understand what you are without resorting to silver bullets and torches. That's where our needs come together nicely."

"I don't understand."

"I'd like you to introduce me to your family."

* * *

Three hours later, I was sitting in the kitchen of a small apartment on the third story of a private residence in the Plaka, not at all far from my hotel and even closer to the Acropolis, which loomed seemingly just overhead. The smell of all of Greece wafted through the open windows every few minutes, and I realized that as much as I longed for the Athens of yore, the present-day version was pretty pleasant, too.

Piotr sat beside me, his head bowed with either shame or exhaustion. Or pain; I pounded him pretty badly. His nose had swelled, although some of that might have been the tissues he'd shoved up his nostrils. I could already see black eyes forming. I imagined under all that hair he had some other bruises as well.

On the opposite side of the table was a man named Nikolaus—Piotr's father. He had just served us some coffee. The Greeks don't do coffee well, in case you were wondering.

"I want to thank you again, Mr. Lenaios," he was saying, for something like the tenth time. "Every night I feared ..."

"Please, Niko, call me Greg."

Nikolaus was aware of his son's so-called curse and had been torturing himself about it for a while. This never translated into much more than praying for his soul nightly and twice on Saturdays, but it was all he knew to do.

Nikolaus stared off into the middle distance, and for a minute there I thought he was going to start crying again. It was shaping up to be a long evening.

"You are a godsend, sir," he whispered.

I sighed. "Niko, what can you tell me about Piotr's mother?"

It turned out this was not going to be as easy as I'd hoped. I learned on our way over from the Gardens that Piotr's mother had died in childbirth.

"Maria?" Nikolaus asked. "My Maria?"

"Yes, her. Did she have a large family?" I was crossing my fingers that at no point in the ensuing conversation would the word *adoption* come up. If it did, I was screwed. And, perhaps, so was Piotr.

Niko snapped back to reality. "I don't understand the question."

"Let's start with her parents," I said. "Are they still living?"

"Yes, yes ... but ... I have not spoken to them since ... you see, they did not approve."

Not a huge surprise. Not because Nikolaus wasn't a prize; I'm sure he was quite handsome in his day. More along the lines of why a Jewish household has a problem with a Gentile in the family.

"But I don't understand," Niko said. "Now that my Piotr is cured ..."

"It isn't that simple."

"But ..."

"Papa," Piotr said, "I am still a Lykanthropos."

"Son ..."

Piotr rolled up his sleeve and revealed the ample body hair he'd developed in just the past few months.

Niko's eyes darted between his child and me. "Then the curse is not lifted?"

"Great Zeus, there is no curse!" I exclaimed. Niko looked like he was about ready to begin a litany of Hail Mary's. "Your son is different. Not cursed. Just very rare."

I had seen this happen enough times to understand the psychology behind it. When Piotr hit puberty and discovered his body changed in quite a few ways differently than any of the other kids on the block, he looked for explanations. The only one that made any sense to him—and to his father, who I think had a hand in the whole idea—was that he was a werewolf.

To that end, they were right. And since all they had going for them was the legends, *like a werewolf* was how Piotr behaved. By the time he ran into me, he'd gotten good at it.

The thing is, we all have a little animal in us, and if you ask us to, we can do a decent job of behaving like one. Hypnotize a guy and tell him he's a bear, and watch him act like a bear. Nothing magical about it, just tapping into an older part of the brain is all. Piotr was lucky I reached him before he got too carried away. Usually, rogue werewolves end up shot.

Nikolaus worked through the problem in his head. This took a minute or two.

"Rare? And you think this comes from Maria's side of the family?"

"It would have to," I said. "They can help Piotr learn to deal with his peculiar condition, and they can also help me."

"How can they help you, Mr. Lenaios? Is there anything I can do?"

"Arrange an introduction, Niko. That will be help enough."

Niko's eyes fell. "I fear you will not find them hospitable." "Let me worry about that."

* * *

From the dialogues of Silenus the Younger, text corrected and translated by Ariadne

DIONYSOS
Silenus, Dionysos, Ambrosia

Dion.

Behold, mighty Silenus, I have returned from many great travels to find you still hale and hearty. How can this be so?

Sil.

My Lord, you speak now to Silenus the Younger, whom you have not met prior to this time.

Dion.

The resemblance is astonishing. And yet hardly possible, for while I did drink much wine and partake of many women with Silenus the Elder, as you must call him, that time was three and more lifetimes ago. You must be Silenus the very much Younger.

Sil.

The lives of Silenii do not conform to human standards, my lord Dionysos. It is indeed true that Silenus the Elder was my own father, and further that I am myself aged beyond one hundred spring times. My father, Silenus the Elder, did pass some forty winters prior, but you may speak to me as you would him, for I bear all of his knowledge as it were my own.

Dion.

You mean by way of anecdote? Silenus the Elder was very long in tale and very short in fact.

Sil.

Silenus the Elder led a great long life of many adventures to which I am faithfully true in the recounting.

Dion.

Then it is to both of you I wish to speak.

Sil.

Would you call forth my father from Hades itself?

Dion.

I would not. But I ask that when next you unburden yourself of one of his tales, first arraign it for its woeful inaccuracies. Thus will Silenus the Elder receive my message.

Sil.

The tales of which you speak would be those that concern your own deeds?

Dion.

Yes those. Although I would call into question any tale passed on by Silenus the Elder. For all who knew him knew of his prevarications in the interest of a more preposterous conclusion.

Sil.

Tell me some of these tales you have heard.

Dion.

But there is no need. They originate with Silenus, and if you speak truthfully as to your direct lineage then the tradition of the telling has passed on to you. Repeating them would serve no good.

Sil.

I see. Do you agree that a tale, once loosed upon the world, can take an existence independent of the storyteller?

Dion.

I do. For man is far better at misapprehending the things before his eyes than any other creature.

Sil.

Then you must know that these tales that have earned your protest may not be the same tales the Silenii have spun.

Amb.

I will speak of these tales.

Sil.

And who are you, fair woman?

Dion.

Ambrosia is my consort. She is quite mad, so take great caution.

Sil.

Is this so?

Amb.

It is, I am mad, but only with ecstasy for my lord Dionysos. Dion. No, she is simply crazed. Keep her hands from the reach of all sharp things or you will not enjoy the same longevity as your father. But Ambrosia does have great affection for these legends.

Amb.

It is told Dionysos's human mother was slain while he was still in womb, and so Dionysos was instead nurtured to term in the thigh of his father Zeus. It is told he was himself murdered by the jealous Titans, chopped up and served in a stew to his own father, only to be resurrected. It is told pirates once took him as hostage and so he turned them into dolphins. It is told he invented wine, and wanders the countryside hiding from jealous Hera and teaching of wine making. It is told he drove the king of Thebes mad when the king dared imprison him, and then the king's women he drove mad also and they tore the king to pieces with their bare hands.

Dion.

That is enough.

Amb.

But there is more. There is Midas.

Dion.

You will please stop. You know I do not care for these tales.

Sil.

But now that I know what stories we speak of, you must explain to me your objections.

Dion.

My objection is these are absurd tales. And wherever I travel now, I am expected by all who know me to act in a godlike manner.

Sil.

And how are they absurd?

Dion.

They are untrue.

Sil.

Ah, but in what sense are they untrue?

Dion.

They did not happen. Is there another sense?

Sil.

Whose truth? By the word of the taleteller these things are true.

Dion.

All but one of these stories was given to Silenus the Elder over many conversations following many more cups of wine. Most are old legends about even older gods whose names are deservedly lost. I am he that spoke them to your ancestor, and I am he that they are now employed to define. There should be no better source.

Sil.

I see. Do you agree that stories such as these serve a purpose?

Dion.

I see no purpose other than the over-feeding of the spirit with fanciful nonsense.

Amb.

I am entertained by them.

Sil.

Ah. And entertainment has value, does it not?

Dion.

If we are accepting the opinion of a madwoman, then yes, it does have a value.

Sil.

What other values have they? Would you say there are lessons to be learned?

Dion.

Certainly. Do not anger a god, do not turn your back on a god, and do not have intercourse with a god. These are not useful lessons.

Sil.

But do you agree that most who hear these tales are not gods?

Dion.

I agree that none who hear these tales are gods.

Sil.

And do you suppose few in this life will have the opportunity to meet a god face-to-face?

Dion.

I do.

Sil.

Then are there lessons to be learned from these tales that have nothing to do with meeting a god?

Dion.

This is a most annoying way to converse.

Sil.

I mean to lead you to understanding, for only by guiding you to your own conclusions can knowledge be attained.

Dion.

And the understanding you wish for me to reach is that in some way these tales, while not being factually accurate are truthful in a sense that reaches beyond mere historical accuracy.

Sil.

That is correct. For knowledge comes in many forms, much as do gods.

Dion.

I am considering a different approach. I wish to lead you to the understanding that I do not wish for these tales to continue. To assist you, I am considering striking you in the face with great force.

Sil.

And would the application of violence lead me to true understanding?

Dion.

The depth and conviction of your understanding is of far less concern to me than the application of your understanding.

Sil.

Ah, but while force may be the preferred method of the gods, does it ever truly succeed? By striking me in the face, will this eradicate the tales from this world?

Dion.

It will not. But I will enjoy it greatly. And in the future, whenever I am asked for details regarding one fantastical happening or another, I will recall this moment with fondness. For I am not a god, and I do not wish for others to know me as such.

Sil.

And you would have me to tell the tale of the god Dionysos who is not a god?

Dion.

You can call it the tale of the god who is not a god who made your nose crooked one summer's day.

Sil.

Before you apply your persuasions to my face, how do you know you are not a god?

Dion.

I know I am not a god because I am not a god and I am the most likely person to know.

Sil.

But you do not age as man does. Is this not so?

Dion.

It is.

Sil.

And you do not become infirm with illness or maladies of the mind and body?

Dion.

I do not.

Sil.

Then you are more a god than any man.

Dion.

If I am a god, I am a god with no power over men, for whom a sword is no less deadly than to any other. If I am a god, I am a weak god who does not wish to be worshipped or challenged. If I am a god, I am a god who would be left alone. As these tales do spread, so too, does the daring of the men who would challenge a god before them, which imperils me.

Sil.

Am I a man?

Dion.

You are.

Sil.

And what if I did not wish to be a man?

Dion.

If this is what you wish, I could strike you lower.

Sil.

Can I say I am not a man, for I wish to be seen as a goat instead?

Dion.

You can.

Sil.

But would this make me no longer a man? Would I then be a goat?

Dion.

I do appreciate your point, but neither goats nor men are expected to survive a blow from a spear, while gods can be slain many times over and arise again.

Sil.

Most men live in fear of gods, and the tales about which you offer protest do only support this fear.

Dion.

You wish for me to encourage these tales?

Sil.

Encourage and respect the tales, as do the other gods. For fear is an excellent deterrent.

Dion.

You speak with the fanciful tongue of your predecessor. You have not met any other supposed gods.

Sil.

Do you believe you are the only one on this earth to live the lives of thousands, to shrug off plague and pestilence, to share your bounty of knowledge with man?

Dion.

Very well. Of whom do you speak? Is it Zeus in a thundercloud? Aphrodite in the eyes of a concubine? I have met many who claimed to be gods that did age and quickly betray their mortality. Ambrosia speaks often of being Artemis when she is less lucid.

Amb.

It is so.

Dion.

Which man or woman has convinced you of their godliness?

Sil.

In the Northwest region, at a harvest festival in her honor, I did meet Demeter. She was luminous and spoke of great beauty with greater wisdom.

Dion.

And did she offer proof of her godliness?

Sil.

She did not need to, for all who laid eyes on her could not question this truth.

Dion.

I do not consider this proven. I have seen many beautiful women, and beautiful beings that were more than simply women but far less than gods.

Amb.

But Dionysos, allow for Silenus to describe this Demeter first.

Dion.

I spent many years with Silenus the Elder. I know well, and distrust better, the slippery poetry of his kind's tongue. But I shall allow for some elaboration.

Sil.

Ah, she was pale as the moon itself. High in cheekbone like none I'd ever seen prior, with eyes the deepest blue of the sky stolen from the most glorious summer day. Her breasts stood firm and her hips swayed gently with each gliding step.

Amb.

And what did she wear?

Sil.

A simple chiton with interlaid gold threading, and a comb of ivory to tame her wild crimson locks.

Dion.
Hair of crimson?

Sil.
Astonishing and bright, it curled as if to shame the serpents of Medusa.

Dion.
Crimson, you say.

Sil.
Like the blood of a thousand ardent men.

Amb.
My lord Dionysos, a change has come upon you.

Dion.
I am convinced. Silenus theYounger.

Sil.
I am heartened. Of what have I convinced you?

Dion.
That you have indeed met another god such as myself. Your interpretation of the tales of Dionysos may continue.

Sil.
You accept also that there is some truth to the legends I speak?

Dion.
I do. And I would like you to repeat them. But if I am to be a god, I would be a fearsome god.

Sil.
You wish to be more awesome and terrible?

Dion.
I have more tales if your skill at invention is wanting. And there is more still you must do for me.

Sil.

What must I do?

Dion.

In two years' time, after your tongue has spread my legends far across these lands and my might and skill are known to all with breath in their lungs and ears on their heads, you will take me to this harvest festival so that I may meet Demeter herself. And in return for this favor, I will not strike you hard in the face.

Sil.

My lord it will be done!

Dion.

You honor me with your compliance, Silenus the Younger. Now tell me much more about this festival.

Chapter Thirteen

The god stepped into the firelight and gave many of his names. A large man, strong in body and in smell, stood in his path and asked how he would know the god spoke honestly.

"The question you should ask," the god replied calmly, "is not whether I am whom I say, but who would be foolish enough to declare themselves to be Dionysos and to not be."

—From the archives of Silenus the Elder.
Text corrected and translated by Ariadne

It was three days before Piotr got back to me. The delay was explained as we met over breakfast in the hotel restaurant.

"When my mother died, they broke off contact entirely," he said, munching hungrily on a sausage. "I never understood why, except perhaps that they had no wish to get to know their grandson."

"Don't judge too harshly just yet." I sipped my orange juice and watched my werewolf friend appreciate his meat. "These are people unlike anyone you have ever known, with old ways that take some work to understand."

More kindly, I added, "It must have been difficult for you to grow up thinking that."

"I don't know that I thought much about it," he said. "Having never known them or my mother. It's just the way it always was. It took some time for us to locate them. Many inquiries were made."

"Your father will not be joining us?"

"He has always felt guilty about mother's death. I don't think he can bring himself to face her parents. Their decision to break off contact was probably the best for everybody."

"Not for you it wasn't."

"I suppose not. But I have you to act as my guardian angel, don't I?"

"Guardian angels aren't in the habit of pummeling their charges into submission."

"Psh. I deserved it."

"How's your nose?"

He was wearing dark glasses to cover the black eyes. But the glasses rested crookedly on his nose, which hadn't set well. He evidently hadn't been to a doctor about it.

"I think it adds character, don't you? And it still works fine. I can smell the kitchen from here."

"Can you?"

My mind did a little back flip, recalling a similar conversation.

"Greg, if you don't mind my asking ... how do you know so much about me? I mean ..."

"I know what you mean. And I'd rather not say. Can you live with that?"

"Of course," he said, smiling. "Angels must keep their secrets."

"I'm not an angel. I may not even be a good person. Now finish up and let's get going."

* * *

We took a cross-town bus to the Kifissia region of Athens. Kifissia was always where one found the wealthier citizens, and apparently that much had not changed, although there does seem to be a disconnect between wealth and acreage nowadays.

We ended up on a tree-lined street with villas on both sides that I was assured by my young companion cost a great deal of money. I have a great deal of money and I own an island. I grant that there are differing degrees of wealth, but still. These were some pretty smallish houses.

The villa we stopped at was a mixture of stucco and yellow panel siding set off from the street by a wooden fence and a small lawn. As with everything else on the street, it didn't look like much.

"We should have called ahead," Piotr said quietly, balking at the last second.

"It'll be much more fun this way. You say they're retired?"

"Yes, for many years."

"Good. Then they should both be home."

I let myself in through the gate, and walked to the front door. Piotr lost his nerve entirely and stayed on the sidewalk.

I do not, as a rule, get involved in family politics. It's almost always messy, generally revolves around distant slights I don't have a hope of understanding, and all parties tend to be ridiculously unreasonable. Plus, depending on the family, it can get you killed. But I didn't have a choice this time, not if I wanted to finish what I came to Greece to do.

I rang the bell. After a moment, a short, elderly woman answered the door. She was plump, with curly hair that had probably been black in some distant past, but had since gone a shade of gray that was very nearly blue.

"Can I help you?" she asked expectantly.

"Hi. You must be Linda."

She looked confused, trying to figure out where she must have met me before. "Pardon?"

"This is the home of Linda and Kargus Iouannou, isn't it?" "Yes ..."

"And you're Linda Iouannou?"

"I-I'm sorry, do I know you? Are you selling something?"

"No, and no. I'm here to help out my young charge, who is standing some distance behind me because he is afraid to come any closer."

She squinted at the sidewalk. "I'm sorry, I don't have my glasses on ... you say you're here to ..."

"Help him. You see it appears he's your grandson Piotr, the child of Maria Iouannou and Nikolaus Mnemnios."

She touched her chin with her hand in a gesture that registered as surprise, happiness, and fear, all at the same time.

"I'm sorry, I ..." she said quietly, haltingly. "I can't. My husband ..."

"Is Kargus home?"

"Yes!" she whispered urgently.

"Why don't you call him? I'm sure he'd like to meet the boy."

"No! He would ..."

"Linda? Who's at the door?" a booming voice asked from within the recesses of the villa.

"It's ..." she started to answer, but then faltered when she realized she had no decent excuse to be standing there, letting the central air conditioning out. He was at the door before she could come up with anything.

"Oh, hello. Can we help you?" he asked, pleasantly enough.

Standing not quite straight, Kargus Iouannou was at least six foot five. He had a jutting chin that was bearded in a lively mixture of dark browns and light grays. His mane of darker hair cascaded over his shoulders despite a receding hairline at the front. He was dressed in a casual shirt and jeans, but I could tell that underneath was an impressive musculature.

I had found what I was looking for: Kargus Iouannou was a satyr.

"Hello. You must be Kargus. Call me Greg."

He looked at me, then at Linda, then back at me again. "And?"

"Oh. Right. I'm here with your grandson. He's a little shy, but he's..."

"No," he interrupted. "No, no. I'm sorry, sir, but we can't help you."

He tried shutting the door, which would have worked better without my foot in the way.

"Piotr, will you get over here?" I called.

Kargus yanked the door back open and glared at me.

"What is the matter with you?" he demanded.

"I could ask you the same," I said. "He's family, and he needs ..."

"I don't care what he needs!" Kargus shouted. "He does not set foot in this house!"

He slammed the door harder, and this time my foot didn't do much to stop it.

"You see?" Piotr said quietly. He'd made it halfway up the path past the gate. "We should go."

"The hell we should. Don't move." I banged hard on the door until Kargus reopened it.

"My wife is calling the police!" he said. "Now get out of here!"

Another reason not to get into the middle of family squabbles is that I just don't have the patience for them. It was at this point that my lack of patience got the better of me. I reached across the threshold, grabbed Kargus by the collar, and yanked him out. Don't ever do this to a satyr.

"You are Kargus of the Iouannou clan from the forests of the Eastern Peleponnese, and you have a responsibility to this child!"

"My back," he groaned. "You crazy ..."

"Look at him, Kargus! Look hard!"

Finally, he did. And when I saw his eyes widen, I let him go.

"Zagreus protect us," he muttered.

"You'd better hope so," I said. "Now can we please enter?"

* * *

Kargus led us past the entryway and into a large dining area that looked out on a back yard taken up primarily by a swimming pool.

The home was decorated sparsely, mostly with religious iconography that the average Christian wouldn't know exactly what to make of. The *pièce de résistance* was a statuette of Dionysos holding his thyrsos and looking very naked atop a dais in a small enclosure built into one wall of the dining room. It was a replica, but a pretty good one. Below it, on the floor, was a wicker kalathos filled with dried fruit. It could have been mistaken as an oddly shaped cornucopia. I was definitely in the right place.

Kargus sat, and so we did as well. Poor Piotr looked terribly confused, and kept shooting me glances. I tried to appear reassuring. In a moment, Linda—having not actually called the police—came in with a tea set. She sat and we all waited for Kargus to do something, but he just sat with his hands over his face.

It took a moment before I realized he was weeping.

"I'm so sorry," he said to nobody in particular. "When I saw the news reports I should have put it together."

"Did you know this would happen to me?" Piotr asked.

"It isn't that simple," I said.

"But you said this came from my mother's side of the family."

"It did, boy," Kargus said.

"My name is Piotr."

"Piotr. Yes."

"A lovely name," Linda said.

I explained, "Piotr, your grandfather is a satyr. Do you know what that is?"

Piotr laughed. "Sure, it's ... but they're myths. They aren't real."

"Just like werewolves?"

"Werewolves?" Linda asked.

"Piotr, when the daughter of a satyr decides to mate with a human male ... usually, nothing unusual happens. That is, she either has a human male child or a human female child. But sometimes she has something different. Sometimes the satyr in her blood makes something like you. It's so rare I'm sure your grandfather didn't even consider it."

"Oh," he said. "Okay."

"No, boy, it's not okay," Kargus said. "I have a sacred responsibility to watch for such an outcome. In the olden days, we would have prepared you for this at a much younger age so you would be ready when it came. So you would not run afoul of your baser instincts. But you must ... when your mother, our Maria died ... we did not want this for her. We wanted her to marry another ... another ..."

"Another satyr," I finished. "To continue the line."

"Yes," he agreed. "I am ashamed. I let my anger at your father affect my judgment. I should have been available to support you."

"That's all right," Piotr said. "I had an angel to protect me."

Kargus looked at me. "He is referring to you?"

"I had what you might call an intervention."

"So you did this to his face."

"Yes. I apologized later."

"I am impressed," he said, adding, "What sort of man are you?"

"I'm sorry to interrupt," Linda piped in. "But did you say my grandson is a werewolf?"

* * *

Once we explained everything to Linda, what followed was one of those lengthy, awkward reunion moments I don't usually have time for, but which couldn't be helped.

I left the three of them alone to catch up, stepping out to the patio to appreciate the magnificent pool. I noted with amusement a large statue dedicated to Poseidon at one end. It was amusing because I never knew a satyr who liked water. I remember a number of them who cursed the sea-gods on a regular basis, especially during floods.

After a time alone on the patio, Kargus stepped out to join me. He had, bless him, an extra beer in his hand.

"I believe my wife will be spending the rest of the day hugging her grandchild," he said with a wry smile.

I accepted the beer. "I'm glad."

"And I am saddened by it. I had no idea how much my decision burdened her."

"You come from a proud people. She knew what she was getting into."

"Indeed."

As he stood beside me, I caught for the first time the telltale bend in his legs where there should not be a bend.

"I wanted to thank you again for rescuing Piotr before he hurt anybody."

"I think he was in more danger of hurting himself than anyone else."

I took a long sip of the beer.

"Besides, I had an ulterior motive."

"I suspected as much," he said.

I smiled. "Kargus, I need to meet with your hierophant."

He stared at me for a long time. "I know of no such person."

This was a lie, but an understandable one.

"I saw the kalathos, filled with the sacred fruits," I said. "And the iconography on the walls. Your kind still practices the Mysteries, as you have for over three thousand years."

"The Mysteries are dead," he said flatly.

"That's what I thought too, but I recently came to believe otherwise."

From my pocket, I extracted the photograph I had taken off Ariadne's wall and handed it to him. He held it for a long time, and if I hadn't known what to look for, I'd have said he displayed somewhere between little and no emotions whatsoever.

You have to spend a lot of time with a satyr before learning how to read one. They are, by human standards, a remarkably stoic race. For instance, a raised eyebrow on a satyr is the approximate equivalent of a man jumping up and down, waving his arms, and screaming.

A couple of hairs on his bushy gray eyebrows flicked in a certain way I'd come to identify as anger, which was not the reaction I anticipated.

His hand was around my throat in half a second. I don't know what he would have done to me had I allowed the hand to remain there, but as I was already jabbing my fingers into a very particular spot just below his ribcage, I didn't have to find out. In people this would be the solar plexus, and I imagine it is in satyrs, too, but it's higher on them as they have a slightly smaller ribcage. You have to know exactly where to hit them. I make a habit of learning as many weaknesses as I can in the non-humans I come across.

All the air shot out of him and he collapsed into my arms, nearly taking both of us into the pool.

"I've got you," I muttered, pushing him back and helping him into a lawn chair. It was right then that Linda popped her head outside.

"Kargus, are you okay?" she asked, alarmed.

"It's his back," I said.

Kargus nodded and waved over his shoulder, which was the only form of communication he had to work with at the time.

"I have him," I reassured her.

"A ... all right." She did not appear mollified.

"I'm fine, woman," Kargus managed to choke out with his first breath of air.

Linda disappeared back inside.

"She's calling my doctor ... right now," Kargus said quietly. He held up the photo. "Are you he that took it?"

"Took the photo?"

"Took the kiste."

I pulled a second lawn chair next to his and sat down.

"It's missing."

"Not missing; stolen," he growled.

I took a drink from the beer. (Yes, I had disabled a six foot five satyr, caught him, and hoisted him into a chair without dropping my beer. If you think that's unlikely, you don't know how I feel about beer.)

"It has been a while since I practiced the Mysteries, Kargus," I said, "but isn't the month of Boedromion soon?"

A little pucker appeared in his cheek, which generally meant surprise. "Who are you?"

"Who I am is something I would rather discuss with your hierophant."

Kargus leaned forward. "You are a stranger to me," he said. "You carry with you a photo of an object only a chosen few even know the existence of. Notwithstanding the kindness you have shown to my grandson, why should I even consider exposing my hierophant to you? She will think me mad."

I didn't particularly want to drop my name if I could avoid doing so, but he made a pretty good point. I also couldn't ignore the gender of his hierophant. Instinctively, I felt it had to be Ariadne.

"All right," I said. "Your people used to call me Philopaigmos the sojourner. Will that help?"

Kargus laughed. "Not another one."

Chapter Fourteen

Dion.

Silenus, I hear word that I am now the god of madness.

Sil.

It is so.

Dion.

Why have you done this?

Sil.

Do you not travel with many mad-women?

Dion.

I have done so, yes.

Sil.

And did you not say to me that you yourself have been mad
on occasions past?

Dion.

I did.

Sil.

And is not the final night of the Northern festival devoted to your drink
and blessed in person with your mad touch?

Dion.

I see your point. But I have also bedded many women. Could you not
have made me the god of that instead?

—From the dialogues of Silenus the Younger.
Text corrected and translated by Ariadne

"When the Romans cut off our access to the Ploutonion and destroyed the Telesterion, the rituals continued, but were adjusted to fit the new reality of the times," Kargus said, over a large draft of beer.

We were sitting in the back of a profoundly disreputable tavern in the center of Athens, well after our confrontation in his back yard. We were waiting to meet his hierophant, who had not yet deigned to arrive.

"That was when? The third century?" I asked. "A.D., I mean."

"Thereabouts," he shrugged.

Incidentally, it's still strange for me to think in terms of B.C. and A.D. (Or, B.C.E. and C.E.) Most modern people look at time as a folded piece of paper, with the numbers running down one side to the crease and up the other side, the crease being the birth of Jesus of Nazareth. I don't see the fold, just one long strip of paper. "But the kiste, the sacred objects ... they never left the Telesterion. Was there warning?"

"In a manner of speaking; we had the prophecies."

Handing him my satyr name—Philopaigmos—had lightened his attitude considerably. Given there was apparently more than one of me, he seemed to be treating this entire matter as something of a joke. It was sort of annoying. I didn't care for him reciting everything in the manner of someone repeating an oft-told lesson. It was clear from his mannerisms that he was sure I knew all of this already and this was some sort of elaborate theater on my part to pretend otherwise. Since it was the only way to get information, I let it slide. Eventually, I was going to have to figure out how to prove I actually was who I said I was without first punching him in the nose. Never punch a satyr in the nose.

"Which prophecies were these?" I asked.

He looked aggravated. Or excited. It wasn't one of their better emotions. "Greg," he said, not willing to call me by my older name, "I don't know where you've gotten your information, but even the real sojourner would know of the prophecies. If ..."

He trailed off, deciding not to finish the sentence. The beer may have been getting to him.

"If he were real," I finished for him.

"My faith does not require that I accept his eventual return," he said simply.

"Is that what the prophet said? That I would return?"

A prophet is kind of like an oracle, except without the drugs. This isn't necessarily a good thing. An oracle needs assistance to get into a special state of mind, and that assistance is what makes it possible for most oracles to lead normal lives outside of work. A prophet spends almost all of his or her time in that special state of mind. In other words, the prototypical prophet is utterly insane. This does not make them very good company. Most prophets I've known led unhappy and very short lives that ended violently. That the Eleusinians had gotten a hold of a good one was lucky.

"Very well," he sighed. "In the final days before the destruction of the Telesterion, two manuscripts from the prophet were prepared. One elucidated all of the greater and lesser Mysteries for the first time so they would not be lost to history. This was in response to her first great prophecy, in which she foresaw that the Mysteries were doomed. The second manuscript was every word she uttered for the next five years."

"That's a lot of papyrus."

I finally understood where the wine recipe Ariadne left in my hotel room had been copied from.

"And at least seven scribes, based on the hand."

"You've seen them?"

"I have. They are largely unimportant. Were it not for the one correct prediction that saved the cult itself, the scrolls would have been abandoned long ago. It was in those scrolls that the return of Philopaigmos was prophesized."

"Just ... a return?"

"No. There was some matter of saving us all. It was interpreted for much of history to mean restoring the Telesterion, but who knows."

I nodded and drank up some of my beer, a strong, dark brew that I liked quite a lot, which was why it was the third one I'd had. "I think I was in Carthage around then."

Kargus made a grunting noise I'd come to associate with disbelief.

"I was," I insisted. "By then Greece was a minor satellite of the Roman Empire, and the Romans were ... well, I didn't care for them. I'm surprised the cults even lasted to the third century."

Kargus scoffed. "You are terrible at this."

"I'm not pretending. Look, to be honest, after I left Athens I figured everyone eventually just gave up and went home. Not that the rituals weren't fun. Do you know what's in the kiste?"

"Excuse me?"

"With your lineage, you must be an initiate. Do you?"

Kargus spoke cautiously, and with a considerable increase in gravity. "I know what we place within the kiste, and why, and what is done when it is removed."

"Ah, but that isn't what I asked, is it?"

At the start of Boedromion—which is the name of a month, not a ceremony—the kiste is supposed to be filled with a variety of foodstuff that each hold ceremonial significance. The food doesn't get withdrawn until the rituals of Eleusis, fourteen days later. But there was something that never left the box, and Kargus didn't know what that was. If he did, it would have made proving my identity to him that much easier.

He lifted an eyebrow ever so slightly. "You are an odd one, Greg."

"Perhaps I am. Now tell me; how many Philopaigmoses have there been?"

He smiled. It's one of the few expressions they have that looks human, because they taught themselves to do that. It's hard to pick up human women if you don't know how to smile on a detectable level. "Dozens. None lasted much longer than it took for those paying attention to recognize the claimant was aging. They ranged from the amusingly misguided to the incredibly dangerous."

"But why?" I asked. "Or rather how? I didn't even realize the Mysteries had survived until recently, so your secret has been ... well kept." Not to say I had been looking. "If it was the satyros that kept the Mysteries alive, how would a human male know enough to make such a declaration?"

"That was the mistake many of our kind made in the past. Who would claim to be who was not? How would they know? But politics are what they are. In the early days, a claimant was generally coached by one of us."

"A puppet." I thought of Pisistratus's temporary Athena.

"Exactly. But now we have many humans in the cult, so there is really no telling. And these things have consequences."

Kargus looked away, and I wondered exactly how much he wasn't telling me. But the pieces were all there, and when I put them together, I got the picture. A man who claimed to be Philopaigmos the sojourner was somehow responsible for the kiste's absence.

"How will the ceremony proceed this season without the kiste?" I asked, after a time.

"We are in the month of Boedromion right now. There will be no ceremony for those of us still in Athens."

"They are taking place elsewhere?"

Kargus grumbled something unintelligible into his beer before looking up again. "There are some that feel the Mysteries should serve a more public purpose. And another kind of god."

That was a statement that deserved much more clarification, but I could tell I wouldn't be getting one, so I tried to find my way around it. "I never saw the gods as being the most important thing about the Mysteries. It's a celebration of harvest, and life. It's not all that versatile."

"Versatile?"

"It used to be a harvest celebration, and now it's being honored by people far from farmlands."

"And nature," he suggested. "And the gods."

"The gods were incidental," I insisted.

Kargus laughed. "My friend, I take back what I said earlier. You make a fine Philopaigmos. I am sure you will do well."

This was sarcasm, which I could live with. It was the rest of it that gave me pause. "Do well? In what sense?"

"There is a process for when one such as yourself turns up making declarations. It's nothing to worry about."

I looked around the room—I'd stupidly sat with my back to the door— and realized we were in the midst of at least three satyrs aside from Kargus, all younger and less likely to be nursing a bad back.

"They will take you to the new Telesterion for the test," Kargus said. "Nothing the true Philopaigmos would have issue with."

Another satyr walked into the tavern. He was older than the rest, but looked supremely fit. I didn't like my chances with any of them. The elder locked eyes on the one nearest to me and nodded. All three satyrs stood.

"Tell me, Kargus. What happens to the ones who fail the test?"

"I don't know, actually," he said, standing as well. "I imagine they just send them on their way."

A hand fell hard on my shoulder, and I stood up to avoid the discomfort of being yanked to my feet. The satyr had a gun tucked into his belt, and he made sure I saw it.

"Send them on their way, you say?"

Kargus smiled. "What else would they do?"

* * *

If you ever wondered what the vehicle of choice is for a party of satyrs, it's a Ford Explorer. And the back seat isn't nearly as roomy as you might think it is when you're the only human in the car and you're crammed between two of them.

It took us a while to clear the city, which was persistently devoured by traffic no matter what the hour was. We were heading north.

The lead satyr's name was Hippos, and that was the extent of what I knew. I tried striking up a number of conversations, but nobody was interested in speaking, or even making eye contact. It was kind of unnerving, and mildly reminiscent of those scenes in mob movies where some unfortunate is driven off to the woods to be shot.

That seemed to be the general idea here. Once we got on the highway, I realized we were heading roughly in the direction of Mount Parnitha. From what I recalled from the various hotel maps I'd had the chance to review, it was one of the few places left in the region that looked vaguely like it did when I last lived here. Woods, in other words.

The young one to my left kept fiddling with the gun in his waistband. It seemed the seatbelt pressing up against it was causing him discomfort.

"I hope for your sake the safety is on," I said, watching him adjust himself.

He glared at me and went back to staring out the window.

"I'm just saying that's not the best place to carry a gun. You should slip it into a pocket or something."

"Be quiet," Hippos hissed from the passenger seat.

"You know your ancestors would be outraged to see your kind with guns," I said to him.

He looked at me with disgust. "Our ancestors were here before there were guns. And what would you know of it, pretender?"

Well. At least he'd gotten around to calling me a pretender. Not that his feelings toward me weren't already sort of obvious. "I know they didn't care at all for metal. I don't suppose these are wooden guns."

"They're very real guns," he countered. "And you should take care not to speak as if you know anything about us. You'll only make yourself look foolish."

I leaned forward, which was more or less the only emphatic motion I had at my disposal. "When the soldiers first came to the great woods with metal swords and armor, the satyros fought them back with sharpened wooden staffs and guile. After the battle, one of the satyr warriors picked up a discarded sword and brought it to the elder of his clan. The elder wondered what type of wood the sword was as he took it in his hands. He noted it was cold to the touch, like water, but hard like rock and sharp like a thorn, and heavier than the hard wood of his walking stick. 'This is a tool of the Duh- ryadyh,' the elder said fearfully. And then he ordered the young warrior to bring it to the edge of the woods and bury it. Only then would the tribe be protected from the wrath of their angry destroyer-god. And for centuries after, each time the satyros found metal in the woods they did exactly that."

Hippos said nothing, but turned to glare at me.

"Don't speak as if you know anything about me," I urged him. "You'll only make yourself look foolish."

* * *

The rest of the drive—it seemed to be over an hour once we hit the highway but was probably less—went by mostly in silence. The main road diverged onto a smaller one, and a smaller one still, and soon we were on a dirt path with trees dangerously close to scraping the side of the vehicle. I couldn't think of a much better place for a body dump, other than perhaps the ocean, which would have been a much longer drive. In my favor, I was nearly positive they weren't going to shoot me in the car.

We attained a flattened clearing, a spot that could hold twenty or thirty cars, but at the time was empty.

It was the cult's new Eleusis. In the old days, the mystai would spend an entire day just walking there; today's version hiked in air-conditioned SUV's.

The satyros had gotten soft, and that was a possible advantage.

The driver—I'm nearly positive they called him Frank, which is not a very popular name for a satyr or a Greek—parked near the opening of a small footpath and shut off the car.

Hippos turned. "Out," he commanded us.

A few minutes later, we were walking up the path. The moon was bright, if no longer full, but it didn't help visibility all that much, as the forest was still impressively thick. Not as overgrown as it had been back in ancient times, but close.

"Where are you taking me?" I asked.

Hippos didn't respond, and the younger ones with him were either not at liberty to speak, or were mute or something. I decided I was tired of expecting a bullet in the back of the head.

Body language in satyrs, as I've pointed out, is a little harder to read than it is in people, but men carrying guns read the same in every species. Specifically, I could tell the one behind me and on my left had never actually fired a gun before and was nervous about having one in his hands. This would be the same one who couldn't decide how to deal with both the gun and the seatbelt in the car. I had no chance at all of overpowering him and getting it, but I didn't have to; I just needed him to keep thinking about that gun rather than me.

When we reached a slight bend in the path, rather than stride forward, I planted one foot and drove my weight backward, then swung my elbow down and made contact with his gun hand. The impact wasn't nearly sufficient to knock the gun to the ground, but it didn't need to be, because for that half second all he was thinking about was not dropping it.

And that was all I needed to disappear.

* * *

If you asked me a week earlier if it made sense to hide from a party of satyrs in a wooded area, I would have suggested you had a better chance of hiding from a shark in a shark tank. But if the modern satyr lives in a city and drives a car, he probably wouldn't be able to hunt for his food or move silently through the forest floor, or vanish into the underbrush like his ancestors.

Whereas I could still do all of those things.

* * *

I left a loud, clean trail for my first thirty seconds in the woods, something anybody with functioning eyes and ears would be able to follow easily. This may seem counterintuitive, but assuming they were smart enough to follow the path, I knew where they were up until they reached the point where the trail stopped.

Had these satyrs known what the hell they were doing, I would have been caught before those thirty seconds were up. All it would have taken was for one or two of them to take to the trees and follow me from the top of the canopy. But the modern versions thought like humans, and humans stay on the ground, hold their guns out in front of them, and run toward the sounds. If I weren't counting on them to be inept, I would have cried.

Predictably, they followed the path, making enough noise to be mistaken for a stampede. Two of them walked right past me, close enough that were I so inclined, I could have grabbed one by the arm. I was not so inclined; they may have gone soft, but I still didn't like my odds in hand-to-hand combat.

"I found his shoes," one declared, which meant he reached the end of my trail. I had to kick off the shoes because it's extremely difficult to move about silently with them on; I needed the feel of the ground under my toes.

My decision to discard footwear was met with great confusion. "Why would he do that?" I heard, followed by, "I have no idea."

I stifled a laugh. Laughter is generally frowned upon when trying to hide.

"Pretender!" a loud, deep voice boomed. It was Hippos, and it sounded like he was still on the footpath. That left one satyr unaccounted for. "You are several kilometers from shelter and the night is cold."

"And he has no shoes!" shouted one of the young ones helpfully.

I made my way closer to the path. One of the tricks to hiding in the woods Is to actually keep moving, especially If someone's actively looking for you. The satyrs of yore could stay motionless for hours and be completely unseen by man or animal, but neither man nor animal was expecting them so it was permissible. In my situation, staying put only meant giving my pursuers an opportunity to find me by process of elimination.

"We have no plans to harm you," Hippos declared. "And you're going to freeze to death out here."

"Do you think I'm an idiot?" I asked.

He and the two in the woods all darted towards my voice, which was fine because I wasn't standing where the voice came from.

(There are a few different ways to do this and it's complicated, but you know how a sand dune will completely mask the sound of the ocean until you reach the top of it? It's like that. Kind of.)

I continued, turning in another direction and offering a new place for them to hone in on. "I survived for over two centuries alone in these woods, satyr. I can last a few nights. Can you?"

It would have seemed as if my voice was coming from four or five different directions. I could see Hippos at the edge of the path, looking up in case I was hiding in the trees. I was actually about ten meters from him, at eye level.

"I can have twenty more here in under an hour, " he countered. "You'll eventually run out of places to hide."

Well that was true enough, especially if one or two of them knew what they were doing. I was sort of hoping someone came to their senses and realized I was who I said I was, so I didn't have to spend the next two weeks playing commando. But Hippos was not going to be the one to make that leap.

I could hear someone coming down the path. At first I thought Hippos's reinforcements had already begun to arrive until I remembered I had been missing a satyr in my head count. He must have been sent ahead. And he'd brought someone with him—someone shorter, and probably human. I couldn't see who, but I had a guess.

A quiet conversation on the pathway ensued, and I could tell by the rising tenor on Hippos's end of it that he wasn't happy. I waited, and listened to the two in the forest as they made enough noise to warn everything with ears in a two-mile radius that they were there. I seriously considered finding a sharpened stick and killing them one at a time just to prove a point.

The conversation ended. I could see long, black hair, and when I moved slightly closer to the path, the rest of her came into view. She was wearing a loose raincoat over a white chiton, and sandals, which was a disconcerting blend of styles.

My favorite memories of chitons on women—and I have quite a few— involved warm weather, a great amount of wine, and a lot of debauching. Ariadne looked like she had stepped right out of one of those memories.

Except for the coat. London Fog, I think. But, it was cool out.

"Sojourner," she called, in English. It sounded strange, as I'd been speaking Greek for the better part of a month. "Adam. You know who I am."

"Hello, Ariadne," I greeted. She lifted her chin at the sound of my voice and smiled.

"That is a clever trick." Ariadne turned to Hippos. "Your ancestors taught him this, Hippos. These are ways even you have forgotten."

Hippos muttered something I couldn't entirely make out, but which included a word that sounded like *ninja*. He didn't look as impressed as he probably should have been.

"Are you their hierophant?" I asked.

Ariadne turned to face the woods again.

"I am."

I took two steps closer to the road. "You're sure about that?"

She glared at Hippos.

"You were in no danger," she insisted. "It's complicated. Let's say that false claimants to your name have proven unusually damaging of late."

"The kiste is missing," I elaborated.

"It's not missing. We know exactly where it is."

Well, that was a mite confusing. "Explain."

Ariadne sighed.

"I'd rather not air our political problems by shouting at a forest all evening, in any language. Why don't you come out and we can sit down and have a proper conversation? Our retreat is just beyond the ridge."

That did sound sort of nice, and much better than spending the night in the woods.

"Tell me first why your adherents believe the kiste has been taken," I said.

"Because it has."

"But not by the hierophant of the order."

"As I said, it's complicated."

I stepped out of the tree line about three meters in front of her.

"You have a schism," I guessed.

She spun at the sound of my direct voice, saw me, and smiled.

"Yes," she confirmed. "Thank you for coming."

She genuflected formally, a gesture more at home in the Christian faith, but nice anyway.

"Don't do that," I said. "But I do have a favor to ask."

"Of course."

"I wonder if one of those satyrs lost in the woods out there could bring me my shoes."

Chapter Fifteen

Sil.

I see, Dionysos, you have returned from the festival.

Dion.

I have.

Sil.

And was it pleasant?

Dion.

It was disappointing. I have little use for ceremony.

Sil.

But you appreciate their importance, do you not?

Dion.

This is not to be an interrogatory discussion. Ceremonies are important because they make man feel better about accomplishing something arbitrary. That is, if he has performed the ceremony correctly, then he must belong. The celebration that follows the   ceremony, when all congratulate one another for doing their arbitrary thing correctly, this is what interests me. It is the celebration that is the true religious event.

—From the dialogues of Silenus the Younger.
Text corrected and translated by Ariadne

For something that was the heart of a religious order, the Eleusinian retreat was surprisingly humble. Were I to stumble upon it independent of my escorts, I'd probably assume it was a summer camp for children, and maybe that was the idea.

"It isn't much," Ariadne said. She was walking next to me. We were flanked by the four satyrs, but now I wasn't quite as concerned about the whole *bullet in the back of the head* thing. "But it beds as many as can attend."

"I think I was expecting something a little more ostentatious," I admitted. "Not the Vatican or anything, but ..."

"Yes, we're trying *not* to draw attention. Don't worry; there's more to it."

The cabins, I soon discovered, were built around a natural depression in the hill we were climbing, which hid the main building from view.

That building was a miniature Telesterion.

From the outside, it might have looked like a temple of some kind, and so it was. But not like any kind of temple someone from the modern world would understand. For one thing, it had no walls. The main structural features were the flat roof and the two-dozen ionic columns holding that roof up. Stairs led up to the floor on three sides, which had the effect of turning the entire interior (if one could call an area with no walls an interior) into an altar. The original structure was a third larger and completely freestanding—this version was built into a hill—but it was a good enough replica to take my breath away for a few seconds.

This was the feeling I wanted when I came back to Greece—the sense of going home to something that had never gotten old and passed away.

Ariadne was staring at me, as I'd apparently stopped walking.

"Better?" she asked.

"Better."

"We were going on some very old descriptions. I always wondered how accurate it was."

"Well done. Except for the curtain."

A white stage curtain was hung just inside the outer ring of columns, hiding the interior.

"Ah, well ... it's cooler up here on the mountainside than in Eleusis. It also affords us some privacy, and keeps in the heat from the fire. We open it on the final night, no matter the weather, though."

"Fire?"

"Dinner, even," she smiled. "Hopefully it isn't cold. I was expecting your arrival to be less complicated."

* * *

Ariadne and I were the only ones to enter the Telesterion. Hippos and his men took positions outside, either to guard anyone else from entering, or to prevent us from leaving. I would have been more concerned with the latter, were I not busy appreciating the interior.

They had done a very nice job of approximating the look, and more importantly the feel of the place. Someone expecting a traditional religious experience would have anticipated chairs or pews, but there were none. Likewise, there was no additional altar. At the center of the vast room was a large fire pit that provided most of the illumination— the rest came from a ring of torches along the outside. The firelight flickered across the columns, which cast a fascinating variety of shadows.

The earthen wall at the far end was wet and mossy, and had a small concavity built into it. It was where the kiste would have rested. I felt its absence acutely, even though I'd never experienced the ceremony here.

Amidst all of this was a discordant domestic setting. Next to the fire was a table and two chairs, and not far beyond that an open bedroll.

"Are you still impressed?" Ariadne walked past me to the table. She picked up a goblet of wine and poured out two glasses.

"I am." Noting the bedroll, I asked, "Have you been sleeping here?"

"Lately, yes." Gesturing to one of the chairs, she added, "Please."

She slipped out of her jacket, dropping it carelessly on the floor. As I had seen when I first glimpsed her from the woods, she was wearing a chiton and plain wood sandals underneath; traditional clothing from a long-gone era. Except the chiton was form fitting, which was a nice modern touch, as was the gold filigree laced into the collar that met behind her neck in a clasp. I watched as she sat down behind her glass of wine. The bottom of the chiton rose to well above mid-thigh, and I remembered exactly how she first caught my attention.

I took the seat opposite her at the table, because standing there and staring was going to end up being unproductive.

Between us was a roasted piglet that smelled amazing. I had to assume a large kitchen of some sort was in one of the surrounding cabins, because otherwise she cooked the pig on the fire pit and I didn't see a spit anywhere.

I sipped the wine and eyed the pig.

"It isn't kykeon," she said apologetically, "but it's good wine."

"I prefer the wine anyway," I admitted. "Never much cared for kykeon."

This was an understatement; kykeon is truly a dreadful concoction. It's a barley-based drink prepared for the final night of the Greater Mysteries. What one does is put the barley stalks into the kiste and leave them there for months until just before Boedromion. The drink is then brewed in a process similar to beer making, except there isn't enough fermentation time and burdock root is used instead of hops. The finished product has a powerful hallucinogenic quality, which is why people tolerate the undeniable fact that it tastes awful.

At the high point of the ceremony, the Telesterion was full of celebrants, and the smoke and firelight and shadows would turn the space into a vivid experience for anyone in an altered state. Without the influence of hallucinogens, I never experienced it exactly the same way, but it sure looked like a lot of fun.

"Eat, please," she insisted, and I wasn't about to wait for a second offer. I began carving off chunks of meat for myself. "And tell me where you'd like me to begin?"

"Start with who you actually are," I asked. "Because clearly there's more to you than ex-government analyst Ariadne Papos."

"This is true," she agreed. "My family name is Papodopoulos. My parents shortened it when they moved to the States. I'm the last of an unbroken line of human keepers of the Mysteries. My family has worked side-by-side with the satyros for over two millennia to keep the secrets safe."

"The last?" I asked.

"My parents died in a fire five years ago, and I'm unable to bear children."

"I'm sorry, " I said. Because that's what one says when hearing something like that.

She shook off the sentiment. "Don't be. I understood it to mean I was the one destined to find you and bring you back. The prophet said as much."

"That must have been one heck of a prophet," I said, adding, "Aren't you going to eat?"

She was drinking her wine and watching me eat instead of having any herself. If I were anyone else, I'd have been concerned that the food was poisoned or drugged.

"No, it's not for me. The prophet was my great grandmother, give or take about fifteen generations. Her specific prediction was that a Papodopoulos would see the sojourner home."

"I didn't know this prophet, did I?"

"No. The sojourner had abandoned the cult by that time."

"Sorry. I had other stuff going on."

She smiled. Lovely smile. After spending all that time trying to catch glimpses of her in Vegas, it was deeply appealing, in a way I can't fully explain, to have her full attention like this. And she certainly did seem preoccupied with me and my feasting. Something about me also seemed to be making her either very nervous or very excited. I had no idea what that was.

She continued, "The reason I'm an American is that my family moved to the Pacific Northwest before I was born. For most of my life, contact with the Mysteries was through the North American Chapter."

I nearly choked. "Did you say chapter?"

"There are a few."

"You people really did take the Mysteries out of Attic."

She looked bemused. "This upsets you. I wouldn't have thought modernization was something you'd find objectionable. Besides, the Eleusinian cult had already left Eleusis. It wasn't a large step."

She had a point. And I was a few generations too late to express an opinion on it.

"All right, so that's you," I said. "What about this schism?"

"The schism is my fault. I had a ... bad period after my parents died, let's say. I fell in love with the wrong man. His name is Gordon Alecto."

I knew the name; he was the eco-terrorist Mike mentioned. "I've heard of him."

She didn't look surprised. "Back then he was a young, charismatic botanist who didn't blow things up. I introduced him to the Mysteries. And he loved everything about it. Soon he was insisting on coming here to experience the real thing. It was a huge mistake on my part; he wasn't ready."

Something clicked. "This is the man claiming to be me, isn't it? You brought him to Greece, and because your connection to me had been prophesied ..."

"Yes. He announced that he was Dionysos himself, the sojourner returned after centuries of wandering, and because he was in my company, the claim was taken at face value. Nobody seemed to mind that he declared it shortly after his first taste of true kykeon and was in a clearly altered state."

"I knew a lot of people who thought they were gods after their first taste. As long as they don't try flying, it's usually harmless. And it usually goes away."

"This didn't. He thought he'd reached a stage of enlightenment, and he kept drinking kykeon to remain in this enlightened state as long as possible. That became much easier after he was granted the title of hierophant, and was given private access to the kiste. And I'm sure you know what constant exposure to kykeon can do to a person."

I did. Like anything that powerful, overuse caused insanity and death. The active ingredient—the part that triggers the hallucinations—is essentially a poison. Small doses at irregular intervals and the body will recover just fine. Regular ingestion is ultimately lethal.

"So his eco-terrorist activity is a part of his burgeoning insanity?"

"It is, but it's much worse than that. He's been having what he calls prophetic visions."

"Oracular?"

"Not that lucid, but similar. The visions are what convinced him to bring the kiste to America."

She stopped to look at the piglet, and my plate.

"Are you done?" she asked with a slight grin.

I had finished eating and was concentrating on the wine, which I quite liked. "I am. It was very good, thank you. You should really try some."

"As I said, it's for you. I'm glad you enjoyed it."

It only then occurred to me why she kept saying that. I'd been taking part in a ceremony. Without the kiste, the celebrants, or any of the other trappings of the harvest festival, it hadn't registered, but the piglet was a part of the traditional feast. If she followed the preparations correctly, it was cooked in the milk of its mother. That's a whole lot tastier than it sounds.

Ariadne got up from the table and reached behind her neck to unclasp her chiton. "Then we should proceed."

"What are you doing?" I asked. This didn't seem like a logical next step in our relationship, per se. But it was the next step of the ceremony, if this was what I thought it was. And her not eating was a good indication.

"You shouldn't have to ask, sojourner." She released the clasp and her chiton fell to the floor. She was naked beneath it, and every bit as spectacular as I'd imagined she would be in that state. Her skin was pale and the firelight licked across her skin and flickered in her eyes.

It had been so long since I'd had anything to do with the Mysteries, I had completely forgotten this part, surprising as that might seem.

Not to be too crude about it, but I managed to include a rule in the rituals that if I show up for the festival, I get fed and I get laid. It was additional incentive for me to show up, and when you have a hand in devising a ceremony, this is the sort of thing you can get away with.

I'm not proud. Although it is kind of genius when you think about it.

Clad only in sandals, Ariadne knelt at my feet.

"You don't have to do this," I said. "It's really okay. This part ... it's an artifact of a different age."

She reached out and took my hand, pressing it against her naked breast. Her nipples were erect, but it was drafty. "I could find dozens of women who would enthusiastically fulfill this obligation. I'm doing it because it's something *I* want to do."

"All the same, I'm sure this isn't necessary."

I did my best to sound convincing. Sex by ceremonial coercion was something I've gotten old enough to feel guilty about. Hard as that may be to believe.

She leaned forward, still on her knees, now settled between my thighs. She kissed my chest. "If you keep talking like that, I'm going to start to feel insulted."

I lifted her chin and looked in her eyes. She gave me a wry smile that was utterly impossible to resist. "If you're sure."

There was more to talk about, like the schism, or what in the world Gordon Alecto was thinking when he brought the kiste to America, but none of that seemed all that important at that precise moment, especially once she undid my belt and snaked a hand down to free me from my pants. Her hand was cool, soft, and wonderful, and I had no remaining objections to voice.

This was *much* better than spending the night in the forest.

I put my hand on the back of her neck and leaned forward, kissing her deeply. I could taste the wine and a trace of figs. Her dark eyes fluttered. I reached my arm and found her ass, and pulled.

"Off your knees," I requested.

"Yes, sojourner," she said obediently.

We stood together, and then I lifted her onto the table. There was the bedroll nearby, but what had begun as a surprising interlude in our conversation a second earlier, had become a very urgent thing that had to be dealt with immediately, and the bed was too far.

With her feet off the ground, she wrapped her legs around me and tilted back, her arms supporting her on the table. She was about to lie down on the remains of the piglet, so I reached past her and shoved the food onto the floor. The plates landed with a resounding crash that was undoubtedly heard outside. She grinned, leaned back further, and pulled me into her.

Taking Ariadne there, in the Telesterion by the light of a brazier, with the smell of roast pig and wood smoke in the air, took me back a lot. I have had sex under many different circumstances, but in some ways the kind offered by the Eleusinian consorts was the most enticing. I've often had sex as a reward at the end of a well-executed pursuit. Only rarely has it been offered as a gift, and I'd forgotten how amazing that was.

Also amazing is sex involving a table, especially one that's just the right height. I pushed forward and we worked into a rhythm, my hand on her tailbone and her heels hooked behind my back. This was not the casual sort of intercourse I could spend a day working through; it was rapid and violent and propulsive.

And for the first time in months, I wasn't thinking about Clara anymore.

"My ... god ..." Ariadne cried between breaths, wrapping one arm around my shoulders and pulling her chest up against mine. She gave in to her orgasm by holding onto me for dear life, every muscle in her body locked up, her head tucked into the crook of my collarbone. And then I joined her.

It was several seconds before either of us relaxed.

She then released me and lay back on the tabletop, panting and laughing. "You know, I did bring a bed."

I smiled. "The table looked sturdy enough."

The wine goblet managed to survive the experience, remaining perched on the edge of the table near her head. I reached across her and rescued it, drinking directly from the mouth as it appeared both of the glasses had been shattered.

She sat up and took the wine from me to have a sip of her own, while I admired her some more.

"How long have you known about the prophecy?" I asked.

"All my life."

"Was what we just did foretold?"

"Not exactly, no. But there was room for interpretation. Help me down?"

I stepped out of my pants so that I could walk without falling over, then lifted her off the table and onto her feet.

"When did you decide to interpret it in this particular way?" I asked, as we negotiated our way around the shattered dishes to the bed.

"When I saw you at the casino, I think." She stepped into the bed and lay down, pulling the blanket partly over herself and holding it open to invite me in. Rather than lie next to her I sat, because between the sex and the wine, the beer from earlier, and the threat of death in-between, I was pretty sure I'd fall asleep immediately. And I had more questions.

She looked disappointed. "Surely you have more than one ceremonial fuck in you, sojourner."

I smiled. "The schism. The kiste in America. You need to explain these things to me."

She sighed. "Oh, all right. The schism is simple enough. The majority of our people still believe Gordon, but he's perverted the Mysteries into something militant. I didn't fully realize how bad it was— how insane he'd gotten—until recently. I tried to re-establish the Mysteries independently, and partly succeeded, which is why I have loyal satyrs here and in the city. But to really stop him, I knew I had to find the man he's pretending to be."

"When did he take the kiste?"

"Six months ago. He's going to hold the ceremonies in America with it for the first time. And he's introducing a new ceremony. Adam, you have to help us stop him."

"From corrupting the mysteries? I think it's too late for that."

"The new ritual is my concern. And recovering the kiste, of course."

"This will be soon?"

"Boedromion ends in two days. We have a flight leaving in the morning."

I stared into her dark eyes, not at all liking the sudden urgency in her request. "What is it you're not telling me?"

She sighed again. I was pretty sure the sighs were a bad sign. "The new ceremony ... Gordon thinks he is going to awaken a god."

"*Which* god are we talking about?"

"A nymph."

"Really."

The nymph, as I understood it, was purely mythological. But I wasn't going to be taking a chance on being wrong, not with an oracle predicting my death at the hand of a god.

"I think I'll stay in Athens. I like it here."

"I was afraid you might feel that way," she said.

"Look, it's ... I mean I didn't even know the Mysteries were still active until ..."

"I understand. But *you* need to understand something. The prophecies foretold of this day. You have to be there, and you will be. That's why Hippos and his men have orders to keep you in here until our flight. If you try and leave, they will do you harm."

"And who gave them those orders?"

"I did."

Still very much naked as she rolled onto her back, uncovered from the waist up and almost daring me to be angry with her while looking so appealing.

"I'm a prisoner?"

"You are. But you have a chance to be an extremely satisfied prisoner. We have until morning."

"You're serious."

"If you're angry, you're welcome to take it out on me in whatever way you deem appropriate."

I considered all the ways I could try and escape, but none of them seemed all that viable, especially since at minimum I'd have to get my pants on first. And sex now, for near-certain death later, was a trade-off I was not entirely unfamiliar with.

So I got into the bed.

* * *

From The Tragedy of Silenus. Text corrected and translated by Ariadne

The festival of Eleusis has ended. Silenus stands with the Hierophant.

Silenus
Grant me audience, great Hierophant. And quickly. My lord approaches.

Hierophant
You have it, Silenus the wanderer. Do you question our ceremony?

Silenus
I do not; it was rare and bold. Two gods answered your call. No other event can boast such a thing.

Hierophant
You look fearful. How can I unburden you?

Silenus
The two gods that graced your festival were gods divided.

235

Hierophant
This is so.

Silenus
Can I ask you why?

Hierophant
The gods come and go of their own initiative. It is not my place to ask.
One leaves and a second arrives and it is so because it is so.
I have no command over either.

Silenus
Truly I understand this, for while I carry the words of Dionysos his
schedule is his alone.

Hierophant
Then why do you question such a thing?

Silenus
When I first came to Eleusis many years past it was said
The goddess herself came and stayed for the whole of the festive
month.
And I came myself and saw it was true, and I met her and asked for her
blessing.

Hierophant
And did she give it to you?

Silenus
She did, and I was greatly enriched. This is not my complaint. I now find
she departs before the final night and more Before my lord arrives.
Thus, is the ceremony split.

Hierophant
It was ever so. The Mysteries celebrate all life cultivated, as tended by
Demeter's loving hand.
Yours is a lord of another domain.
He has no place in our festival save for the concluding bacchanal.

Silenus

No, hierophant, it was not always so.

Hierophant
Then you are truly older than my eyes contend.

Silenus
Indeed I am.
'Ere Dionysos did appear, Demeter saw the ritual's end. This is truth.

Hierophant
It must have been a very different ceremony.

Silenus
Indeed for Demeter, while radiant, is not as boisterous by half as my lord.

Hierophant
I agree.

Silenus
Since no matter when my Dionysos arrives Demeter hastily exits, I ask what should be obvious: Why does she avoid him?

Hierophant
I do not know that she does.
Does Dionysos send you to ask this question?

Silenus
In a manner of speaking
For it was I that told him to seek her out here. Many years have passed since and many are the times I have greeted him with, "My lord, you have only just missed her."
I fear should I respond in this way once more my suffering will be great. And justly so.

Hierophant
But I do not know the answer.
Could your lord perhaps ask her himself?

Silenus
You have missed my point.

Hierophant

But there is Dionysos now!

(Dionysos enters)

Dionysos

Silenus, I would speak to you.

Hierophant

Greetings, mighty Dionysos.

Dionysos

And greetings to you, noble hierophant.

Please do not stand between myself and my herald. That may be the most perilous location for your feet In the whole of the realm.

Hierophant

Then I must take your leave.

(Hierophant exits)

Silenus

My lord, the goddess was here. Had you only arrived sooner.

Dionysos

Had I only arrived sooner she would have left sooner. No, this is not happenstance.

It is not fate. It is not the whimsy of gods

For we are the only gods in contention and I am not feeling whimsical, Although perhaps Demeter is.

Silenus

Forgive my caustic tone

But is it possible Demeter does not like you?

Dionysos

You speak as if we were children.

Silenus

Children mimic adults in play. And sometimes the opposite holds.

It is no less true with gods, I'd wager.

Dionysos

Truly, Silenus, your wisdom is as hard to predict as a storm. But this is
not such a simple dynamic.
I have endured many lifetimes, and all around me has
changed. All but her.
But never in all of these years have I sought her out. I did not need to,
for she was following me.

Silenus

And you did not let her catch you?

Dionysos

She did not wish to catch me. Only to watch. Many were the days I
would turn about and my eyes would settle on her visage.
Always from afar.
I can never close the distance 'ere she disappears again.

Silenus

So, it is she that has sought you out.

Dionysos

But only as a sailor looking on a distant shore. To your point: if she does
not care for me,
Does not wish me to speak to her or seek her out,
Why does she follow me?
You will find me this answer.

Silenus

How? In all your days you have not found this answer.

Dionysos

But you are not I. You will find her, and ask these questions. And you
will return to me with her answer.

Silenus

If I cannot find her? Or if she is found but unswayed?

Dionysos

Then do not return to me at all.

PART Three

The God Reclaimed

Chapter Sixteen

"I have returned from the Northern climes," the god said to Silenus. "Where the women are beauteous and plentiful."

But when Silenus laughed and asked why the god did not take Silenus with him to such a wondrous place, the god shook his head.

"Your kind has never seen cold such as they have there. You that live in the hearth of the world should not venture outside it."

—From the archives of Silenus the Elder.
Text corrected and translated by Ariadne

We were standing twenty yards north of the road that had formerly been known as Route 20, but was now more properly recognized as another treeless flat space in an expanse of growing snowdrifts. I was leaning up against a tree and trying to accustom myself to the harsh surroundings and to the pair of boots I'd been handed an hour earlier.

The boots didn't fit. I give them credit for trying, but my feet are about a half-size smaller, and there wasn't anything anybody could do about it now, given how far away we were from the nearest shoe store.

Ariadne had probably been the one to assess my foot size. Of the four of them, she was the only one who'd met me prior to Athens. For the parka, the snow pants, the gloves, the hat, and the ski goggles, she'd been pretty much dead-on, just not the feet.

I do enough hiking outdoors to know that it's never a good idea to put on a brand-new pair of boots right before going on a long walk. One has to break them in first, or risk major blisters. Granted, most of my hiking days pre-date the advent of footwear, but when it came to rocky or snowy terrain, I was never one to shy away from innovation. And I always made sure the damn things fit.

One might think I'd have other things to complain about. I was, after all, still a captive and heading to certain doom, if the last thing I heard from Cassandra Jones was in any way accurate. Worse, I hadn't found time to have sex with Ariadne since we left Athens.

"We go northwest from here," Hippos shouted, in Greek. He was holding a small GPS device, which I presumed worked in a similar fashion to the one in Mike's car.

Since arriving in the States, Hippos had spoken English almost exclusively. Part of it was probably force of habit—he'd been to the U.S. on more than one occasion—and part of it was to help Staphus and Dyanos, neither of whom were fluent and thus needed all the exposure they could get. The two of them were mainly there to guard me, so far as I could tell.

The heading we were electing to follow took us on a path diagonal to the storm, which was blowing in from the northwest and carried a high velocity mixture of snowflakes and ice pellets. Something I picked up on long ago was that the bigger the flakes, the shorter the storm. These were tiny flakes, so we were in for a long day.

With Hippos leading the way, Ariadne following close behind, and me flanked in front and back by my two satyr guards, we started marching uphill through the trees. We were making our own path rather than following one that had been established by the park, which made it slow-going and rife with various, and somewhat literal, pitfalls. That's the problem with any forest floor; tree roots and water erosion combine to make for a consistently uneven walking surface.

"Do you know how far we have to go?" I asked Dyanos—who was behind me—in Greek. He was wearing a parka with the hood up and pulled tightly against his face. The parka was nearly as ill fitting as my shoes, not quite covering his wrists. He actually looked sort of funny, and if I knew him a bit better, I'd have said so.

"Half a day's march," he shouted, because you have to shout to be heard in a blizzard.

"Half a day under what conditions?" I asked. *"Was snow factored in?"*

He didn't bother to respond.

Self-evidently, the prophet made no predictions regarding the weather, as the storm was a surprise to everyone concerned. I give them credit for the winter gear—this was September, in the North Cascades—but their plan clearly did not have enough time built into it. We were going to be hard-pressed to reach the ceremony before all the fun began. And that was fine with me.

Another indication that this plan wasn't working out was sitting in a snow bank on the road behind us.

We were met at the airport—on the tarmac, as we never entered the terminal—by an Econoline van. It was the kind of vehicle you take if you're following the Grateful Dead, and less than ideal in adverse weather conditions as opposed to, say, an SUV. With Hippos driving, we barreled along Interstate 5 in our van and directly into the teeth of the storm, which turned from rain to sleet to snow as we went. By the time we reached the turnoff for Route 20, we were the only vehicle on the road. And that is almost never a good sign.

But a far more ominously bad sign came when we reached the entrance to the park proper, just past Marblemount. It was there that we discovered the rest of Route 20 was closed.

The large signs posted on both sides of the roadway indicated that every season, usually sometime in November, the highway passage through the center of the North Cascades National Park is closed down. The normal seasonal weather here was bad enough to make the roadway entirely impassible for six months out of the year. Incidentally, this is how you know you've put a road in a bad place.

It was not November, but obviously somebody in the park office had seen the weather report (which we, equally obviously, had not) and concluded that shutting down the road early would be prudent. A large metal rail had been pushed across the road, blocking the way.

But Hippos wouldn't be deterred. He and Staphus climbed out, and with a little work, managed to reopen the road by pushing the rail aside. I suppose it was foolish for the park rangers to not have a car out at the barrier, but conversely who would be stupid enough to ignore a warning like that? Other than us?

We made it another ten miles or so before the predictable happened and Hippos lost control of the van. To his credit, he had been able to keep us on the road in very bad conditions for nearly three hours before this happened, and in a fairly judgmentally impaired state. (From Athens to Seattle, we'd been traveling for twenty-four hours and I don't think he got any sleep at all. I had; I slept on the plane. But satyrs don't need much sleep.) We skidded and fishtailed along the empty, snow-covered road before crashing softly into a snow bank on the northern side, which was good as the southern side consisted of a steep drop directly into the Skagit River. Equally good, he missed all the trees. But the van ended up stuck.

This put Hippos in an even fouler mood.

* * *

We got in a good hour of off-path hiking before hitting a real trail. This was a cause for celebration, and a chance to stop for a minute and get our second wind.

Ariadne sat down in the snow against a tree and pulled back her hood to shake some of the sweat loose from her long, black hair. I sat down beside her.

"Where are we going?" I asked.

"Azure Lake," she said quietly. "It's not far from the base of Mount Terror."

"Mount Terror? You're kidding me."

"Nope."

She reached inside her voluminous parka and emerged with a bottle of water. It took an effort to get the cap off with snow-covered gloves, but she managed it eventually.

"Have you ever walked through a storm like this?" she asked.

"Sure. Before the glaciers over Europe receded, I spent a lot of time hunting in these conditions. Not the sort of thing you do unless you really have to."

She stared at me. "You lived through an ice age?"

"I was born at the tail end of one, yeah, but in central Africa. Much nicer weather there."

"If we both survive this, you'll have to tell me about it."

I laughed. "This was your idea. You make it sound like we're both captives."

"I'm trying to save something important. If I could do that from a warm bed, I would."

Hippos, who had been looking at a trail map that was being slowly taken apart by the wind, stepped up and said, "We take this path for a ways, until it branches off here." He tried showing this to Ariadne on the map, but it was impossible to hold it still.

"I'll take your word for it," she said.

"Are you ready to continue?"

He and the other satyrs didn't look at all winded. Forest travel for them was in their blood, although their people didn't historically have to deal with conditions like this.

"Yes," she said.

He pulled her to her feet. I had to stand up on my own, a matter that my thighs disapproved of. That's where you feel it when you walk in the snow—the thighs. The pain comes from having to lift your whole leg up just to take another step forward. I also had wind burn on parts of my face, and I hadn't felt my fingers for more than an hour. About the only thing that was working out was that I'd lost feeling in both feet, which made the blistering from the oversized shoes less painful.

"And you," Hippos said, "you can continue?"

"Would you consider seeking shelter until the storm passes?" I asked.

"I would not."

"Then lead on, ambassador."

Ambassador was my new name for Hippos. It seemed to annoy him, which worked fine for me. I started calling him that as soon as we got aboard the 727 from Athens, which happened to be a private jet owned by the Greek government. It turns out Hippos is the deputy ambassador to the United States. That was how they managed to get someone whose wrists were lashed together with twine into the country without having to answer awkward questions at customs. I was tempted to write my congressman about the lax security, but I'm not really a U.S. citizen and thus don't have a congressman.

With Hippos again leading the way, his GPS device apparently frozen to his right hand, I fell in line with Ariadne and continued the slow march. Neither Dyanos nor Staphus seemed concerned enough about this to say anything.

"Still worried you're about to die?" she asked, without looking. "Cassandra could have been wrong."

"Oracles aren't wrong, they're just misinterpreted," I said. "What did she tell you, anyhow? You seemed to have gotten a much more detailed prophecy than I did."

"It was longer than yours, certainly," she agreed. "Detailed? Not really. But I'm working with two prophecies. There wasn't much overlap between them, and I have a lifetime of experience interpreting the subtleties of prophetic statements."

I considered pointing out that I've had two or three lifetimes' worth of experience doing the same, but that would have just led us back around to the fact that I was expecting to die, which I didn't feel like talking about anymore.

I changed the subject. "Here's something I'm not clear on. What does your ex think this nymph is going to do for him?"

"Defend the natural world in a way he can't."

"What happens if it doesn't feel like doing that?"

"He seems to be under the impression that he is you, and that you can control a nymph." She looked at me directly, which is difficult with a hood. "Can you?"

I laughed. "Of course I can't. I've never seen one. I don't even know if they exist."

She stared at me.

"What?" I asked.

"It is *very* hard to tell when you're joking."

She marched ahead before I had an opportunity to figure out what that meant.

* * *

The storm only got worse.

I have been in plenty of hairy situations in my life, weather-wise, and truthfully this didn't come all that close to any of the nastier ones, but that didn't mean it had no ambition in that direction.

Twice we strayed from the trail and didn't realize it for several minutes and were forced to follow our own steps back. As I was in the middle of the pack, it was possible for me to see both Dyanos in front and Staphus in back, but I seriously doubted whether Staphus could see Dyanos or vice versa. And when the wind really picked up, I couldn't see anyone.

Despite this, I got the sense that we weren't entirely alone. Every now and then, I'd catch a whiff of campfire smoke, but nobody was going to be getting a fire up in these conditions so it had to be an old one. Wind direction indicated the source was to our left.

I was pretty sure I could track it.

I wasn't thinking about escaping, per se. The problem with conditions this severe, is that it's really difficult to survive in them alone with no provisions, and the satyrs had all of the supplies. So while I was heading to what I thought was probably my own death, death by exposure was much more definitive. But, if whoever was out there had a link to the outside world, that could prove useful. I didn't know if I had the resources to stop the impending ceremony, but I knew someone who might.

As we progressed, I allowed myself to drop behind Ariadne just enough to stretch the line in which we were traveling thinner. Checking Staphus's progress behind me, I identified a large tree stump on the side of the path and then counted the number of seconds it took before he passed by the same tree stump. It was a ten-count. Then I waited until we reached a rise, a point where the trees offered less protection from the winds.

A quick leap off the path, and onto a downward slope, and in a couple of seconds I was in the trees. Even though I fell over twice—a combination of numb feet and an uneven surface—I still managed to reach a dense copse before I even finished my ten-count, and then I ducked down and waited.

Incidentally, this was not the same thing as vanishing into the woods near Mount Parnitha. I was good, but I couldn't make footprints disappear and once they noticed I was missing they'd be able to double back and find my trail. If I were a satyr, I could resolve this by climbing a tree and jumping from limb to limb, but that wasn't happening.

Once I was certain nobody was tracking me, I sniffed the air to see if I could pick up on the campfire again. This would have been easier if I had a werewolf's nose, or a satyr's, or really anything but a frozen human nose. Still, after a few shifts in the wind I picked it up; it was downhill from where I stood, in a small ravine.

I stumbled down the hill until reaching the bottom of the ravine, then leaned up against the nearest tree and tried to quiet my breathing as I listened again for a sign of someone following me. I didn't hear anything. However, my ears were covered by a fur-lined hood, it was windy, and satyrs can still move pretty fast, so there was no telling how long I had.

And then I did hear something. It wasn't coming from the top of the hill, though; the noise was a few yards further along the ravine.

"Someone here?" I called out. No answer.

I pushed ahead toward the noise. As I got closer, I realized I was listening to a radio. Classic Rock, it sounded like, or whatever passes for it now.

It didn't make any sense. Who would leave behind a radio?

I crested a small rise and saw ... well, it wasn't pleasant. It appeared somebody in the woods was a very messy eater, and the meal had been two, or possibly three, human beings. I could see the remains of a tent, a toppled Hibachi, a sleeping bag that would be of no use to anybody any longer, and various and random people parts covering everything.

Whenever coming across a scene like this, there is one important rule to keep in mind: find out if whoever or whatever did it is still there. So I crouched down exactly where I was and watched for signs of movement while my thoughts raced through the land animals with which I was familiar that would be capable of such a thing.

A bear seemed obvious, but most self-respecting bears were sleeping this time of year. A lion or a tiger perhaps, but the last time I checked there weren't any in North America outside of the zoos. It actually looked like the work of a dragon, but I hadn't seen one since the fifteenth century and I didn't think anyone else had either. That left only one animal—man. But it'd have to be one huge man.

Although it was possible a demon had done it. They were big enough, strong enough, and vicious enough to cause this kind of damage. But it didn't feel right for a demon. Usually the violence they commit is of the brute force variety. These people had been sliced up like someone was trying out a large *Ginsu* knife on them.

It could also have been a vampire with very poor impulse control or a profound hatred of Classic Rock, but the attack had happened within the past hour and it was daytime. Granted, the sun was blocked by clouds, but I didn't know of any vampire who would take a chance like that.

I knew how recent the attack was because of two things. One, it had been snowing all day but the blood was mostly on top of the snow rather than covered by it. Two, the bodies were steaming.

There was no sign of the attacker, so I got up and walked into the center of the clearing, and checked out the massacre up close.

It had been three people: two men and a woman. I determined this by counting heads. My guess was they left the path to get away from the wind—the ravine offered a lot of protection—started a fire and planned to wait it out. The fire didn't last long, but the rest of the plan was solid, except for the part where they were torn into pieces.

Up close, it looked more and more like somebody used a knife of some sort. Or a sword, actually, given the amount of damage.

Had there been a fourth member of the party? Someone who likes going out into the woods with a katana, maybe? But I saw no tracks leading to or away from the bodies—they were all within ten feet of one another—other than mine. There were these odd spots in the snow where grass poked out, but those hardly qualified as tracks.

Something else caught my attention. It was their expressions. All of them died with their eyes open, which is unusual enough but more so in this case because *each* of them bore a look of surprise. I could understand if the first victim was surprised, but the other two would surely have had time to register a different emotion before their heads were separated from the rest of their bodies. How do you surprise three people that completely? And permanently?

"A nymph," I muttered, remembering what Ariadne said. A terrible idea began to take shape. I tried to ignore it.

I eventually found the radio, which had moved from E.L.O. to a portion of the Bachman-Turner Overdrive oeuvre. It was hitched to the back of one of the men's backpacks. I turned it off and then riffled through the rest of the bag, which was fortunately intact.

Settled at the bottom, under a set of spare clothes, I found a satellite phone.

It took a minute to dig the card out of my pants—underneath the snow pants— quietly thankful both that I hadn't changed out of the jeans and that Hippos never ordered anybody to go through my pockets.

I dialed Mike Lycos's number.

And that's exactly where my luck ended.

"Hi, you've reached special agent Mike Lycos. Please leave a message and a contact number and I'll get back to you as soon as I can."

Beep.

"Mike, it's Adam. I'm in the North Cascades. Get to Azure Lake as soon as you can and you'll find Gordon Alecto and Ariadne Papos. Bring lots of very big guns. I'm going to ..." And then something hit me hard, knocking me several feet away and onto my ass, the phone spinning off into a snowdrift.

I looked up at Staphus staring down at me with fury in his eyes.

"You monster, what did you do to these people?"

Chapter Seventeen

Silenus:

I even spoke with a god of the woods.

King Laios:

And what did you learn?

Silenus:

Alas, I said I spoke. I did not say the god spoke back.

—From The Tragedy of Silenus.
Text corrected and translated by Ariadne

"I found them like this," I started to say, but he sprang at me before I could elaborate. I took a hard punch in the chin, and then he had me by the coat.

"How could you?" he demanded, hoisting me up in the air and preparing to fling me several yards into Zeus only knew what. He didn't seem to want to calm down long enough to figure out I couldn't have done this to three people with my bare hands, and I wasn't going to last long if I stayed in his reach. So when he bent his arms to push me off, I swung both of my fists as hard as I could into the sides of his head and boxed his ears.

He shoved me away—not nearly as violently as he wanted—and grabbed his head.

"You need to calm down and think, Staphus," I suggested, scurrying

to my feet and looking about frantically for something I could use as a makeshift weapon. "*I didn't do this.*"

He roared incoherently and charged hard, so hard that when I dropped to the ground, he passed directly overhead. My hands found a tent stake half-buried in the snow.

Staphus skidded to a stop and turned completely around faster than I thought anyone could in heavy powder. He came at me again as I yanked up the stake. But just before he reached me, he was tackled from the side.

Dyanos had arrived, and was thinking much more clearly. The two satyrs disappeared into a snow bank.

"Don't move!" I heard Hippos bark. Looking around, I saw he had just reached the edge of the clearing. Ariadne was still climbing down behind him.

The two satyrs burst free of the snow bank, Dyanos restraining Staphus.

"*Look at what he has done to these poor people!*" Staphus shouted.

"*Use your head, brother,*" Dyanos said. "*He has no blood on him. Nor weapon. Something else did this.*"

"*That's what I've been trying to tell him,*" I said.

Ariadne reached the clearing, and screamed.

"What happened here, imposter?" Hippos asked, walking slowly to where I was standing and assessing the damage as he went.

I should note that upon learning of my reluctance to voluntarily attend the ceremonies, Hippos had taken to calling me imposter again. He seemed to have reached the conclusion that the real Philopaigmos would have been happy to attend, and therefore I am not he. I couldn't tell if he was serious about it or not, but it got annoying.

"Something big and scary went on a frenzy here. I've never seen anything like it."

"Nor have I," he admitted. "Did you witness it?"

"No. But whatever did this can't be far. Track it if you want. I plan to go in the opposite direction of wherever it's headed."

Hippos crouched down and examined one of the victims.

"There is no scent," he said.

"Maybe the snow is screwing that up?"

"Perhaps," he mused. "I can understand Staphus's reaction. He would have picked up only your odor and that of the dead. It should have been the correct conclusion."

"You think I'm capable of this?" I asked. "I mean, this fast?"

"No. If you were, you would have done it to us long ago."

Staphus, finally calm, walked over and held out his hand.

"*I am sorry, I should not have attacked you in that manner.*"

I ignored his hand.

"*Don't worry about it.*"

"*Thank you for understanding,*" he said.

"*Don't thank me.*" I held up the tent spike. "*Thank Dyanos. He saved your life.*"

"What did this to these people?" Ariadne asked, trying to maintain her cool. She wasn't coming any closer than the edge of the campground, and I strongly suspected that while we were talking she had been vomiting behind a tree somewhere.

Hippos addressed her question.

"A wild animal," he said. "Nothing we will not be able to cope with should we encounter it."

"Don't be ..." I started to say. Hippos cut me off.

"Silence, imposter."

He shot me a look, but the look didn't say *shut up*. It said *we both know something else did this, but let's not talk about it, okay?*

He continued, still talking to me, "We must move on. You will swear to me that you will not run off again, and I will allow you to walk with us. Or I can have you bound and dragged the rest of the way. Is that fully understood?"

"Sure," I said. And I meant it. If we came across the thing that had slaughtered the campers I'd much rather be with three satyrs than alone.

"Good. *Staphus! Give him an ice pack for his chin before the swelling gets worse.*"

He gave me an appraising look. "We will talk more later on this," he said, meaning the stew of dead people around us. I didn't get a chance to reply before he walked away, heading down the ravine and holding up his GPS.

"Are we going back to the trail?" Ariadne shouted after him.

"No need," he said. "The imposter has led us to a much better path. This valley is more direct, and out of the wind."

Ariadne fell into step behind him, and Staphus, after dropping a chemical icepack in my hand (ironic given the weather, but useful as I *was* starting to swell) followed her. Dyanos came up beside me.

"*You will be dropping that spike here, will you not?*" he asked.

"*Of course.*" I flung it into the snow, not far from where the satellite phone had disappeared.

"*Very good,*" he said, nudging me forward.

As I stepped past the last spatter of blood in the snow, the words of the oracle rang out in my head.

Red on white.

* * *

It was getting dark.

We had left the Seattle airport around mid-morning. I gathered that under optimal conditions we'd have reached the campground at Azure Lake by nightfall, but the storm screwed that plan to hell.

"Hippos!" Ariadne called. The winds had died down, so there were no longer whiteout conditions to combat. She could see, as I had, that our guide had picked up the pace. It was difficult for humans to keep up with him.

He stopped, reluctantly, and glanced down at his GPS.

"If we hurry, we can still reach the camp before morning," he said.

"No," she said "The sun is setting and it's getting too cold. We have to stop."

"We have a schedule to keep."

"Then radio the hierophant and tell him we will keep it tomorrow," she said.

I did a double take.

"Hippos. Please," she said. "We have been hiking all day. I need rest."

He stared at her, possibly considering whether she was light enough to carry the rest of the way. "All right. We'll make camp here."

I pulled Ariadne aside.

" 'Radio the hierophant?' "

"We had to find out where the ceremony was being held," she explained. "This was the only way."

"We're expected."

"Yes."

"All of us?"

She couldn't look me in the eye. "We told Gordon we're coming to reconcile the schism. You're part of the reconciliation."

I looked around and wondered how far I would get if I started running. Probably not far. "So in addition to the whole raising-a-god thing, I'm being handed over to a crazy man who thinks he's me and has his own army. That's fantastic. What if he decides to have me shot before the ceremony even begins?"

"It won't come to that," she insisted. "I still have some sway over him."

"He's insane, Ariadne. The only thing holding sway over him at this point is his own delusions."

"He will listen to me. I promise."

I stared at her for a long second, wondering if she really believed what she was saying, or if she just knew how little choice she'd left herself and was hoping for the best.

"I'm going to help build the camp," I said. "And then I'm going to see if we've brought any beer, because I'd like to spend my last night on earth drinking, if that's at all possible."

* * *

An hour later, the only tent in the party had been pitched, and we'd started a small fire to keep warm by. There were no sleeping bags and we had only one day's supply of food: dried meats and fruit. And no beer whatsoever.

Ariadne and I sat up next to the fire and made an effort to regain some basic sensation in our extremities while Dyanos and Staphus searched for more wood to burn and Hippos stepped away to contact Gordon on his own satellite phone.

"This is turning into a disaster," I said to her—quietly, in the off-chance Hippos was in earshot.

"We're just stopping for the night."

"Bet that's what the campers said. 'Let's just stop here and wait out the storm.' "

Her face turned grave. "I'm trying not to think about them."

"I can't help it."

Hippos returned.

"He will postpone the ceremony for a day."

"Can you do that?" I asked. The Greater Mysteries at Eleusis always took place at the same time, every year. If you missed it, you were out of luck.

"You understand little," Hippos grunted, settling to the forest floor beside the fire.

"Then enlighten me," I said. "And try to sound like you're on our side instead of his. I'll sleep better."

Hippos and Ariadne shared a meaningful look.

"The reason I'm here is my loyalty to the line of Papodopoulos," he explained. "That doesn't mean I disagree with what Gordon Alecto intends to do. And if you are who she says you are, you might agree as well."

"I know only that he plans to revive an old god. Why don't you help me better understand that decision?"

Ariadne shot Hippo a look and shrugged. "Go ahead."

"He is reinventing the Mysteries," he explained.

"Reinventing how?"

"Into something more meaningful for the satyros. It was our line that kept the Mysteries alive all these centuries. Gordon would take us back to our roots. You saw for yourself how far we have strayed from our origins."

"So you would do... what? Divest your worldly possessions, shed your clothes and live off the land? I don't think that's possible anymore."

And we're all better off for it. I complain from time to time about the lack of a genuine forest to visit, and I do feel the loss, but at the same time, living off the land kind of sucks.

"This is true," Hippos agreed. "Which is why he is seeking help from the old gods. The forests of the world are dying. Only they can help."

I glanced at Ariadne. "He's kidding."

"No, that's about right," she said, a slight smile on her face.

"The Greeks called them nymphs," Hippos added helpfully. "They were our gods before we came out of the woods."

"Duh-ryadyh," I said.

Hippos looked surprised. "In the archaic tongue, yes. Dryads. Wood nymphs."

Before I had an opportunity to react appropriately to this, a high-pitched scream echoed through the valley. Ariadne jumped.

"What was that?" she asked.

"Staphus," Hippos said, leaping to his feet. "That sounded like Staphus."

"Put out the fire!" I started throwing snow on the fire as quickly as I could, not bothering to put my gloves back on first.

"What are you doing?" Ariadne asked. "Stop that!"

I ignored her and kept digging for more snow. The fire was smoking, but didn't appear to be going anywhere.

"What could have happened to him?" Hippos asked.

"Staphus is dead, ambassador," I said. "Now help me put out the fire."

"Hippos!" Ariadne called. He finally noticed what I was doing.

"We need the fire, you fool!" he said, stepping in front of me. "Have you gone mad?"

"Actually, no, I'm the only sane one here." I got to my feet to meet him face to chin. "Your ancestors didn't *worship* the gods of the wood, you ignorant Athenian."

To call a satyr an Athenian was a greater insult than referring to one as ignorant. In the old days, the satyros who left the forest and established a life in the city were looked down upon. Hence, it didn't happen all that often.

"What do you know of it!" he roared, and for a second I thought he was about to hit me.

"Do you know what the gods were to the satyros?" I asked. "They were terrible things. Things that were so terrible the old tribes—your ancestors— feared them like they feared no other thing on this earth."

Hippos looked a bit less certain.

"I don't believe you," he said.

"It doesn't matter if you do or not. But what you do need to believe, right now, is that there is something out there that is not afraid of us. The fire is a beacon."

He looked off in the middle distance, expecting, I suppose, for Staphus to walk into the camp and explain that he'd been frightened by a bunny, and was sorry for the gut-wrenching scream.

"Yes ... yes, I do believe you are right."

He stepped into the middle of the fire and kicked the wood across the snow, while I shoveled as much powder as I could onto the embers.

"Now what do you recommend?" he asked.

I pulled the still-addled Ariadne to her feet. "We move into the woods. Quickly."

I led us away from the campsite and into a thicket, huddling atop one another in brambles that effectively hid our existence from a casual prying eye.

After a few minutes of silence, Hippos said, "Somebody is coming."

"I don't hear anything," I said.

"You are human," he muttered.

"Fine. Then what does your satyr nose tell you?"

"It is still full of smoke from the fire."

There was indeed something in the camp. We held our collective breath as it felt its way around the remnants of the fire. And then it spoke. *"Hello?"*

It was Dyanos. We called him over.

"What are you doing in there?" he asked. *"And where is Staphus? I thought I heard something."*

* * *

The four of us remained huddled in the brush for the entire evening, using body heat for warmth. It was a poor substitute for a fire, but it kept us breathing and all of our body parts remained attached, which was a decent trade-off. On the plus side, the storm ended and the wind died down during the night and it even started to warm up a little. I managed to sleep with Ariadne on top of me, which would have been considerably more fun if there were less clothing involved, not to mention the threat of impending death awaiting us if we made too much noise.

I stepped out into the open in bright sunlight and stretched the kinks from my muscles. I was one big kink, and I imagined so was everyone else.

"It's beautiful," Ariadne commented. She was right; it was. I pulled open the parka and took off the hood and the goggles. It felt about forty degrees, and the sunlight through the ice-covered tree branches around us reflected kaleidoscopic rainbows.

"Look here," Hippos called. He was standing near the tent. I walked over. "Something did come for us in the night."

The tent was slashed apart. It looked as if four parallel knives had been used. Or more obviously, four very sharp and very long claws.

"That's what we'd look like if we had been in there."

"Yes," he agreed grumpily. It must have been killing him to concede any point to me at all.

"I heard no sounds during the night," he said. "Did you?"

"No. We must have slept through it."

"I didn't sleep," he insisted.

On the ground near the tent were more of those peculiar bare spots I'd seen at the earlier campsite. Hippos took note of them as well.

I toed the bare patch with my boot. "You ever see that before?"

"No. It must be heavy for Its footfalls to reveal the bare grass... whatever it is," Hippos said.

Dyanos, who had been the first of us to leave the brambles at daybreak, returned.

"*I've found him,*" he said simply. That Staphus was not standing beside him as he said it spoke volumes.

"*Where?*" Hippos asked.

"*Over the rise. I can lead you.*"

"*You stay with her,*" Hippos ordered. "*We will go and see for ourselves.*" He was referring to he and I.

"No," I said. "*Pack up; we should all go together.*"

"She does not need to see this," Hippos argued, switching to English.

I shook my head. "Actually, I think she does."

He twitched an eyebrow, but didn't argue further.

Ten minutes later, we'd packed all the goods that hadn't been destroyed during the night and Dyanos led us to the final resting place of Staphus.

He'd been caught from behind just as the dead campers had, killed by a single swing at his back that nearly cleaved him in two. Several other cuts were inflicted after fell face-first into the snow, possibly after he was already dead. There was viscera everywhere, and it hadn't snowed hard enough during the night to cover much of it.

I caught the look of sorrow on Dyanos's face.

"*He didn't suffer much,*" I said. "*It was the first blow that killed him. That was when we heard him cry out.*"

He nodded, but I don't think my consolation helped much.

Ariadne refused to come close enough to see what had happened to her satyr friend.

"Hippos," I said, "get her over here."

He walked to her, put his arm around her shoulders, and led her to the scene. Nobody seemed all that bothered by the fact that I just issued an order to my erstwhile captor.

"I can't look," Ariadne cried. "It's so ..." She pushed away from Hippos, but I caught her by the wrist and spun her around.

"Look at him," I insisted.

"Why?"

"Because you knew this was going to happen."

"What? How could I ..."

"Peter Arnheit, Ariadne. Don't pretend you've never heard the name."

It was probably the phone call I'd placed to Mike's cell phone that got me thinking about Peter again, but it didn't really come into focus until I was huddled in a bush, in the dark and terrified for my life, while trying to get some sleep.

She jerked her wrist from my grasp and ran for the trees. We followed, catching up when she stopped for a session of dry heaving.

"I don't know who you're talking about. I swear."

"You're lying," I said.

Hippos asked, "Who is this Peter?"

"He's a fugitive," I explained. "Part of the California Mystery Cult. A year ago, he and a friend visited the Amazon rainforest, but only Peter survived the trip. Isn't that right, Ariadne?"

She was sitting in the snow and wiping away tears, declining to play a meaningful role in this discussion.

"What I haven't figured out yet is how much of this has been an act."

Ariadne reacted as if I'd slapped her. "How can you say that?"

"You put Gordon in charge. And when he became impossible to control, you found me. Maybe Peter's trip was your idea, too."

"It wasn't ..."

"You're the only one who benefits at the end of the day. Maybe we're as much puppets in this as Gordon is."

"It wasn't like that!"

Hippos put a hand on her shoulder and spoke. "Yet there is much you have kept from us, Papodopoulos. Now would be the time to share it."

She shook her head. "No, Hippos, you don't ..."

He stared in a way that caught her up short. I decided he must make for one hell of an ambassador with that stare.

"Okay, okay," she said quietly. After a few calming breaths, she continued. "Peter was investigating the jaguar myths of the Yanomamo Indians of the Amazon. That was why he and Lonnie went there. Gordon was going to go, too, but ... he was busy traveling with me to Athens. But this was something Peter and Gordon had been doing for years.

Gordon said they were looking for the Great Protector."

"The what?" I asked.

"Syncretistic versions of the nymph myths. The Great Protector is a god-thing that defends the forests from the non-natural world."

"From humans?"

"Or human designs, yes. I never thought much of it. Not until Lonnie was killed."

Hippos asked, "So this man, this Lonnie, he was killed by one?"

"When Peter emerged from the rainforest, he knew two things," Ariadne said. "One, he'd learned from the Yanomamo how to awaken the jaguar god. Two, when it's awake, it's angry. But I didn't ever think..."

"... that there were two of them," I finished her thought.

"Gordon was overjoyed," she said. "He was sure all he needed was to get to another forest and Peter could do whatever it was he did in the Amazon to awaken the god of that forest. Gordon wants to do this in every heavily forested region on earth."

"The ecologist's ultimate revenge," I said.

"I thought he was crazy to believe any of Peter's story, but Gordon's not listening to me anymore. Please understand that I never thought this would come about. You should have heard how insane the whole thing sounded when they explained it to me."

Hippos's expression got stony. Even for a satyr.

"I take it you didn't know about all of this," I said to Hippos.

"We were told the dryad could be awakened," he said, "and that it would bring about a great change. That such a thing was an indiscriminate killer was omitted. How did the hierophant hope to survive this experience?"

"He thinks he can control it. Remember the prophecy?"

"Hold on, what prophecy are we talking about this time?" I asked.

" *'The sojourner ascendant will tame the wild, the flock to be restored',*" she recited, in nearly perfect archaic Greek. "Gordon took it to mean that only he, as Philopaigmos, can command the dryad."

"So if I have this right, Peter woke up the dryad of the North Cascades, and now he and Gordon are calling it to Azure Lake, where Gordon plans to ... tame it?"

"Yes."

"How many people are there with them?"

"At least fifty," Ariadne said. "Possibly more. Some families."

"It'll be a slaughter. And we're heading right into this."

"It's not too late. If we can just get there before it does ..."

"Then what?" I asked. "Tell the dryad to go away? Give it a sleeping pill? What?"

"Then you will stop it yourself, Philopaigmos," Hippos said.

I looked at him. "What did you call me?"

He knelt down.

"Forgive me for doubting you," he said. "It is Gordon Alecto who is the imposter."

He noticed a confused Dyanos out of the corner of his eye. *"Kneel, you fool. It is he."*

Poor Dyanos, having no idea what any of this was about, knelt nonetheless. For my part, this sort of thing always made me more than a little uncomfortable.

"Get up, both of you," I said.

They pulled themselves up.

"What do you want us to do?" Hippos asked. "Should we leave this place?"

I turned to Ariadne.

"Families?"

"Probably, yes," she said.

"Children?"

"Yes."

I don't like playing hero. I never have. Some of the worst experiences of my life have come about largely because I fooled myself into thinking I had to act in some sort of heroic manner, but the truth is, the life expectancy of a hero is considerably worse than that of the pragmatic non-hero.

But a valley full of people who thought they were worshipping in my name, were about to be slaughtered in my name. (That they were worshipping in my name at all was another issue. Given my significance to the early formation of the Eleusinian Mysteries I could understand it, but still; if I'm at the center of your religion, something has gone horribly wrong with your religion.)

I'd spent most of the past two days trying to figure out how to escape my apparent fate, and now that I was in a position to do just that, I realized Ariadne had been right all along. I couldn't let this continue.

Gordon Alecto had to be stopped, and I was the only person qualified to do it.

"I guess we better get there before the dryad does," I said.

Chapter Eighteen

Dion.
We can take shelter in the wood.

Sil.
It is a great army; no woods will be enough.

Dion.
The trees cannot defend us, but nothing man has ever wielded is a match for the satyrs of the forest.

> —From the dialogues of Silenus the Younger.
> Text corrected and translated by Ariadne

After debating the merits of attempting to bury or ceremonially cremate Staphus, we decided to leave him where we'd found him and return later for more appropriate respects. There was just too much risk involved in sticking around. So after a few quick, but solemn words, we covered his body with snow, noted the GPS coordinates, and moved on.

"Tell me more about the prophecies," I asked Ariadne a couple of hours later, as we trudged along after Hippos. We were following a path that ran along Stetattle Creek and straight to Azure Lake, but it was slow going, even without the storm conditions. The snow that the storm had dropped everywhere was still something to contend with, and the sun wasn't doing a lot of damage to it.

"What do you want to know?" she asked.

"I'm thinking specifically about what else might have been included in that passage you quoted."

"There isn't anything else. That's the full extent, so far as they concern this particular moment in time."

"Nothing in there about *how* I'm supposed to tame this thing?"

"It was always understood that your superior nature would naturally make you the victor."

"Great. So what does follow the passage?"

"It's the last line of the scrolls."

"You're joking."

"No. We've been arguing for hundreds of years about whether she stopped there because that was where it ended, or whether she simply died or otherwise lost the gift and couldn't continue."

"Seems abrupt."

"Yes. But prophetic declarations very rarely end with *and they lived happily ever after*."

"That's because nobody ever does."

Ahead, Hippos stopped and waved us over.

"If I am reading this GPS device correctly, the lake is just over there."

"If you're reading it correctly?" I asked. "You mean there's a possibility you don't even know how to use that thing?"

"It is the technology I doubt, not my eyes. Are you prepared for this?"

"Not even slightly. Tell me more about what we should expect."

"The agreement we brokered was to deliver you unharmed to Gordon. It was our understanding that you would be put to the task by the dryad itself; it would choose whether you lived or died," Hippos said.

I glared at Ariadne, who I was still sort of upset with.

"I thought you knew how to tame a nymph!" she said defensively.

I turned to Hippos. "I think we all know where the dryad will be falling on the question of whether I live or die, so maybe we should find a way to keep things from getting to that point. How many of your kind are here?"

"Only ten," he said. "But they are armed."

"Fabulous."

I wondered if one of them had been the shooter in back of Ariadne's house outside of Sacramento. It would explain the ease with which he escaped from Mike. Then I wondered if Mike had gotten my message, and that kind of wondering didn't help me at all with my current problem, so I let it go.

"Where's their loyalty? Can you command them to recognize me?"

"Gordon's hold is very strong," he said. "I doubt my opinion will sway them."

"And they've already rejected me as their hierophant," Ariadne added.

"I have to convince fifty or sixty total strangers that their god is about to turn them into bite-sized pieces. I can't do that on charm alone; give me something to work with."

Hippos asked, "What proof have you that you are the god returned?"

"What, like a birthmark? Nothing. What convinced you?"

"No one thing," he admitted. "You do know more about the old gods than I do, and I would not think that possible for an imposter."

"That won't help." I looked around. "Hey, where is Dyanos?"

"I don't know," Hippos said, looking as well.

"You know what just occurred to me? We've been talking in English a lot lately. How much English does he even understand?"

"Practically none," Ariadne said. "But he's loyal to Hippos."

"You're sure of that?"

Hippos turned his nose up into the air. He was sniffing something.

"Oh dear," he said.

In the woods on the left of the path, six satyrs emerged holding TEC-9s.

"I've heard enough," one of them said, in perfect English. A seventh satyr appeared behind him, unarmed. It was Dyanos.

"*You were right, brother,*" the satyr with the good English said, in Greek. "*They have betrayed us.*"

"Boehan, I can explain," Hippos said. "Give me a hearing."

"No need, traitor," Boehan replied. To the others, he said, "*Bind their hands.*"

"I guess we don't have to worry about how we're getting into the camp now," I muttered to Ariadne.

* * *

Azure Lake looked like it had been formed long ago by run-off from the mountains—Mount Terror, presumably—on the far shore. As lakes go, it wasn't particularly large and was mostly frozen. I expected it would be fully solid by nightfall, given our elevation. The tree line reached the water in a couple of places, disappeared completely in a few other places (like where a sheer mountain face met up with the water) and receded enough to provide a small beach in another spot. It was a really pretty scene, and I was having trouble imagining it covered in blood.

The beach was where we were headed. For some ridiculous reason Boehan—the lead satyr—insisted our hands be bound with twine. But since we needed to walk and keep our balance, our hands were in front, and the binding was loose enough that if I got a hold of a gun I'd have no problem firing it.

Not that I would. I was surrounded by a pack of armed satyrs; that would be suicide. Which is why the twine wasn't necessary in the first place. Besides, I'd just gotten through twenty-four hours (on the trip from Athens) with the same kind of twine on the same wrists, and they were still raw and itchy from that experience. I didn't recall a preference to twine in the history of the satyros; maybe there was just a sale on the stuff.

Ariadne looked much more miserable than I was. Whether that was because of the twine, or the whole impending doom thing, it was hard to say. Hippos just looked stoically indignant, like he always did.

When we first entered the camp, I thought we were in pretty good shape, body-count-wise; it seemed hardly anyone had showed up for Gordon's big adventure in god-waking. But Ariadne drew a lot of attention—a legacy member of the California Chapter escorted as a prisoner will do that—and as soon as word traveled, people popped up to see for themselves. They had sought shelter in the trees. And there were a lot of them.

It was clearly more than fifty people. This was going to be awful.

Sixty paces along the shore was an altar, which looked to be our destination. Not much more than a wooden stage, it was situated just at the point where the ring of trees sloped back toward the water, so that standing on the stage one would have the lake on one's left and the trees on one's right. Atop the stage was an enclosed tent.

At the foot of the altar were a dozen closed wooden crates. I had yet to see a truck, a car, or any tire tracks; the crates were brought in on foot. Even in good weather, it was a half a day's walk from the highway.

"How'd they do all this without anybody noticing?" I asked Ariadne.

"The supplies have been coming in for months. The stage was built last week where it stands. I have no idea how all the people got here without drawing attention, but it's a big park."

"Quiet," Boehan hissed. We complied.

It had to have been a logistical nightmare, getting all of those people to the lake without the rangers knowing about it. I would have thought it was impossible, unless they'd been filtering in for weeks and just living in the woods. That would require a greater level of devotion than your average weekend retreat does, which also meant Gordon was not your everyday charismatic cult leader.

There was no way I was going to be convincing these people to abandon the camp. The risen Christ wouldn't have been able to, and he was better with crowds than I am.

* * *

We didn't end up stopping at the altar. Instead, we were led into the woods behind it, to a large tent pitched in a small glade. But not a regular camping tent; the kind you own as an adjunct to an enormous camper with a TV and a microwave. That anyone who thought they were me would insist on such creature comforts on a beautiful day like this was downright insulting.

"Inside," Boehan commanded, pushing aside the tent flap.

Ariadne and I entered. Hippos was retained outside, probably to receive a private dressing-down. I hoped they weren't planning on hurting him too badly.

The interior of the tent was bright with electronic lights, heated, and dry. In one corner was an army cot beside a portable refrigerator and a ham radio. The bed looked particularly comfortable, as would anything horizontal and not covered in a layer of snow, given what I'd been through in the last two days.

Standing at the center of the tent beside a card table and four folding chairs, was a tall man who got his grooming tips from Yul Brynner. He was barrel-chested, a fact that he was clearly proud of, as his loose-fitting white robes revealed quite a bit of his pectoral splendor. His head was shaved bald, and he'd gone that extra step and also shaved off his eyebrows, which looked silly and had me wondering if he'd shaved his body hair in the less visible places. (I've done it; it itches like hell.) In one hand he held a thyrsos, a staff that was topped with a pinecone and some elegantly twisted vines. It was the ancient symbol of Dionysos.

In ceremonies, the thyrsos was used to anoint celebrants with water, much in the same way holy water is spattered on Catholics during the Easter mass. For practical purposes, it could also bear small amounts of water to plants and in a pinch could be used for a decent torch. It was what Karyos and I used to water our grapevines.

"Hello, Gordon," Ariadne said to the bald man. "How've you been?"

Sitting in a chair at the table was a second man. He was much less impressive-looking, and dressed in normal clothing for this climate. Thin, pale, and looking very worn out, I recognized his face from the pictures in his file. It was Peter Arnheit.

"Welcome home, Ariadne," Gordon said gravely. "We have a lot to discuss." He had a lovely speaking voice that was deep, resonant, and powerful. I could imagine what he must be like in front of an audience. He also seemed utterly sane, which was disappointing. I don't know what else I was expecting, though gibbering and drooling topped the list.

Gordon turned his attention to me.

"Is this him?" he asked.

"Hi," I said, waving with my bound hands.

Gordon turned to look at Ariadne. "He doesn't look like much."

"I forgot my robes. Didn't know it was going to be a costume party."

He gave me another once-over, and then gestured to the table.

"Sit," he commanded.

We settled into seats at the card table. Gordon took the fourth seat.

"Hello, Peter," Ariadne said. "How have you been sleeping?"

"Not well," he answered, rubbing his forehead apprehensively. Peter was sweating quite a lot. When he disappeared, he had still been under a doctor's care, and I wondered if he was fighting a residual infection.

Gordon waved to one of the satyr guards and a moment later had a mug in front of him.

I knew it could only be one thing.

"Kykeon."

"Yes," Gordon answered, taking a deep draught.

I extended my hand. "May I?"

He fixed me with a stare, but then slid the mug across the table. I picked it up and sniffed the concoction. Then I took a sip. It was fresh.

"The kiste is here," I said. "On the altar, right? Inside the tent?"

"And you know this by tasting the kykeon?"

"Only the grains aged in the kiste taste like that. Do you know why?"

He snatched the mug back. "Why don't you tell me?"

"No. I don't think I will."

For just a half second, the resolve in his expression wavered, and a little bit of the crazy snuck in.

"Your question is meaningless," he decided. "The gods fill it with power."

"Well that's *almost* right."

"You haven't coached him very well, Ariadne," he snapped.

She stammered, "I haven't ... Gordon, please, what you're doing ... the thing that Peter has called is not what you think it is."

When she mentioned his name, Peter stiffened. If I'd seen the destroyer god of the satyros up close, I guess I would be a little edgy too.

"It's a new Eden," Gordon said. "We talked about this, Ari. I don't understand why you choose to turn your back now, when we're almost ready! We planned this for years!"

"Tell me, Gordon," I interrupted, "ignoring for now the confusion you're making out of your mythologies, how exactly did you envision this new Eden coming about?"

"The vengeance of the old gods is considerable," he said. "They will frighten away anyone who would dare to harm their forests."

"By killing people. Am I right?"

"By killing anyone who doesn't show respect."

"Uh-huh. What's your take on that, Peter? Did you and Lonnie neglect to bow down properly before the jaguar god of the Yanomamo?"

"That was unfortunate," Gordon answered for Peter. "An accident."

"Is that what it was? Peter?"

Gordon scoffed. "Yes. Had I been there ..."

"You would what? Wave your second-rate thyrsos in the air and hypnotize it? It's going to kill everything that isn't rooted into the ground, Gordon. That includes you, me, and every other person in this camp. And it's already headed this way."

Gordon looked askance at Peter. "We began calling it three days ago. How could you know this?"

"It killed Staphus," Ariadne said. "And three campers whose bodies we found on our way here."

"That's wonderful!" he said.

"I just told you it killed four people!" she snapped.

"Yes, and that's ... I am sorry about Staphus. He was a good soldier. But it worked! Peter, we've done it!"

Peter didn't look happy about this at all. He looked terrified.

Gordon continued, "We must finish the preparations for the ceremony!"

"Gordon, what you have to do is get these people out of here!" Ariadne pleaded.

"Only the impious have anything to fear," he said, draining the rest of his kykeon.

"You would have been right at home in the witch trials," I said. But he wasn't listening to me anymore. Or to anyone else.

He leaned back, his eyes rolling around frantically, and then he started convulsing. Peter saw it happen first and called for Boehan, who ran in and held Gordon down.

Ariadne and I jumped to our feet and backed away from the table before it was upended by the satyrs that were trying to keep Gordon from convulsing right out of the tent.

"Does this happen a lot?" I asked Ariadne.

"It used to be once a week at worst," she said. "I'm told it's now a daily occurrence."

"Twice daily," Peter amended while struggling to hold Gordon's arms still. Gordon was a much bigger and stronger man; I wagered that Peter would have to actually sit on him to accomplish this.

"And this is divinely inspired, you say?"

"So he believes," Ariadne said.

Gordon's body stiffened and rocked, and if he had anything revelatory to say, he wasn't going to be well-understood, as one of the satyrs had managed to work a piece of wood between his teeth.

I'd seen this sort of thing before. There was a cult of Christians who called themselves Ecstatics who spent the better part of the fourteenth century having public fits in front of confused townspeople. Back then I could understand somebody labeling it the work of a divinity, but I expected modern man to be beyond such hoodoo. I had a name for it too, and I know next to nothing about medicine.

It was a *grand mal* seizure, and Gordon was having them because he'd been poisoning himself. How that wasn't obvious to everybody else in this bastard Mystery Cult was anyone's guess.

The Greeks were accustomed to drink that was lethal except in extreme moderation; their wine was cut with water, and their kykeon was only drunk once a year. Gordon Alecto imposed no such limitation on himself and now his mind was being rotted out from the inside. And as far as I knew, there was no going back.

Once the fit passed he was led to the cot. As he lay down, Gordon whispered something to Boehan.

"We must prepare you for the coming of the Great Protector," he said.

"Shouldn't you get him a doctor first?" I asked. "That looked pretty bad there."

"The divine spirit inside of him is sometimes too great for his physical form to bear," the satyr said gravely, without giggling or cracking a smile or anything. Religion is still the very best way to get someone to accept something unabashedly ridiculous; don't let anyone tell you otherwise.

* * *

"So what's the answer?" Ariadne asked.

We were sitting in a tent in semi-darkness, and had been for hours.

They were kind enough to bring us some food and water, but beyond that, nothing. We couldn't even tell if it was sundown yet—when the ceremony was scheduled to begin—because the guard had zipped the door closed.

"The answer to what?" I asked.

"Why the kykeon tastes the way it does. I know it doesn't have the same properties when the grain is kept elsewhere. I just don't know why."

"No hallucinations."

"Yes. And the fruits we store in there have the same property. I never understood why."

I lay down on my back and tried to stretch my legs. I hated this waiting. "That manual you've got," I said, "the one where all the old ceremonies were written. You've seen it, right?"

"You know I have."

"Right. You gave me a page of it."

"That was from the copy made for our California branch. What about it?"

"The kiste is mentioned there?"

"It is."

"Including how to open it."

"A series of metal bolts have to be slid into place in a specific order before the lid can be opened. It's a remarkable piece of craftsmanship."

"Thanks."

"You built it?"

I couldn't see her expression, but she sounded impressed.

"I designed it. Someone else built it. Is that the only procedure you can remember?"

"That's the only procedure at all. Are you saying there's another way to open it?"

"No, I'm not saying that."

"So answer my question."

"The question being what makes the foodstuff stored in the kiste special?"

"Yes."

"It's a gift from the gods."

She sighed.

"Look, if you don't want to tell me, just say so."

I just smiled.

* * *

From The Tragedy of Silenus. Text corrected and translated by Ariadne

(Silenus walks alone through the wilderness.)

Chorus

There he is, poor old Silenus.

His clothing ragged, his back stooped.

Pray that the goddess Demeter might end his woeful suffering.

He spoke to the wind and to the sea.

To the sun-kissed city of Athens he begged pleasure, And for solace from the satyrs of the wild.

He sang to a dryad and scaled Olympus, For naught.

Delphi is closed to his entreaties, Thebes lays silent,

And Sparta has never known his gods.

O lament! Where does Silenus go now? Is Hades where his quest will end?

But look! The goddess approaches!

(Demeter enters from the chorus)

Silenus

Goddess!

(Silenus falls to the ground.)

Demeter

Please rise.
You owe me no allegiance.

(Silenus rises)

Silenus

But I will gladly swear it.

Demeter

I expect none.You ally with Dionysos; I would not contradict that.

Silenus

It is true that my journeys began at his noble feet, But many decades
have passed since I enjoyed
My lord's radiance.
I fear my allegiance is for barter
In these, my last years.

Demeter

You are a sturdy breed.
You have many days left. I do demand an oath of you, but no loyalty.

Silenus

What oath would you require?

Demeter

You have spent much of your span seeking me out
And I have decided to hear your words
For I can no longer bear watching you suffer.
But the price for my response is your oath:
Never are you to return to Dionysos.
Swear this.

Silenus

But that my quest is of two parts.

First, to find the goddess Demeter and ask a question. Second, to return
to Dionysos with her reply.
This oath will bring me no peace
And I will greet Charon unfinished.

Demeter
I know this.
Would you rather satisfy one part knowing the second
Will not be done? Or complete no parts
When the completion of the first is in your hand?

Silenus
Then I swear your oath.
For I shall not willingly choose ignorance.

Demeter
Then ask.

Silenus
I have sought answers from all men and creatures,
Gods and beasts.
Three times have the oracles entertained my quizzes,
And responded with three quizzes of their own.
But none can answer this:
Demeter watches Dionysos from afar
But does not approach.
Why is this so?
Dionysos, when spying the goddess,
Does approach. And then Demeter is absent.
Why is this so?
Demeter would see the god but not be seen.
Dionysos would approach the goddess but is not approached.
Tell me, goddess, why is this so?

Demeter
There are things you must understand first, Silenus the wanderer.
The one you call Dionysos strode this realm
Long before there were gods. As did I.

He is not as he seems.

Silenus
In what way?

Demeter
Look around you. See the death.
See the violence that man brings with him,
And to others like him,
And to the trees and the beasts you claim to speak to.
Look at all of the things you would call terrible or evil. Understand that
Dionysos is the bringer of all these things.

Silenus
But this is not so!
My lord is the god of madness and mischief, But also wine and song and
stage.
He deceives, but there are many godly deceivers.
And there are gods that are rightly called evil, Or whose actions bring it
about.
Dionysos is no such god.

Demeter
I speak only of things that are true.
You color your argument with legends and the spirited dreams of
mortals.
Name a god and turn his face,
And you will be staring at your lord's countenance.

Silenus
He does not speak these facts, or even claim true godhood. I would
even call him humble, in his way.
Are you sure we speak of the same being?

Demeter
We do. And he is more a creator of this world
Than anyone else you could meet.

Silenus

More so than you?

Demeter
Indeed. And my influence wanes daily as his grows.

Silenus
But, even if true, this does not answer my question.

Demeter
Can the winter meet the summer?
Or the sun meet the moon?

Silenus
Unless you would also be Selene and my lord Helios,
Or Boreas and Aura,
Your comparisons offer no illumination.

Demeter
Even now I seek to evade your question, fair Silenus,
For I do not wish to hear my own voice speak these words. But I will talk
more plainly:
I watch him only to witness his downfall.

Silenus
His downfall?
You wish this upon him?

Demeter
I do.

Silenus
But why?

Demeter
I have already told you.
This world is his, and it was not meant to be.
I would see him fall by his own hands so that I may know peace myself.

Silenus
And how do you suppose this will happen?

Demeter

I do not know, but it will one day.

You and your elder have spoken for him for many years.

Is this not true?

Silenus

It is.

Demeter

And you have spread word of his greatness across the lands.

Throughout the world now, wherever he strides,

He is said to possess true godly power.

A day will come when he must employ this power

And it will be his undoing.

Silenus

Do you speak prophecy?

Demeter

Perhaps I do. Perhaps I simply know of older gods than   either of us.

Gods who reject this world he has created

And who will make their displeasure known.

Silenus

You utter the words of one enraged

But not so in tone.

Does your hatred burn so softly that it no longer animates you?

Demeter

I am more at peace in his world than he is himself.

But do not mistake my interest.

The reason I do not speak to Dionysos

Is that I do not wish to.

I do not wish to speak to him because of my hatred for him

And for the things he has done.

Silenus

And does he know this?

Demeter

He knows. But he may not remember.

Silenus

A riddle.

Demeter

Knowledge and awareness need not be the same.

No man knows all that governs his actions,

But that governance still comes from within.

Do you now understand?

Silenus

Yes.

But goddess, what can I do now?

I am sworn to get your answer, and your answer is that he knows the answer himself.

You tell me he has done things he does not know he has done

And created a world he does not act as if he created.

Yet if he is a creator god, he is somehow one who wields no godly power

And who can be felled by mortal hand

Or by the will of these unnamed older gods.

Not any of this makes sense.

Demeter

It is all the plain truth.

And I ask you again to remember your oath.

Silenus

I remember. But that I hoped your answer would give me some measure of peace.

Instead it has inflamed my curiosity.

I burn to return to my lord for elaboration

As I now have as many questions for him as I have still for you.

Demeter

I will answer no more of your questions.

It is as clear as I can make it.
Now go, Silenus.

Silenus
But where?

Demeter
I do not care. Live out your days however you will.
Only do not return to Dionysos and speak my truth to him. Neither will any of your progeny,
For I will know if this is done, and my vengeance will be terrible.

(Demeter exits)

Silenus
O gods! What is there left for Silenus
Except to carry this burden to death?

Chapter Nineteen

Dionysos:
I am here as promised, on this, the final day.
Let me shake my thyrsos, and bless you with my madness.

—From The Tragedy of Silenus.
Text corrected and translated by Ariadne

Sunset on Azure Lake made for a beautiful picture, though it was slightly marred by a small army of eco-religious fanatics—and their kids—in brown robes, chanting ancient Greek blessings and stomping up and down in what I believe was an effort to exhaust themselves into a state of ecstatic frenzy. Or, they were trying to keep warm in unison.

The crates before the altar had been opened. Out of the first came crude wooden bowls, which were passed around to the celebrants. Then the men, women, and children waited for their bowls to be filled with the contents of the other crates, mainly kykeon. It had been prepared beforehand and shipped in vats. The ancient priestesses of Eleusis could be heard rolling in their graves.

It was so far removed from any proper Mystery ceremony I had ever witnessed as to be something entirely different. For starters, it's warm in early October in the Attic region, warm enough for all of the celebrants to be naked on the final night. Brown robes covering parkas, heavy pants and hiking boots didn't come close to being correct. It also made the whole crowd look like a monastic football team, but that's more of a sartorial observation than a religious one.

Also, we never indoctrinated children into the way of the Mysteries. Are you kidding? The Greeks didn't even *like* children, but they would still never give a child a hallucinogen on purpose.

And there were never this many mystai.

Ariadne explained that all of the people in attendance had been accepted into the California version of the Mysteries already, and were no longer technically considered mystai, which meant that none of them should have been participating in this part of the ritual. But since Gordon had taken his oaths in the U.S. and then traveled to Greece to retake them, he felt that everybody else should experience the same thing, and bringing the kiste, the center of the Greek Mystery Cult, to the U.S. was easier than bringing the U.S. members to Greece. Thus, a hundred new mystai.

We didn't have a role to play for the bulk of the ceremony, so we got to sit in the snow on the forest floor next to the stage.

Hippos had rejoined us, his hands also bound. It looked like his experience as a prisoner had been much worse than ours.

"Nice eye," I muttered.

The left side of his face was swollen, and the eye was nearly shut.

"Thank you," he said. "I fear my people are not going to be very helpful regarding your cause."

"I get that, yeah. Anything broken?"

"Bruised ribs, but I don't believe any breaks."

"I still have that icepack in my pocket, if you want it."

"I'll be fine."

Gordon was standing atop the altar in front of the tent, which was still closed. Gesturing with his thyrsos and wearing his loose white robes (cold weather doesn't seem to bother the insane as much as it does the sane for some reason) he led the chants. It was in Greek, but nobody seemed to be having trouble repeating it. I wondered if they even knew what they were saying.

From our vantage point we could also see Peter. He was sitting underneath the stage and doing something with his hands. I couldn't quite make it out.

"What's he doing under there?" I asked Ariadne, who was slightly closer.

"I think he's calling the dryad."

"But how? I don't hear anything."

Gordon reached the benediction and signaled to Boehan, and then the satyrs were traveling down the rows with the kykeon. The momentary quiet just emphasized the point that if Peter was calling the dryad, it wasn't with an audible sound.

Or perhaps it was a sound that wasn't audible to humans.

"Do you hear it?" I asked Hippos.

He nodded. "It's some manner of woodwind, but nothing I have ever heard before."

Peter who was rocking side to side in a vaguely rhythmic fashion. The torchlight from the stage was not helping my night vision at all, but I did finally catch a glimpse of the stick in his hand.

"It's a recorder," I said.

"A tape recorder?" Ariadne asked.

"No, no, like a flute. I guess a Pan flute would have been too ironic."

The distribution of the kykeon was carried out quickly and efficiently, and soon each of the mystai had a bowl in front of them that was at least half-full of the awful stuff.

In the old days, the bowls were filled one-by-one and blessed individually. Here the entire community held their bowls over their heads and waited for the hierophant to utter the sacred words—a phrase that literally meant "swallow for your life", but had an idiomatic meaning along the lines of "drink up!" It had no formal ceremonial purpose. It was like having the priest shout *Cheers!* before drinking the sacramental wine.

As I thought about how amusing this was, and how difficult it would be to explain why it was amusing, someone caught my eye.

It was one of the mystai. The front row was only about twenty feet away and with everyone dressed with their hoods up, robes on, and their winter clothing underneath, I could barely tell male from female. But since they were all acting in some measure of unison—bouncing up and down together, chanting together, kneeling together—any variation was immediately notable.

A few rows in and just to my right, there was a man who didn't want to try his drink. He acted like he was drinking, but what he was really doing was pouring it into the snow in front of him. I looked around at the satyrs, but it seemed I was the only one who caught it.

I was nearly certain he had wanted me to notice.

After polishing off their kykeon, the mystai placed their bowls before them and huddled down on their knees, heads bowed and chanting as they waited for the visions, which would be coming along presently. I stayed focused on my new friend. He prostrated himself along with the others, but after a ten count he lifted his head slightly and locked eyes with me, or so I assumed since the hood still blocked a decent view of his face.

From somewhere in the crowd, a woman screamed. She sat up and started babbling—what the Christians might call speaking in tongues, but which sounded to me remarkably similar to an old Slavic dialect. Then came the moaning, the laughing, and the shouting, as the others began their own spiritual journeys. I remembered how incredibly funny a crowd of hallucinating people could be. It was one of the best parts about the Mysteries. Much better when they were also naked, but whatever.

The prostrate supplicant who'd discarded his kykeon took his cue from the people around him and started flailing about and acting goofy. And in the middle of his gyrations, he tossed something. It struck me right in the chest—which hurt—and fell in the snow between my crossed legs.

I picked it up. It was a pocketknife. Inscribed on the side were the initials *M.L.*

Mike Lycos had made it to the party.

"Ariadne," I muttered, "take this. Cut me loose."

Gordon began chanting something new. This wasn't from the text of the Mysteries.

"Bring forth the old gods!" he boomed, in English and then in Greek and back again. Peter, still blowing away on his flute, made some changes to his finger work.

Hippos reacted.

"Did the sound change?" I asked.

"Yes," he said. "It is more ... urgent now. I expect the first melody was to awaken the creature and this new piece is to call it."

Ariadne opened the knife.

"Where did this come from?"

"It apparated here from the spirit world," I said.

"No, really."

"I'll explain later. Start cutting."

Gordon's chants got faster and louder, which was amazing given the lack of a microphone. Then I realized he wasn't the only one chanting. The satyrs had joined in.

"They are following the rhythm of the flute," Hippos related.

"Even though Gordon can't hear it?"

"Perhaps he can."

"Okay!" Ariadne said. I pulled my wrists apart and the twine fell away.

"Thanks. Wish me luck."

I rolled heels over head backwards into the temporary shelter of the woods and found my feet.

The satyrs were too busy chanting loudly and stomping their feet— Gordon was now keeping time with his thyrsos as well—to notice I was missing. If ever there was a time to disappear into the woods and save myself, this was that moment.

I wish I could tell you I never considered it.

* * *

Getting under the altar was pretty easy. It was really just a set of planks holding up a small wood platform, with four steps in front leading to the center of the stage. Peter was sitting directly beneath it and behind the stairs. In the shadows of the torches on the stage, he was nearly invisible. This worked out fine for everybody. Gordon, in particular, benefited from the impression he was calling the god of the forest all on his own.

I stepped past a wooden support beam and came up right behind him. He needed to be stopped, but there was a risk that the satyrs—and possibly mad Gordon—could hear the flute's music. They would notice if I stopped it. But at the same time, it couldn't continue.

I had to hope all the noise they were making was enough to drown out the sound in their own ears. I only needed a few minutes.

Peter was concentrating so hard, he didn't know I was there until my left hand was covering his mouth and my right hand was snatching the flute. I tossed it to the ground and held him while he struggled, taking care to keep his mouth shut. He was feverish and weak and easy enough to contain. Then, in time with Gordon's rhythmic pounding on the stage, I put my right hand on the back of Peter's head and drove his face into a support beam.

He crumpled to the ground, unconscious but alive. (Probably.) I figured Mike would want him when we were all done. I removed his brown mystai robe and slipped it on.

The flute was interesting. It was a small hollow stick that had been carved with great care by somebody who had obviously done it a few times before. I wondered if Peter had simply stolen it from the Yamomamo, or if they'd given it to him; I suspected the former. It was made of a light wood and was very easy to snap in two.

Hopefully, I'd stopped him in time.

I snuck out from beneath the stage. Nobody was waiting there to kill me, and Gordon and the satyrs were chanting merrily along. So far, so good. I hoisted myself up behind the tent and lifted the corner of it to get inside.

I was the only one in the tent, thank goodness. It was just me and the kiste.

Even in the meager light from the torches on the other side of the tent walls, I could see that it had survived the centuries well; nearly as well as I had. Being considered important by a religious group is an excellent way to travel through time.

"Hello, old friend," I greeted. It didn't answer, but it was just a box.

I felt around the front for the locking mechanisms.

Ariadne was correct in that it took a very specific combination of switches to unlock the box. These switches—which looked like simple iron bars installed to support the front—were slid left and right in a certain order to allow the top to be opened. But there were two combinations. I worked the second one, and felt the bottom quarter of the front of the box fall open like a mail chute.

I reached inside.

After all these centuries, the secret of the kiste was still there.

I re-closed the box but left the locks as they were. Then I took a better look at the inside of the tent on the off-chance someone left a spare TEC-9 for me.

It was a square framed street fair-type tent, the kind you usually find someone selling homemade jewelry out of. It was held up by lightweight metal bars and had no floor. Removing it was going to be a fairly simple matter. I just wasn't sure what to do after that.

Right on the outside of the tent was a well toned madman with a cadre of armed satyrs at his beck and call. I couldn't take all of them out at once, but maybe I didn't have to. If I could disable Gordon—or kill him, although that would probably take too long with my bare hands— the shock of the act might buy me a little time.

Reaching under the robe, I felt around until I found the zipped inner pocket of the parka I'd been wearing for the past couple of days and pulled out the now-body-temperature chemical icepack. With the sharp end of the broken flute I poked a hole into the center of the pack and squeezed until some of the contents started to drip out. Holding it in my right hand, I took two deep breaths, said a quiet prayer to the oldest god I could remember, and lifted the square base frame of the tent.

The tent flew up and fell off the back of the stage and nobody shot me, which was great. It probably helped that with my hood pulled up they didn't know who I was.

Startled, Gordon stopped chanting and banging his thyrsos, and when he stopped, so did the satyrs. The mystai, in the middle of their religious epiphanies, took very little notice.

I tossed the pieces of the flute at Gordon's feet.

"Who dares?" he raged loudly. He swung the thyrsos at me, which I anticipated, catching it with the palm of my left hand.

With my right, I slammed the chemical pack into his face.

I don't know much about chemistry. The last time I was given a primer on the subject was in the fifteen hundreds, by an alchemist who later died of mercury poisoning. I have to think his knowledge was far from comprehensive, or necessarily correct. What I do know is that it's almost never a good idea to get chemicals in your eyes.

Gordon grabbed his face as I yanked the thyrsos away. At first he just looked sort of surprised that his face was wet. And then he started screaming and clawing at his eyes. He fell to his knees. With a kick, I knocked him off the stage altogether.

I heard a rustling of robes to my right as one of the satyrs drew on me.

"Stop!" I commanded, pointing the thyrsos. Behind him, I saw Mike sprint for the edge of the woods. I didn't see Ariadne or Hippos anywhere, but I was now surrounded by satyrs holding semi-automatic weapons, and other than possibly getting in front of bullets for me, I didn't expect any help from them.

But the order worked, for the moment, as nobody fired. With a flourish, I held the thyrsos up and smashed the pinecone end against the stage until it shattered.

"Who are you?" Boehan shouted.

I took two steps back so that I was standing beside the kiste. "*I am Epaphios Choreios!*" I shouted the words in Greek, trying to sound as impressive as I could. "*I am Thyoneus Lyseus! I am Philopaigmos Agrionos! I am Dionysos the sojourner and I have killed more of your kind than you can ever imagine, satyr Boehan!*"

I slapped the top of the kiste and the front popped open again. Thrusting the end of Gordon's staff into the opening, I pulled out the secret of the kiste, now attached to the top of the stick. It was the Hammer of Gilgamesh. I pulled back my hood.

"Now bow before your god!"

297

* * *

Back when people in Greece actually called me by all of those names on a regular basis, just about the only god-like thing I had going for me—aside from not aging—involved my thyrsos. It was actually Gilgamesh's Hammer shoved onto the end of a stick, as he'd suggested so long ago, and I hung onto it because I liked the idea of having something that was unequivocally unique, at least as far as I knew at the time.

So I never carried a true thyrsos, which is not to say a thyrsos wouldn't have made for an excellent symbol for the god of wine.

What I failed to appreciate for all of those years was how constant exposure to the rock had driven the king of the Sumerians insane, and how that insanity would also impact anyone who hung out with me for too long. It's why most of my relationships for a few centuries ended with the sentence ... *and then she just went crazy one day*.

It wasn't until a particularly drunk bacchanal celebrant asked me to bless his drink that I figured it out. I waved the rock over his wine, he ended up hallucinating, and I smacked myself in the forehead for being so dense.

My blessing the drink of the Eleusinians—then an early stage Dionysian Mystery Cult— became a regular feature of their biggest seasonal event, but the problem was remembering to show up. I wasn't always in the area, and there were no calendars worth a damn, or timepieces, and forgetting about a ceremony put together to worship you is just embarrassing.

So after I nearly missed one entirely, I asked the hierophant to build me a box. And thus was the kiste—which, by the way, just means *chest*— created.

The box was built with a false bottom with small holes in the floor, and Gilgamesh's rock was put in the gap. Knowledge of the secret compartment died with the box's manufacturers and the hierophant, leaving me the only owner of the information.

From that point onward, foodstuff kept in the box had a special kick, and when one enterprising hierophant decided to bastardize Egyptian beer with barley stalks—wine grapes didn't keep well enough—kykeon was born.

It's actually sort of amazing nobody had found the secret of the kiste after all this time, but then tinkering with sacred objects is generally frowned upon.

* * *

Hippos stepped forward from behind the stage. His hands were freed, no doubt thanks to Mike's pocketknife.

"*He speaks the truth!*" he barked. "*Bow down, you ignorant fools.*"

Ariadne appeared beside me.

"Nicely done," she whispered.

"Not too corny?" I asked.

"A little corny."

"*This is the man who was brought into camp this morning,*" Boehan shouted. A few of the satyrs had complied and were kneeling, but Boehan was having none of it. "*He is no god!*"

To prove this, he raised his weapon and prepared to open fire. Before he could, a shot rang out, and he fell forward. I looked in the direction of the shot and saw Mike down on one knee, with his revolver drawn, standing just beyond the tree line.

Seizing the opportunity, I shouted, "*You see what happens when you doubt?*"

Hopefully, most of the satyrs were too confused to notice the guy in the corner with the gun.

The gunshot caught the attention of a few of the mystai, who couldn't have followed most of what we were saying in Greek. They were high on kykeon, but a gunshot is a gunshot. A murmur went through the crowd and I prepared to address them in English. Hopefully,

I thought, there was time to get these people out of here.

But it was too late for anything like that.

A loud shriek pierced the air. Actually, calling it a shriek is misleading. It sounded like two oaks being rubbed together.

I looked in the general direction of the sound, but couldn't see anything except trees.

And then one of the trees moved.

Chapter Twenty

The god smiled at Silenus. "I can best a man in combat, or teach him to make wine and drink with him until the sun rises, sets, and rises again. But if his mind is set, I can no more change it than command the forest to walk. Such is the stubbornness of mankind."

—From the archives of Silenus the Elder.
Text corrected and translated by Ariadne

It probably hadn't been standing there for very long, mainly because it didn't seem like the type of creature who spent a lot of time deep in thought. Perhaps its first instinct, when coming upon the campfires, was to camouflage itself.

It was quite a remarkable camouflage. The dryad looked to be about fifteen feet tall. When motionless, it appeared to be nothing more than a wide-based tree trunk, the top of its head obscured by the low branches of the pine trees. But when it moved, it ... unfolded.

Its center expanded like an accordion until it was twice as wide, with long, thin arms stretched from the center of its torso. The hands looked like long thin twigs. It stood up on squat legs that had been tucked underneath. There was no telling where the torso ended and the head began until it opened its mouth to emit another shriek.

Everyone in the compound turned with the second roar from the dryad. (This one was deeper, and sounded like high winds racing through a hollow log.) Even the drugged-out mystai seemed to understand that this was not simply another hallucination, as those closest to it began to scatter, and a loud murmur of crowd panic settled upon the scene.

"Yes ..." I heard Gordon whine. He was lying on the ground, just at the edge of the stage. He'd covered his face in snow in an effort to neutralize the chemical bath I'd given him. "The Great Protector comes!"

The dryad put one hand on the trunk of the nearest tree, and immediately the nub of a branch sprouted out. All at once those patches of grass we'd found in the snow made perfect sense. It wasn't that the creature's footsteps were revealing the grass; the grass below was growing up towards the creature's feet.

And then it sprang forward.

I have seen things in my lifetime that move quickly, are deadly, and very large. Vampires, old ones, can move extremely fast and are known to be deadly when provoked. But they tend to be man-sized. Dragons were capable of growing to nearly the same height as the dryad, but the larger they got, the slower they moved. I'd never seen anything move like this god of the woods.

Its motion was jerkily unreal, like a stop-action monster from a fifties movie. But it was decidedly efficient. It covered twenty feet in only a few seconds. The twig-like fingers lashed out and raked through the crowd of people—they were already running and screaming, as one does—and struck down four with one blow. Blood arced through the air.

Hippos jumped to the forest floor and picked up Boehan's gun.

"*Shoot it, you slugs!*" he shouted. He began firing over the heads of the mystai, trying to hit the creature without hitting them. These poor people didn't know which way to run; away from the killer tree or away from the loud semi-automatic.

The other satyrs were torn between bowing to me, shooting me, and wondering what in Zeus's name was bearing down on the crowd. Hippos' entreaty seemed to help them resolve this confusion. They joined in and began shooting as well.

It didn't appear to make any difference. TEC-9's are not the sort of thing you use to gun down something from a distance, but I had to think at least a few of the bullets were finding their mark, and yet the dryad continued its charge into the crowd.

It was a slaughter.

We had to get everyone to safety first and then worry about how to kill it. But where are you safe from a forest god in the middle of a forest?

"On a lake," I said to myself.

I jumped off the stage and found Hippos.

"Get the people onto the ice!"

He stopped shooting long enough to think about this.

"Yes," he agreed. "I believe you are right."

Hippos, I decided, would make a great field general. Seconds after handing me his gun, he'd gotten the other satyrs organized. Four of them positioned themselves between the dryad and the fleeing crowd, while Hippos, Dyanos, and the other four started to corral everyone onto the lake.

"Adam, what in Christ's name is that?" Mike asked. He'd run to the altar when the shooting began and basically looked like he just found out the Easter Bunny was real.

"A dryad," I explained. "It's the same kind of thing that killed Lonnie Wicks."

"A dryad? Seriously. Isn't he supposed to be a naked girl or something?"

"You can tell it that if you want."

"No thanks. How do we kill it?"

"Working on it."

The bullets were definitely impacting the dryad, but they were about as effective as they might be to a real tree. The creature's claws, meanwhile, were devastating. One of the satyrs protecting Hippos' back stood still for a half second too long and had his head removed with a backhand swing. This inspired the remaining satyrs to move more quickly while still shooting. Meanwhile, Hippos was finding it difficult to convince all of the stoned mystai to get onto the ice, and probably wished he'd kept his gun. Fortunately, Dyanos and the others still had theirs, and began firing over people's heads to convince them to congregate in the proper direction.

Then a second satyr from the defensive line fell. With the guns doing no damage, the only thing keeping the creature from the mystai was all the jumping around the satyrs were doing. And that was only working because they were really annoying it.

"What do we know about it?" Mike asked. "It has to have a weakness."

"Gordon," I said, as another of the satyrs fell, or rather flew.

We were going to run out of satyrs soon.

Gordon was still on his knees at the foot of the stage. Ariadne was beside him. When Mike and I reached them, she was calmly wrapping a cloth around his eyes.

"He's blind," she said.

"It's so beautiful," Gordon babbled happily.

"He's not deaf, right? He can hear the screams?"

"The Great Protector will save us all," he insisted.

"Not deaf, but maybe delusional," Ariadne offered.

I knelt beside him.

"Tell me more, Gordon. Tell me all about the Great Protector."

"She Is In touch with all the plants of the world. She wills life from lifelessness, green from brown ..."

"Yeah, okay, I've seen that happen already. But how do you kill it?"

"Why would I want to kill her?"

"Because she's about to kill you!"

He bowed his head for a second, a gesture of resignation. "She can't be killed. As long as her forest lives, so does she."

"Great. Where's a logging company when you need one?"

In the field of battle, Hippos and his men had managed to get the last of the living congregants onto the ice and had gone back to shooting at the dryad full time. There were only four satyrs left. If they were smart, they'd get on the ice with the others and leave us to fend for ourselves.

Thankfully, they were not smart. Quickly running out of land, Hippos gave the signal and he and the other three living satyrs—Dyanos, I noted, was not among them—broke off the attack and ran, leaving nothing but a little ice between the dryad and over eighty defenseless people.

"If it crosses the lake, they are all dead," Hippos shouted at me as soon as he was in earshot.

"It won't."

The dryad did take one step onto the ice, which seemed to hold under its weight. But it hesitated.

"Why's it stopping?" Mike asked.

"The water is the realm of the onead, and the mountains belong to the naiad. I figured if dryads are real, there's probably some truth behind the boundaries as well."

"So I guess we can't hope it trudges into the center, breaks through and drowns, huh?"

"I'm pretty sure it doesn't breathe," I said.

Stopped at the water line, the dryad howled again with the sound of a hurricane wind shearing off a tree branch, and turned around.

I shifted uneasily. "Uh-oh."

"The water looks like a good idea from here," Mike said.

"I agree."

But this was not a stupid dryad. It put itself between us and the lake.

"Well, shit," Mike said.

I took a look around to see who was left. Peter, I could see, was still unconscious underneath the stage. With his luck, he'd probably be the only one to survive this attack. Gordon and Ariadne remained where they were, useless but good targets for the dryad. That left me, Mike, Hippos, and three satyrs who were probably almost out of bullets.

Nobody had a howitzer or a small nuclear device, which was just poor planning.

We could probably delay the inevitable by scattering, but I didn't care for the odds. And once it was done with us, it could sit on the shore and wait for sunrise to melt the lake if it wanted to. Maybe that was giving it too much credit, but maybe not.

The dryad started marching our way, slowly.

Hippos turned to me. "Now would be the time for an idea, sojourner!"

"I'm working on it."

Cassandra's prophecy came to mind:

The tree of life will strike, red on white, red on white!
Godhood reclaimed marks the sojourner's end and the pretender's fall.
Seek the source!

I'd sought the source by visiting Greece, so that was pretty clearly done. And the tree of life stood before me now, spattering red blood on white snow all over the place, so there was nothing much left to say about that. But the middle sentence was tricky. If the pretender was Gordon and the sojourner was me, the dryad was the one reclaiming godhood, in which case I was screwed.

Except the dryad already had a starring role in the first sentence. And ten minutes earlier, I'd stood on the stage and reclaimed my erstwhile godhood about as clearly as it can be reclaimed, so maybe I was looking at it all wrong. Maybe the end of my sojourn was simply the day I rejoined the Mystery Cult.

If that was the case, nothing Cassandra said could help anymore because the prophecy was complete. All I had left to go on was Ariadne's prophet insisting I could tame a dryad, and I still didn't have a clue how to do that.

"We will get you some more time," Hippos said. He took back the TEC-9 I was holding for him, walked twenty paces and took up a position between me and the dryad. The other three satyrs followed suit.

Then Gordon started crying.

He'd probably been doing it for a while, but it was the first time it was quiet enough for anyone other than Ariadne to hear.

"I am here," he repeatedly chanted, and it finally caught the dryad's attention.

Gordon began walking towards the creature. What was worse, Ariadne was still beside him.

"Ariadne, get out of there!" I shouted.

"I'm trying!"

She was pulling Gordon by the arm, but he was too strong and too crazy. And the blindness probably didn't hurt, because no matter how insane you've become, if you could see what the dryad looked like, you wouldn't be walking toward it.

"Let him go!" I said, which was not nearly as effective as Mike's reaction. He left my side and reached her in a matter of seconds, nearly tackling her.

"But it'll kill him!" she screamed.

"Yes, it will," Mike said. "But you don't have to die with him."

"I am here to do your bidding, O Transcendent One!" Gordon shouted, spreading his arms wide and walking toward where he imagined the dryad must be standing. He was a little off, but the creature took care of that by taking two giant steps toward him. "I am Dionysos, and I am pure!"

Ariadne was still fighting Mike, and he didn't much care to be directly behind Gordon for what was bound to happen next, so rather than wait for her to regain her senses, he threw her over his shoulder and carried her back behind the satyr line of defense.

Meanwhile, Gordon and the dryad were sharing a moment.

Gordon was standing still, arms outstretched, a look of ecstasy on his damaged face. Not knowing quite what to make of a human that wasn't running and screaming and bleeding, the dryad cocked what passed for its head, puzzled.

"Philopaigmos," Hippos said. "Should we ... do something?"

"I don't know. This is different though, isn't it?"

For just a few seconds, I thought maybe Gordon had been right all along; supplication was the key to survival. And that would have been really embarrassing.

The dryad held out one of its hands, looking at it first like it was going to pick up Gordon, or pet him. But then it put one pointed claw tip on Gordon's chest and pushed. Slowly.

It sounded a little like a sword being sheathed. Gordon gasped as his lung was punctured, and then let out a meager scream that became a gurgle. The dryad held him up and watched him die. Then it flung the body into the woods.

"Gordon ..." Ariadne cried. She was at my feet by then, as Mike had brought her to me and dropped her in the snow there.

"Hey," Mike said as Gordon flew over our heads, "would this be a bad time to tell her she's under arrest?"

"Probably."

With Gordon dispatched, the dryad turned to look at us again.

"Sojourner ..." Hippos said. His men were ready to fire.

I shook my head. "Not yet."

It tilted its head this way and that, looking carefully at each of us, almost as if it just noticed we were there. And again I wondered if we were being granted a reprieve of some kind.

"Hey," Mike muttered, "stupid question, but that thing is made of wood, right?"

Hippos heard this, and he and I both turned to look at what Mike was already staring at—the torches on the altar.

Hippos glared at me meaningfully.

At around the same time, the dryad decided that whatever it wanted, we didn't have it.

Arching its back, it tilted its head toward the sky and let loose the loudest and most horrific sound I'd ever heard. (It's beyond my ability to adequately describe the sound. But late at night, I still hear it sometimes.)

"Go," I said. "Hurry."

Hippos tossed his TEC-9 to Mike. "Keep it occupied!" he ordered.

Mike and the three satyrs opened fire. It was no more effective than at any other time, but it gave Hippos an opportunity to reach the stage and grab one of the torches without the dryad noticing.

Of course, when you're a living tree, you tend to be more actively interested in the current location of all sources of fire, so Hippos didn't remain unnoticed for long. About to attack the firing line, the dryad abruptly shifted direction and lunged at the stage. But Hippos was already on the move, and if there's one thing satyrs are naturally good at, it's leaping to the tops of trees.

With a tremendous jump, Hippos landed on the dryad's back and touched the flame to its skin.

"*More torches!*" cried one of the other satyrs, and they quickly scattered to find new sources of fire. Hippos, after starting three hotspots, found the creature's back too perilous to remain upon; he launched himself off, landing only a few feet from us.

"Will this work?" Mike asked.

"It *is* made of wood, half-breed," Hippos said. "I felt the bark myself. And wood burns."

The dryad's back was blazing freely, and once the other three satyrs got into the act, so were one of its legs. It shrieked in pain and stomped around the snow-covered beach furiously, trying to put itself out. And it refused to use the available water source right behind it.

It was soon fully engulfed in flames, and we were fresh out of extra satyrs; the chaotic motion of the dryad was too difficult to predict and one by one they'd ended up kicked or stepped on. But the thing was burning.

And then the oddest thing happened. It stood still—looking a bit like a gigantic effigy—and it started to sing.

"What is that noise?" Mike asked, covering his ears.

"Maybe ... it's dying?" Ariadne offered, getting to her feet and deciding, I guess, to finish mourning Gordon later.

"Maybe," Mike said.

It wasn't dying.

"It's healing itself. Look!"

The flames started to flIcker out. Grass all around the dryad's feet sprang up from the ground and in a widening circle. In the spots on its body that were no longer afire, I saw a thick layer of sap pouring from the creature's body.

It was re-growing itself.

"It is as self-healing as the forest itself," Hippos said. "We cannot possibly kill it, anymore than we could kill nature."

Ariadne said, " 'In touch with all the plants of this world.' "

That sparked a thought. "What was that?"

"Just something Gordon said."

"That's the answer."

"What is?" she asked.

I strode forward purposefully, holding the thyrsos above my head.

"Dryad!" I shouted, as loudly as I possibly could. I wanted its attention. "*I am Dionysos Lyseus! I am your destroyer!*"

So saying, I snapped off the long part of the staff that was holding Gilgamesh's rock, leaving only a short haft.

My declaration got the creature's attention. I stepped to the edge of the new grass the dryad had grown, and stopped.

It showed no particular interest in kneeling before another god, nor did it act as if it planned to run away anytime soon. Instead, it raised itself up to its full height and bellowed. I don't speak dryad, but I imagine it was saying something along the lines of *oh yeah?*

The open maw of the creature presented a very appealing target. I threw the Hammer of Gilgamesh into it.

The dryad's roar was cut short by the sudden and unexpected introduction of a rock to its mouth. It looked surprised—a really fascinating expression for a dryad—but no less interested in killing me than it was before.

"Oh please, oh please, oh please," I said to myself. I'd pray, but to which god?

It lifted its arm, sap flying off in every direction, preparing for the killing blow. I stood my ground, figuring if I was going to die anyway, better to look good while doing it.

But before it could administer my final moment, it stopped. Its hands reached for the spot I took to be its neck, and started digging. It made a sound that was almost a wheeze.

"Is it choking?" Mike asked.

I hadn't even noticed him joining my side.

"No. Not exactly."

A greenish-brown moss started spreading from the dryad's mouth, across its face and down its arms and legs.

"Um, we should step back," I said. "Quickly."

"Yeah. Actually, maybe running would be good."

We spun around and started running toward Hippos and Ariadne.

"Move!" I shouted. Hippos, who could see the same thing we had, swept up Ariadne and bounded toward the shelter of the woods. Mike, alas, wasn't nearly big enough to carry me, or we would have been right behind them.

I snuck a glance over my shoulder. The dryad looked a lot like a rooted tree that had been stuffed with an angry rhino. It bulged and splintered and groaned under the pressure and then ... it exploded.

I dove forward, smacking Mike in the back to push him down, and the two of us went face first into the snow as dryad body parts—excellent projectiles—flew in every direction.

And then, silence. Blissful normal forest silence.

"You hurt?" Mike asked.

"Don't think so." I rolled over and sat up. Mike got to his feet and helped me to mine.

"What'd you throw in there, a grenade?" he asked.

Ariadne and Hippos emerged from the woods, looking as stunned as the two of us must have looked.

All that was left of the dryad was its feet, which looked like hollowed-out tree stumps that had stood there for decades, and in those decades had been covered with a brownish green moss. In fact, the moss was everywhere.

I walked into the middle of the carnage and reached into one of the legs, pulling out Gilgamesh's rock.

"He was right all this time," I said to the others.

"Who was right?" Ariadne asked.

"The man who gave this to me. He insisted until the day he died that it was a weapon. He was right."

"What manner of plant is this?" Hippos asked. He was examining the moss.

"Don't touch it," I said. "In fact, all of you should back away from here; some of it may be airborne."

"Poisonous?" Mike asked.

"No," I said, "but it'll give you one hell of a trip."

* * *

Several hours later—by then past midnight—the first outside authorities began to arrive. Mike radioed them in, explaining he was at a scene that had multiple injuries and over two-dozen deaths. That got helicopters into the air pretty quickly.

I was sitting beside the kiste, drinking a lukewarm cup of coffee and watching the proceedings. Peter—finally awake and very confused— and Ariadne and Hippos were all being led away in handcuffs by representatives of the state police. They would be flown off just as soon as all the wounded were evacuated. Meanwhile, the stoned-out mystai had been helped off the ice and were being administered to by park rangers who arrived by snowmobile from all over the place.

Mike cordoned off the grassy area by placing torches around it and tying ropes from torch to torch. It wouldn't be necessary for much longer; the moss was already dying.

When enough people were present to ensure that things could run smoothly, he joined me on the stage.

"We had to arrest them," Mike explained without being asked. "The big Greek guy ..."

"Hippos."

"Yeah. He'll probably end up on a plane in a day or two, seeing as how he's an ambassador and all."

"And how he didn't commit a crime?"

"Oh, there are plenty enough crimes here to go around. One or two would stick if we wanted them to. Kidnapping, for instance. He told me he brought you here against your will. In fact, he went out of his way to make sure I understood that. Seems he wants to keep you out of trouble."

He sat down next to me. "Is that true?"

"That I was kidnapped? Yeah."

"You gonna press charges?"

"Hadn't planned to, no."

I sipped my coffee. "And Ariadne?"

"She's in a lot of trouble," he said. "But we'll see. She might come out of this okay."

"Peter?"

"Do you care?"

"Not really, no."

"He's a fugitive. The trial might go his way, but there is the matter of him skipping bail."

"Think a jury will believe his defense that it was a nature-beast from hell who killed his friend?"

Mike smiled. "I think you'd be surprised at the things a jury will believe."

We sat quietly for a while. I was thinking how great a beer would taste.

"So how'd you know?" Mike asked. "How'd you know that would work?"

"You saw how it was healing itself, right? It was drawing from the plants around it and incorporating the healthy plant matter into its own body. I figured that was something it couldn't just turn off like a switch."

"That mossy stuff grew out of the rock, just like the grass," Mike said. "Fine, but why did that hurt it?"

"It's like Gordon said—it was in touch with all the plants of this world."

"And?"

"And that moss wasn't from this world," I said. "The rock came from space."

"No shit?"

"No shit."

"That's quite a find," he said. "I have a bunch of scientists on their way here to figure out how a tree managed to walk around and kill people. I bet they'll find that even more interesting. You don't happen to know where this rock might be now?"

"Back where it should be."

"In this here box."

"Yeah."

"The box is evidence."

"Good luck opening it," I said. "Let them study the moss on the ground if they want. Just make sure they're wearing gas masks or something, or they'll be one loopy set of scientists."

"Right. So what should we do with the box, anyway? Do you want it?"

"No, but I can tell you who to ship it to. Guy named Kargus. Lives in Athens."

"I'll see if the FBI feels like springing for international postage."

"Hey, how'd you get here so quickly?" I asked. "It took us a day just to get to the lake from the Seattle airport. Granted, we had a storm to contend with, but still."

Mike smiled. "Cassandra Jones."

"Another prophecy?"

"I went back to question her, like I said I would, and ended up getting a reading of my own from her. 'All paths end in terror's shadow.' "

"Mount Terror."

"Crazy name, right? It's like someone called it that just so it would sound scary when coming from an oracle. So yeah, I was at a ranger's station on Route 20 trying to figure out the quickest way to get here when I picked up your message. I ended up borrowing a snowmobile."

"You couldn't have maybe called a few more agents?"

"I did. But I don't usually travel with a battalion. Takes a while to put this big a response together in a blizzard, you know. Plus I'm not entirely good with my people yet."

"This should help."

"This should help a bunch. Anyway, when I got here, I saw you tied up and the place guarded by guys with big guns. Didn't seem like the best time to show off my badge. So I found an extra robe and joined in the fun."

"Lucky for me," I said.

"No such thing as luck. Just who you know. I'm glad you called. I was going on the word of a stoned hippie before that message."

He reached into his pocket and pulled out a pack of cigarettes. I took one, and we both lit up and sat quietly for a while, basically just appreciating the fact that we weren't dead. This is the sort of thing better done with a bottle, but we had what we had.

Looking over the scene, my eyes scanned the trees, half expecting to see another one of the conifers uproot and start walking. It might be a while, I decided, before I could spend a lot of time in another forest.

I spotted her almost as an afterthought. She was standing alone at the base of a distant tree, dressed in a long coat and a white turtleneck, nearly looking like she belonged there. Her red hair stood out like always.

The Eleusinians would have been pleased to learn that two gods had shown up for their ceremony this year.

"Did I tell you my grandparents are Greek?" Mike asked.

"No kidding," I mumbled.

She was looking straight at me. Traditionally, in a moment such as this, my next step would be to run toward her as quickly as I could, but it had been a hell of a day and running to catch her never worked before, so I just smiled and gave her a little nod.

"Big time," Mike said. "Made me learn the language and everything."

"That's interesting."

He followed my gaze. "Who's she?"

"I don't think you would believe me if I told you." She smiled back at me and bowed her head slightly; an ancient greeting.

"I could just go ask her myself," Mike said. "If she's connected with this ..."

"She's not. Besides, she's already gone."

Mike looked back to find she had indeed disappeared.

"You were saying?" I asked.

Mike shook his head. "Yeah. Greek. So if I'm remembering the language right, when you were up on the stage here you called yourself Dionysos."

"I did, didn't I?"

"And again when you were threatening that thing with your magic rock."

"I might have done that, yes."

"So ... can't believe I'm asking this ... are you some sort of god? Is that your deal?"

"Depends on who you ask."

"I'm asking you."

I grinned.

"Mike, sometimes a god is just somebody who's been around for a long time."

"Is that a yes?"

"That's the best answer you're getting."

"Huh. I don't know if I can accept that."

"You know, you're pretty talkative for a werewolf."

He stared.

"What did you just call me?"

Epilogue

In the aftermath of the incident at Azure Lake, I half expected to end up in custody myself. But Mike had enough pull to keep me out of major trouble and I was able to depart on my own terms. It probably helped that as the only FBI agent on the scene, Mike Lycos was credited with having brought down, single-handedly, one of the most feared eco-terrorist groups in the Western hemisphere. That kind of thing will get you far.

I returned to my island in the Queen Charlottes. From there, I followed the case as well as I could in the news.

Peter Arnheit returned to California and pled out rather than stand trial for the murder of Lonnie Wicks. Thanks to what happened in the North Cascades (I assume) he managed to get sent away for manslaughter, rather than murder in the first degree.

Among the living members of Gordon Alecto's eco-terrorist group, he was lucky. Seventeen others connected directly to the group were successfully convicted of the murder of three people, plus destruction of property, acts of domestic terrorism and a few other things. This stemmed from an incident a year earlier, wherein a bomb was set off in the headquarters of an Oregon mining company. They'd done it on a weekend when they figured nobody would be there. They were wrong.

Both Hippos and Ariadne stayed out of the news, so I didn't know what happened to them up until the day the helicopter arrived on the landing pad in my back yard.

I was in the shower at the time. I've found that even when living alone it's a good idea to shower at least once or twice a week, provided a shower is available. And with the water running, I didn't hear the rotors. Fortunately, I'm not actually completely alone as I share the place with a pixie named Iza. She was kind enough to interrupt my bathing to inform me I had a guest.

Throwing on a pair of shorts, I stumbled outside just in time to see the helicopter fly off. Resting on the side of the pad was a large crate. Sitting on the crate, wearing jeans, an oversized sweater, and a heavy parka (it was February) was Ariadne Papos.

* * *

"I figured you'd be in prison somewhere," I said.

We were in my kitchen drinking coffee and listening to a very annoyed pixie fly around. Iza had a problem with a woman being in the house that wasn't Clara. It was kind of weird for me, too.

"So did I," she said. "But my testimony helped put away the rest of Gordon's crew, and a mutual friend of ours testified on my behalf."

"That was very kind of this mutual friend."

"I thought so, too. Speaking of." She reached into the oversized bag at her feet and pulled out a very large folder. "This is for you."

I opened the folder and found a note, which read:

Enclosed you will find a hard copy of every scrap of information currently available on the unknown subject called Adam. Handle with care, as the electronic file was somehow purged due to a computer malfunction. If this were to suddenly fall into a fire, the United States Government would no longer be aware of his existence. And that would be a terrible shame, wouldn't it?

—ML

"Good news?" Ariadne asked.

"A returned favor," I said, closing the folder.

"He also told me to tell you ... how did he put it ... something about not financing terrorists after this or it was his ass."

I laughed. "I'll try and remember that. So are you still a government employee?"

"Nope. I'm considered a security risk. But it turns out the Greek ambassador to the United States has use for a computer analyst."

"With optional helicopter access?"

"No, that was a charter. I'm on vacation."

I smiled. Iza buzzed angrily and I continued to ignore her.

"So what's in the crate?" I could see it from the kitchen window, still sitting on the helipad.

"It's the kiste," she said.

"What's it doing here?"

"It belongs to you."

"It belongs to the Eleusinians. I never wanted it. And you can't have your cult without it."

"That's sort of the idea. Hippos and I agreed that if we were to continue, it would have to be with your blessing."

I got up and walked to the window.

The whole thing was dizzying. A few thousand years earlier I inadvertently helped found what was perhaps the oldest ongoing religious ceremonial tradition in the history of mankind, and the future of that tradition was now sitting in a wood crate outside my door. If I were to throw it in the same fire that consumed my FBI file, would the world be better or worse for it? Or different at all? Considering how I feel about religion in general, it was a strange place to be.

"I'll have to think about that," I said.

"You have time. And I have another gift."

She reached back into the bag and pulled out second folder.

"One of the cool things about being the hierophant was access to all of the Cult's private documents." She slid the papers across the table. "I found this in the archives. I think it might be more important to you than it is to us."

I sat back down, flipped open the folder and saw ancient Greek in longhand. It was a copy of the original scrolls, clearly, but it appeared the originating text was well preserved, which is pretty rare when it comes to copying.

The first name I saw caught my eye.

"Silenus."

"One of them. There were at least three different ones, based on the handwriting from the originals. I read through all of it, and translated some. You'll probably have an easier time than I did. You figure prominently in most of that."

"From what I remember, Silenus the Younger disappointed me."

She nodded. "Just read through it. He found your Demeter, whoever she was. But he promised her not to tell you what he learned. It looks like his descendant figured out a solution and embedded the information in a play, imagining you'd end up seeing the performance."

"God of the theater and all that," I said.

"Exactly. Except the play was probably never performed. You know how the Cult was with secrecy."

I fingered a corner of the ream of pages. It was hard to say what was more enticing: the potential knowledge that lay within, or the guest at the other end of the table.

"By the way," Ariadne asked, "what was he?"

"Silenus?"

"He had a longer-than-normal lifespan and is described as a creature a few times. But I've never heard of him outside of the Dionysian mythos."

"He was an imp. Most of them are more mischievous than his line. But maybe not as clever."

I closed the folder. There would be time to go through it later.

"So, vacation?"

"A whole month."

"Where's your luggage? Or is this just a day trip?"

She grinned. "I have a few necessities in my bag. I travel light."

"Very light."

"I don't know about you, but I've found the best vacations are ones where clothing isn't entirely required."

She pulled a white cloth from her bag and held it up against her chest. It was a chiton.

"And you would be amazed at the number of situations in which this is considered perfectly acceptable attire."

"Hmm. Do you have the sandals in there as well?" I asked.

"Why, yes, sojourner, I believe I do."

"Well, then. I think you'd better start vacationing immediately. Let me show you where you can get changed."

ABOUT THE AUTHOR

Gene Doucette is an award-winning screenwriter, novelist, playwright, humorist, essayist, and owner of a cyclocross bike, which he rides daily. A graduate of Boston College, he lives in Cambridge, MA with his family.

Also by Gene Doucette

The Spaceship Next Door

The world changed on a Tuesday.

When a spaceship landed in an open field in the quiet mill town of Sorrow Falls, Massachusetts, everyone realized humankind was not alone in the universe. With that realization, everyone freaked out for a little while.

Or, almost everyone. The residents of Sorrow Falls took the news pretty well. This could have been due to a certain local quality of unflappability, or it could have been that in three years, the ship did exactly nothing other than sit quietly in that field, and nobody understood the full extent of this nothing the ship was doing better than the people who lived right next door.

Sixteen-year old Annie Collins is one of the ship's closest neighbors. Once upon a time she took every last theory about the ship seriously, whether it was advanced by an adult ,or by a peer. Surely one of the theories would be proven true eventually—if not several of them—the very minute the ship decided to do something. Annie is starting to think this will never happen.

One late August morning, a little over three years since the ship landed, Edgar Somerville arrived in town. Ed's a government operative posing as a journalist, which is obvious to Annie—and pretty much everyone else he meets—almost immediately. He has a lot of questions that need answers, because he thinks everyone is wrong: the ship is doing something, and he needs Annie's help to figure out what that is.

Annie is a good choice for tour guide. She already knows everyone in town and when Ed's theory is proven correct—something is apocalyptically wrong in Sorrow Falls—she's a pretty good person to have around.

As a matter of fact, Annie Collins might be the most important person on the planet. She just doesn't know it.

* * *

The Immortal Novel Series

* * *

Immortal

"I don't know how old I am. My earliest memory is something along the lines of fire good, ice bad, so I think I predate written history, but I don't know by how much. I like to brag that I've been there from the beginning, and while this may very well be true, I generally just say it to pick up girls."

Surviving sixty thousand years takes cunning and more than a little luck. But in the twenty-first century, Adam confronts new dangers—someone has found out what he is, a demon is after him, and he has run out of places to hide. Worst of all, he has had entirely too much to drink.

Immortal is a first person confessional penned by a man who is immortal, but not invincible. In an artful blending of sci-fi, adventure, fantasy, and humor, IMMORTAL introduces us to a world with vampires, demons and other "magical" creatures, yet a world without actual magic.

At the center of the book is Adam.

Adam is a sixty thousand year old man. (Approximately.) He doesn't age or get sick, but is otherwise entirely capable of being killed. His survival has hinged on an innate ability to adapt, his wits, and a fairly large dollop of luck. He makes for an excellent guide through history . . . when he's sober.

Immortal is a contemporary fantasy for non-fantasy readers and fantasy enthusiasts alike.

* * *

Hellenic Immortal

"Very occasionally, I will pop up in the historical record. Most of the time I'm not at all easy to spot, because most of the time I'm just a guy who does a thing and then disappears again into the background behind someone-or-other who's busy doing something much more important. But there are a couple of rare occasions when I get a starring role."

An oracle has predicted the sojourner's end, which is a problem for Adam insofar as he has never encountered an oracular prediction that didn't come true . . . and he is the sojourner. To survive, he's going to have to figure out what a beautiful ex-government analyst, an eco-terrorist, a rogue FBI agent, and the world's oldest religious cult all want with him, and fast.

And all he wanted when he came to Vegas was to forget about a girl. And maybe have a drink or two.

The second book in the Immortal series, Hellenic Immortal follows the continuing adventures of Adam, a sixty-thousand-year-old man with a wry sense of humor, a flair for storytelling, and a knack for staying alive. Hellenic Immortal is a clever blend of history, mythology, sci-fi, fantasy, adventure, mystery and romance. A little something, in other words, for every reader.

* * *

Immortal at the Edge of the World

"What I was currently doing with my time and money . . . didn't really

deserve anyone else's attention. If I was feeling romantic about it, I'd call it a quest, but all I was really doing was trying to answer a question I'd been ignoring for a thousand years."

In his very long life, Adam had encountered only one person who appeared to share his longevity: the mysterious red-haired woman. She appeared throughout history, usually from a distance, nearly always vanishing before he could speak to her.

In his last encounter, she actually did vanish—into thin air, right in front of him. The question was how did she do it? To answer, Adam will have to complete a quest he gave up on a thousand years earlier, for an object that may no longer exist.

If he can find it, he might be able to do what the red-haired woman did, and if he can do that, maybe he can find her again and ask her who she is . . . and why she seems to hate him.

But Adam isn't the only one who wants the red-haired woman. There are other forces at work, and after a warning from one of the few men he trusts, Adam realizes how much danger everyone is in. To save his friends and finish his quest he may be forced to bankrupt himself, call in every favor he can, and ultimately trade the one thing he'd never been able to give up before: his life.

* * *

Immortal Stories

* * *

Eve

"…if your next question is, what could that possibly make me, if I'm not an angel or a god? The answer is the same as what I said before: many have considered me a god, and probably a few have thought of me as an angel. I'm neither, if those positions are defined by any kind of supernormal magical power. True magic of that kind doesn't exist, but I can do things that may appear magic to someone slightly more tethered to their mortality. I'm a woman, and that's all. What may make me *different from the next woman is that it's possible I'm the very first one..."*

For most of humankind, the woman calling herself Eve has been nothing more than a shock of red hair glimpsed out of the corner of the eye, in a crowd, or from a great distance. She's been worshipped, feared, and hunted, but perhaps never understood. Now, she's trying to reconnect with the world, and finding that more challenging than anticipated.

Can the oldest human on Earth rediscover her own humanity? Or will she decide the world isn't worth it?

* * *

The Immortal Chronicles

* * *

Immortal at Sea (volume 1)

Adam's adventures on the high seas have taken him from the Mediterranean to the Barbary Coast, and if there's one thing he learned, it's that maybe the sea is trying to tell him to stay on dry land.

* * *

Hard-Boiled Immortal (volume 2)

The year was 1942, there was a war on, and Adam was having a lot of trouble avoiding the attention of some important people. The kind of people with guns, and ways to make a fella disappear. He was caught somewhere between the mob and the government, and the only way out involved a red-haired dame he was pretty sure he couldn't trust.

* * *

Immortal and the Madman (volume 3)

On a nice quiet trip to the English countryside to cope with the likelihood that he has gone a little insane, Adam meets a man who definitely has. The madman's name is John Corrigan, and he is convinced he's going to die soon.

He could be right. Because there's trouble coming, and unless Adam can get his own head together in time, they may die together.

* * *

Yuletide Immortal (volume 4)

When he's in a funk, Adam the immortal man mostly just wants a place to drink and the occasional drinking buddy. When that buddy turns out to be Santa Claus, Adam is forced to face one of the biggest challenges of extremely long life: Christmas cheer. Will Santa break him out of his bad mood? Or will he be responsible for depressing the most positive man on the planet?

* * *

Regency Immortal (volume 5)

Adam has accidentally stumbled upon an important period in history: Vienna in 1814. Mostly, he'd just like to continue to enjoy the local pubs, but that becomes impossible when he meets Anna, an intriguing woman with an unreasonable number of secrets and sharp objects.

Anna is hunting down a man who isn't exactly a man, and if Adam doesn't help her, all of Europe will suffer. If Adam *does* help, the cost may be his own life. It's not a fantastic set of options. Also, he's probably fallen in love with her, which just complicates everything.

* * *

Other works

* * *

Fixer

What would you do if you could see into the future?

As a child, he dreamed of being a superhero. Most people never get to realize their childhood dreams, but Corrigan Bain has come close. He is a fixer. His job is to prevent accidents—to see the future and "fix" things before people get hurt. But the ability to see into the future, however limited, isn't always so simple. Sometimes not everyone can be saved.

"Don't let them know you can see them."

Graduate students from a local university are dying, and former lover and FBI agent Maggie Trent is the only person who believes their deaths aren't as accidental as they appear. But the truth can only be found in something from Corrigan Bain's past, and he's not interested in sharing that past, not even with Maggie.

To stop the deaths, Corrigan will have to face up to some old horrors, confront the possibility that he may be going mad, and find a way to stop a killer no one can see.

Corrigan Bain is going insane . . . or is he?

Because there's something in the future that doesn't want to be seen. It isn't human. It's got a taste for mayhem. And it is very, very angry.

* * *

Surviving Hector

"You can call me Hector. Nobody else does, and I only thought of it three seconds ago, so you will not find anything about me by knowing this. It's better than you with the gun, however."

Before leaving work for the weekend, Anita's boss gave her a file for safekeeping. Now the killer sitting in her bedroom wants the file, and is willing to kill Anita and her wounded, unconscious husband if he doesn't get it. But if she hands it over, he might kill them anyway.

Alone, unarmed and dressed for bed, can Anita save her husband and herself? Can she survive Hector?

Made in the USA
Lexington, KY
27 January 2019